THE AIRLOCK DOOR OPENED . . .

and a trio of Cardassians stepped in, weapons raised.

Commander Sisko started to speak, but a phaser blast from the foremost Cardassian silenced him. Crimson sparks fell from the ceiling where the bolt struck.

Phaser fire from both sides lit the passageway. A bolt scorched across the wall centimeters from Sisko's shoulder. The defenders of *Deep Space Nine* retreated as the Cardassians moved toward them . . .

Look for STAR TREK Fiction from Pocket Books

Star Trek: The Original Series

Star Trek: The Next Generation

Star Trek: Deep Space Nine

Star Trek: Voyager

STAR TREK
DEEP SPACE NINE®

VALHALLA

Nathan Archer

POCKET BOOKS

New York   London   Toronto   Sydney   Tokyo   Singapore

An *Original* Publication of POCKET BOOKS

POCKET BOOKS, a division of Simon & Schuster Inc.
1230 Avenue of the Americas, New York, NY 10020

This book is published by Pocket Books, a division of Simon & Schuster Inc., under exclusive license from Paramount Pictures.

ISBN: 0-671-88115-9

First Pocket Books printing April 1995

10 9 8 7 6 5 4 3 2 1

POCKET and colophon are registered trademarks of Simon & Schuster Inc.

Printed in the U.S.A.

VALHALLA

CHAPTER
1

THE ALIEN SHIP came in hot and fast, popping out of the wormhole like a champagne cork from a bottle, the strange, smooth hull as blue as the eerie, swirling discharge of the wormhole itself.

Display screens in the operations area of the station called *Deep Space Nine* lit with warning sensor readouts—ship's surface temperature 3500 degrees Celsius, radiation output well into the lethal range for all known humanoid life-forms, velocity a respectable fraction of the speed of light.

At the science workstation of the main operations table, Lieutenant Jadzia Dax scanned the messages quickly, displaying no sign of surprise.

Dax was a Trill—a merged being. Her outward appearance was that of an attractive, dark-haired young woman, indistinguishable from a humanoid being save for an odd mottling of her skin along the sides of her head, and the Jadzia half of her was

1

exactly that—but the other half, hidden inside her, was an ancient creature, a sexless wormlike being three centuries old that had learned to be surprised by very little.

A neutrino surge had provided a warning that something was coming through the wormhole, but until the alien had actually appeared Dax had assumed that the new arrival would simply be a recent Ferengi trade mission returning ahead of schedule. Given that that particular Ferengi captain's plans had struck Dax as being hopelessly optimistic, she had rather expected an early return.

This ship, whatever it was, was not the Ferengi trader she had expected. It was completely unanticipated, and totally unfamiliar in design.

Dax looked up from the panel and saw that Commander Benjamin Sisko, the station's top authority, and Major Kira Nerys, his second-in-command, were still closeted in Sisko's office, arguing vehemently about the latest crisis in relations between the Bajorans and the Cardassian Empire.

Dax therefore took it upon herself to scan the alien vessel thoroughly without consulting the station's harried commander. Benjamin didn't need the added headache just now.

The Dax part of the Trill had known Benjamin Sisko in its previous symbiosis, when it had been not Jadzia but Curzon Dax, and it knew Sisko to be a good man, a strong and intelligent man—but one who let his responsibilities weigh heavily on him. She had no desire to add to that burden.

Dax scanned the reports with practiced ease. No life-forms were aboard the intruder, according to her readings—but that flood of hard radiation was interfering enough that she couldn't be sure those readings were correct. The object was coasting, not moving under power; perhaps it wasn't a ship at all, despite its appearance and velocity. It wasn't responding to the station's hail—but then, if there were no life-forms aboard, that was hardly surprising.

If it was a derelict, some bit of space junk that had fallen into the wormhole by accident, it might be interesting to take a good close look at it. It might call for a study team when Dax, as *Deep Space Nine*'s science officer, had the time to spare from her regular duties—as she did not just now, since she was committed to a conference with the personnel of an Ashtarian expedition to the Gamma Quadrant, just as soon as her shift in Ops was over. There was some sort of problem about allowing the Ashtarian ship through the wormhole, one that the station's technical crew had been unable to resolve.

Dax doubted that the problem, whatever it was, would prove as interesting as studying this mysterious new arrival, but the Ashtarians were impatient, and there was no need for any great hurry in dealing with the unknown object.

At least, not if it was going to drift on harmlessly, but she couldn't take that for granted.

Dax touched controls to call up a plot of the new arrival's path, and discovered that if left to itself, and assuming it was actually powerless and wouldn't change course on its own, the object would cross into Cardassian space within hours.

That changed things. Given the present rather tense political situation, anything that would involve the Cardassians, even peripherally, was important enough that Commander Sisko had to hear about it.

Dax had a strong suspicion that Commander Benjamin Sisko did not *want* to hear anything more about

Cardassians, but really, he had little choice in the matter. She tapped her communicator badge.

Benjamin Sisko glowered down at Major Kira. Ordinarily he found her pleasant enough to look at, with her reddish hair and almost-human features. Her ridged nose and clan earring provided an interestingly exotic touch.

Just now, though, all he could see was her damnable Bajoran stubbornness.

That stubbornness might have helped the Bajorans survive the long Cardassian occupation of their planets, but it still wasn't any joy to deal with.

"Major," he said for the third time, "I refuse to start a war between the Cardassians and the Federation."

"I'm not *asking* for a war!" Kira shouted at him. She realized how wild she sounded, caught herself, clenched her teeth to regain control, then said, with rigid calm, "I am only asking that you stop these incursions."

"And do you really think that I can do that *without* starting a war?" Sisko demanded.

"Yes!" Kira shouted. "Maybe," she added, before Sisko could reply.

"Major," Sisko said, "I would like to oblige you, and I agree that the Cardassians have no legitimate business making these sorties into Bajoran space, but so far their ships have done no harm. They have not fired a shot. They have not landed on Bajoran territory."

"Done no harm!"

"Not deliberately," Sisko amended.

"But they've intruded on Bajoran space!"

"Where, under the terms of the agreement they

4

made with both the Federation and the Bajoran provisional government," Sisko reminded her, "they have the right of passage so long as they obey interstellar law."

"That agreement was designed to give them access to the wormhole and Gamma Quadrant, Commander; it wasn't to allow them to terrorize Bajor. And with the *Defiant* off at—"

"Nonetheless," Sisko interrupted, "they have remained within the letter of that agreement, and while they have undoubtedly violated Bajoran statutes, they have so far obeyed interstellar law."

"And is it obeying the law to cruise over our cities at rooftop level, running high-intensity sensor scans of every building and vehicle?" Kira demanded. "Because that's exactly what they've been doing!"

Sisko frowned, and Kira pressed her momentary advantage. "Commander, they've shorted out precious equipment with their sensors, they've terrified innocent people. . . . I don't think you appreciate what it's *like* for us to see Cardassian ships overhead."

"Perhaps . . ." Sisko began, but Kira cut him off. She wasn't finished speaking.

"We all lived under the Cardassian occupation," she said. "Some of us grew up in their relocation camps, or worked for them as slaves. Some of us saw our families tortured or killed there. Some of us remember all too well when those ships were collecting prisoners instead of information, and using phasers instead of sensors. Seeing those ships in the sky brings back all those memories, Commander— it's not as if these were Federation ships, or some other civilization's; they're Cardassian, and that means something very definite, and very terrible, to every Bajoran. So far there hasn't been any wholesale panic or rioting, but it's only a matter of time. And the Cardassians have no *right* there!"

"It's a violation of Bajoran airspace, yes . . ." Sisko began, trying to calm his first officer.

"It's not a mere *violation,* Commander! It's a calculated attack, a campaign of terror!"

Sisko's expression, which he had tried to keep carefully noncommittal up to that point, hardened into something harsher. What Major Kira said was largely true, and it was quite clear that the Cardassians were being deliberately provocative, but he could not allow Bajoran patriotic fervor to drag the Federation into an unnecessary conflict.

This improvised situation he had been thrust into, where a Federation commander ran a Cardassian-built station now owned by Bajor, was a constant invitation to trouble, and Sisko wondered, not for the first time, how the Federation Council could ever have thought it was a good idea.

Of course, if not for the Federation presence, some trigger-happy Bajoran terrorist would probably have started a war of revenge by now, and in retaliation the Cardassians would have wiped out the Bajorans once and for all.

Major Kira was not particularly trigger-happy, and was no longer a terrorist, but at the moment she seemed determined to start a war anyway.

That might well be exactly what the Cardassians wanted. Maybe they thought that if they could provoke a Bajoran attack on them, the Federation would not defend Bajor from the inevitable counterattack.

Or maybe, far more frighteningly, the Cardassians thought they were ready to take on the Federation.

"Major, it is *not* an attack," Sisko said. "Not from the Cardassians' point of view, nor from the Federation's. It is a violation of agreements, yes, and it will be dealt with—but through the proper diplomatic channels, with a demand for an apology and a further demand for reparations for any damages. Using this station or Federation ships to shoot down the intruders, or to launch a counter-raid into Cardassian space, as you suggest, is out of the question."

"This station is Bajoran . . ." Kira began.

Sisko's communicator chirped, and he held up a hand as Dax's voice said, "Dax to Sisko."

"Sisko here," he said, as he tapped the badge.

"My apologies for interrupting, Commander," Dax's voice said, "but we have an intruder . . ."

"Another Cardassian?" Kira asked quickly.

"No, from the wormhole," Dax replied. "The design is unfamiliar. It emerged approximately three minutes ago, and is headed for Cardassian space."

Sisko glanced quickly at Major Kira; for an instant he had an irrational suspicion that this was her doing, that somehow she had arranged for this ship to pop out of the wormhole as part of a scheme to retaliate against the Cardassians.

The idea was absurd on the face of it—but she had been a part of the Bajoran resistance; she might still have contacts within the remaining underground groups, the terrorists who hadn't dared surface when the Cardassians had left and the provisional government was formed.

But an alien ship appearing from the wormhole— surely that was beyond anything the Khon-ma or others of their ilk could arrange!

It had to be a coincidence.

It was a damnably annoying one, though.

"Is it a Tosk vessel, by any chance?" he asked. That, at least, would be a known quantity; the station's first

7

visitor from Gamma Quadrant had been troublesome, mostly through ignorance, but in the end no serious harm to the station or Bajor had come of it.

Other arrivals from the wormhole had presented no great difficulties as yet.

"No, sir—totally unfamiliar. Sensors indicate no life-forms aboard."

"A derelict?"

"Or a missile," Kira suggested.

Sisko threw her an angry glance. "I'll be right there," he announced; he headed for the door of his office.

The door opened directly into the Operations Center—the Cardassians who built the station had considered that a basic element of efficient design. Sometimes Sisko wished they hadn't been quite so efficient; having a few steps to gather his thoughts, without being in full view of the Ops crew, would have been welcome.

The Cardassian designers had also been irrationally fond of steps. While putting the prefect's office—now the station commander's office—on a higher level, to symbolically emphasize his authority, might be an interesting concept, Sisko did get tired of climbing up and down the short flight every time he wanted to go anywhere.

And the steps to the transporter pad and the turbolifts seemed downright silly. He supposed they were intended to keep people from accidentally stepping into the lift or the transporter while the devices were operating, but still . . .

Well, no one had ever said the Cardassians thought like humans. Anyone who looked at the way they had laid out the station's interiors, at the odd curves and peculiar angles and dull colors, would know the

Cardassian sense of aesthetics was different from anything human.

The station's design worked adequately, though. And putting Ops at the top of the station's central core was good sense, as was arranging Ops around a central operations table where all the essential services worked side by side.

Dax looked up at him from the operations table, and stepped aside so he could see the readouts for himself.

Major Kira watched the station commander march down the steps into Ops, but took a moment to compose herself before following.

Bajor's lost religious leader, Kai Opaka, had told her that she had to move beyond her violent past, and she was trying to do that. She wanted to appear calm and reasonable. She wanted to appear as logical as a Vulcan.

For one thing, emotional pleas didn't seem very effective on the big, dark-skinned Earthman.

It was hard *not* to give in to emotion, though. Even the Kai would have seen that here. This was a return of the bad old days, and Kira had to fight to resist the bad old ways.

She was trying hard, but didn't seem to be able to make Sisko understand—her people were under attack. *Her* people, the rightful owners of this station, were being harassed by their old enemies, their former self-appointed masters, the people who had blithely killed any Bajoran who inconvenienced them.

This time the Cardassians weren't shooting anyone, they weren't landing, or taking slaves, or killing—yet.

But they were Cardassians. And they were back in Bajoran space. That was enough; that was intolerable.

Maybe the Federation thought a formal protest was

9

enough of a response, but Kira's entire upbringing told her otherwise. If the Cardassians weren't stopped *now,* it *would* take a full-scale war to stop them, she was sure of it. Just sitting back and letting them do as they pleased would only encourage them; only a show of force, strong enough that they would respect it without being intimidating enough to frighten them or destructive enough to anger them, would stop them.

The Bajoran provisional government wasn't doing a damn thing about it, of course; they just debated endlessly, going nowhere. Half of them were terrified that any action would bring the Cardassians back, and the other half didn't dare do anything without Federation support.

And meanwhile people were being hurt, both physically and spiritually.

She had to make Sisko see that. He was an Earthman, not a Bajoran, but there had to be some way to force him to understand how important this was. She had to convince him to bring in Federation starships.

This thing from the wormhole was just a distraction; the Cardassians were what mattered. The sooner the intruder was dealt with, the better.

Her expression artificially calm, she walked down the steps into Ops, a few paces behind Sisko.

CHAPTER
2

"TRACTOR BEAMS," Sisko ordered, as he watched the alien ship on the main viewer. "Bring it in."

"Sir, it's highly radioactive," Dax pointed out. She was back at her own station at the operations table.

"It should be safe enough at the end of upper docking pylon two," Sisko said. "Or would you rather we let it continue on into Cardassian space?"

Dax didn't answer; instead she tapped at the tractor-beam controls. Chief Miles O'Brien, alert but calm, and Dr. Julian Bashir, excited and nervous, had arrived in Ops a moment earlier; now both men watched over the Trill's shoulder, studying the readouts on the alien ship.

"Locked on," Dax reported. "Bringing it in. Still no signs of life or power aboard."

"This might be a trick," Kira said as she came up behind Sisko. "A trap of some kind."

"Oh?" Sisko said, turning.

"It might be a Cardassian construct," Kira insisted.

"Some sort of weapon or booby trap. And we're bringing it right here to the station. There could be something aboard—a tailored virus, even a simple bomb big enough to wreck the station, and if anyone protests *that,* the Cardassians will just shrug and say it's a part of the dangers out here. And meanwhile the wormhole and the entire Bajoran system will be sitting here unguarded, waiting for them to move in."

"And how would the Cardassians have managed this?" Sisko asked. "Dax saw that ship emerge from the wormhole; I doubt the Cardassians are operating munitions factories in Gamma Quadrant."

"But how do we *know* that they aren't?"

"Because we've watched every ship that's passed through, Major," Sisko replied wearily. "You know that as well as I do. And there certainly hasn't been time for any Cardassian ship to have reached the Gamma Quadrant *without* passing through the wormhole."

Since the Gamma Quadrant was at the far side of the galaxy, seventy years away in normal space for even the fastest starship, that was inarguable, but Major Kira did not look convinced, and Sisko suppressed a sigh.

She was obsessed with the Cardassians. That was hardly surprising, given her background, and usually she kept it under control, but during this latest crisis . . .

It would be helpful, Sisko thought, if they actually knew just what was going on in the Cardassian Empire that had prompted the raids into Bajoran space. The Cardassians had behaved themselves for months, after all, and now there were these sudden intrusions—not attacks, Major Kira's opinion notwithstanding, but what appeared to be searches of some kind. *Something* must have happened to cause them.

Rumors had reached *Deep Space Nine,* in the form of bits of talk over the subspace communication bands, or impressions picked up from passing travelers. There were the rumors, and a few fragmentary reports, but so far, despite requests for information from Starfleet, nothing more than that.

The reports and rumors were consistent, though. Some sort of political crisis was going on on Cardassia, and that was somehow responsible for the intrusions.

To Sisko it didn't seem to make much sense, but it all seemed to have started with the death of a rising young politician named Kag Duzek. Within hours of the first reports of his death there had been Cardassian ships cruising through Bajoran space, and before long they were approaching the Bajoran worlds in a series of ever-bolder incursions.

Starfleet had been informed immediately, and had promptly relayed what information they had in their computers that hadn't been classified as secret—but Sisko, after looking those transmissions over, was fairly certain no human being had bothered to look at them before they were sent, as they were so vague and incomplete as to be useless.

And beyond sending the data, Starfleet had as yet done nothing about the intrusions—and Major Kira blamed him, Commander Benjamin Sisko, Starfleet's local representative, for that inaction. She wanted him to stop the raids *now.*

Although just how he could do that, what she expected him to do . . .

His thoughts were interrupted by Dax.

"Docking complete, Commander. I've raised the

emergency blast shields around the airlock; the ship appears stable, but the radiation levels are *very* high."

"Good work, old man."

Sisko noticed Dax smiling slightly at that, and knew that it was because no one else on *Deep Space Nine* thought of her as anything but a young woman; only he had known her during her previous symbiosis.

"Commander, I'd like permission to board the alien vessel and take a look around," the Trill added.

Sisko glanced at her, startled.

"This is a great opportunity, sir," Dax explained. "That ship is our first contact with a new culture."

Sisko thought, but did not say, that at this particular station that was not especially unusual. This unique access to the Gamma Quadrant that the wormhole provided had already brought about several first contacts.

"It's also deadly, isn't it?" he said.

"Obviously, I will take all necessary precautions," she said.

Sisko supposed that Dax couldn't have lived for three centuries without learning some elementary caution. If any of them would be safe aboard the alien vessel, she would.

"Sir," O'Brien said, "I'd like to accompany Lieutenant Dax, if I may. The engineering on that ship . . ."

Sisko interrupted him, before he could complete the sentence, to ask, "Do we know for certain whether there's anything aboard, other than the radiation, that might be dangerous?"

"The sensors show no life-forms," Dax said, "but the radiation may be blocking our readings."

"And of course we have no way of knowing about any purely mechanical devices there might be," O'Brien added. "But all the same, sir . . ."

"There may be injured beings aboard," Dr. Bashir interrupted.

That decided it. "You will all wear full protective gear and carry phasers," Sisko said. "Stay together at all times; assume the ship is hostile."

"Yes, *sir!*" Dr. Bashir answered, smiling.

Sisko watched the three of them hurry to the transporter platform, Dax moving with calm grace, O'Brien with brisk efficiency, and Bashir with reckless speed, and he sighed. He glanced at Major Kira, but she was reading a display at the science station and showed no sign of resuming the argument this new arrival had interrupted.

That was just as well; it gave him a chance to do a little more research. He really needed to know what was going on on Cardassia, and his only solid clue was a single name that had cropped up twice in the Starfleet reports. Until now he had been too busy to check on it, but perhaps it was time to give it a higher priority.

He stepped to his own workstation at the operations table. There, with practiced ease, he brought up everything the station's computer had on file about Kag Duzek.

CHAPTER
3

THE SHIP'S DESIGN was completely unfamiliar, but Miles O'Brien thought he knew an emergency manual release when he saw it, and that was what he found just to the left of the airlock's outer door.

The airlock was built into a sort of niche in the ship's side in such a way that the outer hatch faced directly forward, oriented so that what appeared to be the top was pointed toward the ship's long axis, while the bottom was toward the ship's outer circumference. That, combined with the general shape and appearance of the vessel and the results of the scans he had run on it, had convinced O'Brien that the aliens did not have artificial gravity aboard, but instead had rotated the ship, so that centrifugal force would serve as an adequate substitute for gravity.

That was a fairly primitive solution to the problem, and in general the ship did not appear terribly advanced.

That was something of a disappointment; the possibility of discovering some major improvement on Federation technology was one of the lures of any first-contact work.

The door itself was low and wide, slanted forward, the sides sloping in to form a trapezoid; O'Brien had never quite figured out why so many starfaring races used trapezoidal doorways, but he had long ago become accustomed to it.

This particular doorway, though, was only a little over a meter high, and almost three meters wide at the bottom, which would obviously not suit humans at all; O'Brien therefore suspected that this vessel's builders had not been even remotely humanoid.

And whether they were humanoid or not in their general build, the grip on the emergency release certainly wasn't designed for human hands; a tentacle would have fit it better than the armored gauntlet of O'Brien's radiation suit.

He almost sprained his wrist discovering that the release ratcheted back and forth along a ninety-degree arc, rather than turning steadily, but after a moment he got the hang of cranking it. With each tug the door slid down, centimeter by centimeter, into its slot in the ship's blue ceramic outer hull.

When the seal first broke and the ship's atmosphere spilled into the station airlock, the temperature read-out at the top of O'Brien's faceplate almost immediately registered the rush of hot gas from the ship's own airlock, and alarm lights indicated toxic elements. His suit's climate control prevented him from feeling or smelling a thing, though; he had to rely on the gauges.

On the other hand, O'Brien thought he could almost feel Dr. Bashir's impatient breath on his back as he worked the lever. He knew that was impossible through their bulky protective suits, but the doctor's eagerness was *so* obvious that it was painful to see.

Someday, O'Brien thought, that lad is going to get himself killed if he doesn't learn to rein in his enthusiasm. He was like a cocker pup tripping over his own ears.

O'Brien paused to adjust his grip on the uncomfortable handle, and Dr. Bashir proceeded to duck down and squeeze head and shoulders through the narrow opening.

"Hey!" O'Brien protested.

Bashir paid him no attention whatsoever, and with a suppressed sigh O'Brien resumed cranking.

A moment later the three of them crouched in the airlock, unable to stand upright in the confined space; the chamber was unlit, and their own bodies blocked the light from the station's docking airlock, making it impossible to see the controls until O'Brien turned on the lamp on his helmet.

When he did, something whirred, and pinkish light sprang up. O'Brien glanced quickly at Dax.

She seemed unperturbed.

Dr. Bashir, however, started at the sudden illumination and stared about wildly.

"It seems that she's not totally dead," O'Brien remarked calmly.

"The sensors reported at least partial function in several systems," Dax replied.

"So I might've saved myself some work with that damned lever if I'd known what button to push," O'Brien said.

"Possibly," Dax acknowledged. "But your approach was unquestionably safer, Chief."

"But if the machinery is working, surely this must be the cycle control," Dr. Bashir called, pressing a large red button beside the inner door before either of the others could move to protest.

O'Brien bit off a shout as the outer door slid

upward, sealing them into the pink-lit chamber. The lad might well get *several* people killed, at this rate, but the damage was done, and there was no use in yelling at him, any more than there would be in yelling at a puppy. O'Brien unclipped his phaser from his tool belt and held it ready.

The airlock did seem to be cycling normally, but O'Brien couldn't resist commenting. "Dr. Bashir," he said, a bit wearily, "you're a doctor, not a first-contact specialist. It's quite obvious that you haven't met any of the galaxy's more paranoid inhabitants. Among the xenophobes of Darius Eleven, a big, obvious control like that is wired to an explosive of at least a ten-kiloton yield."

O'Brien watched through the faceplate as Bashir blinked, startled. "Really?" he said.

"I have heard that, Julian," Dax confirmed.

Something thumped, and machinery growled. Bashir turned back to the inner door as it began to descend. "Well," he said, "whoever built this ship wasn't quite so unfriendly as all that." He added, in a tone that was apologetic, "But I will try to be more careful in the future."

O'Brien noticed that this promise didn't hold Bashir back from bending down and stepping through into the ship's interior the moment the door had opened sufficiently. With another sigh, this one not suppressed at all, O'Brien followed.

The three of them straightened up in a broad passage, lit the same odd pink; the top of Bashir's helmet scraped the ceiling, startling him, while the corridor was easily five meters wide. The golden walls curved slightly; so did the floor and ceiling, but that was simply because of the ship's cylindrical design, while curving walls were more likely to be an aesthetic choice.

"Not designed for humanoids, I'd say," O'Brien said. He glanced at the nearest wall, then stopped and looked more closely.

Bashir and Dax were already moving down the passageway as O'Brien stepped up and stared at the tiny ripple in the corridor wall. He ran an armored finger along it, stopping at a spidery junction.

"Conduits," he said to himself. "Now, why would anyone put those out here, instead of inside the bulkheads?" He studied the bluish stud atop the junction, then took a step back and looked at the surrounding tracery of ridges in the material, ridges that were so small as to be almost invisible—unless one was looking for them.

Circuitry, plainly—but constructed in a way he had never seen before. And the pattern had something strange about it, something almost familiar—but not something from any technology he knew. . . .

At last he placed it: the circuits were arranged like the nerve cells in certain species.

An interesting design, certainly. He wondered how it would work—didn't it mean the ship's systems would operate in a nonlinear net? That would call for some tricky balancing in the data flow—in fact, thinking back, hadn't this been attempted long ago, and never made to work?

Whoever built this ship had made it work.

And O'Brien remembered now that this sort of design *had* been attempted, several times—because if it worked at all, it would be incredibly efficient, and would create computers capable of amazing feats. . . .

"Chief!" Dax called; O'Brien abandoned his study of the circuitry, turned, and hurried down the passage to rejoin the others.

* * *

A few moments later Dax and O'Brien watched silently as Bashir knelt over an inert alien, awkward in his heavy suit. Bashir held his tricorder in one heavy glove, while the armored fingers of the other hand pressed gently against the pseudo-crustacean's ugly purple flesh.

The chamber they were in was tilted at an uncomfortable angle; DS9's artificial gravity did not match the ship's no-longer-present centrifugal force.

"It's dead," Bashir said at last, stepping back slightly. "I'd say it's probably been dead for two or three days, though it's hard to be sure with something so unfamiliar. If there were some sort of preservation in use, it could have been much longer."

O'Brien looked at the thing, trying not to be relieved that it was dead. He had dealt with aliens for all his adult life, including some that were fairly repulsive, and he thought he had gotten over this sort of reaction, but this creature looked unusually nasty.

It was vaguely crablike, with half a dozen barbed and jointed legs that would presumably have supported its body when it was alive, and with a row of manipulative members along the front of its torso that resembled forked tentacles with elbows in them. Four black pits arranged above the manipulators were apparently eyes, or the equivalent.

The low, wide shape of the thing would fit the corridors and doorways well; it seemed a safe bet that this was the species that had designed the ship, and not some interloper that had acquired it later.

"It appears to have died of asphyxiation," Dr. Bashir added, as an afterthought.

Dax considered that, then asked, "What atmosphere did it require, Julian?"

Bashir frowned through his faceplate at his

tricorder. "Hydrogen-methane, mostly—and before you ask, that's exactly what's all around us."

"Then what killed it?" O'Brien asked. "Did someone smother it? Where's its nose, or its mouth?"

"It appears to have breathed through spiracles along either side," Bashir said. "Fourteen in all. I admit I don't quite see how anyone could block all of them without a great deal of struggle."

"I see no sign of a struggle," Dax said, looking about the room.

O'Brien looked about as well.

The place was so alien he really couldn't say whether there was any sign of a struggle or not. Nothing was obviously out of position, but since he couldn't tell what half the objects in the room were, that didn't mean much. The short red cylinders along one wall were all still in a neat row, and must be held in place somehow; the tangled black tubes that were spilling from a thing like a square bucket appeared to have been affected only by the room's angle.

But were those two flat brown disks supposed to be on the floor? If not, had they fallen with the shift in gravity, or had something flung them?

Was that octagonal panel in one wall supposed to be open? Were those things behind it where they should be, whatever they were?

What *had* killed the alien? Was whatever had killed it still aboard?

"Let's move on," O'Brien said.

Bashir looked to Dax; she didn't answer, but simply walked on.

A few moments later they found the ship's bridge—at least, O'Brien assumed that it was the bridge. There were control panels and viewscreens in sufficient numbers for a ship's bridge, recognizable despite their alien construction—and their arrangement suggested to O'Brien that he had been right about the ship's computer design.

This room happened to be the right way up, which was convenient—and which also implied that it might be important, a place that would be used both in flight and when the ship had landed.

There was another dead alien here, of the same vaguely crablike species as the first—though this one had dark green speckles on its purple integument that the other had not possessed.

Bashir had his tricorder ready and working before anyone could say a word.

"Asphyxiation again," he said.

Dax looked at O'Brien. "Could there have been a life-support failure, perhaps?"

O'Brien frowned and glanced at his helmet readouts. The air was hydrogen and methane and while it would be deadly poison to anything human—or Trill—the pressure certainly seemed adequate, and it should be capable of supporting the sort of life these crab things appeared to be.

Some of the other readings, though, were far less hopeful. "Doctor," O'Brien said, "are you *sure* they asphyxiated? Might it have been radiation poisoning?"

"Well, it might be, I suppose," Bashir admitted, considering the suggestion. "I don't know that much about the species, and perhaps hard radiation breaks down the gas-transport capability of their circulatory fluids. I see no tissue degeneration, however, and that's a symptom of radiation sickness in most species."

"The air in here seems just fine," O'Brien said. Then he hastily explained, "I mean, for them it's fine, it'd kill any of the three of us dead as mackerel in half a minute. But that's chemically—as far as radiation goes, it's toxic soup. We're taking a few hundred rems every minute, or we would be if we weren't in these suits." O'Brien shook his head. "Not a healthy environment for much of anyone—but it's not breathin' that would be hard."

"There *are* species that thrive in radioactive environments," Dax pointed out.

"I don't think this particular species was one of them," Bashir remarked.

O'Brien didn't reply; instead he glanced about, looking for some clue to the mysteries here, and spotted something he recognized.

This ship might represent an alien technology, and might be designed for a nonhumanoid species, but there were always *some* things that translated readily; the illuminated diagram on the big panel on the starboard bulkhead was unquestionably a ship's status display. O'Brien knelt and studied it.

Those blue lines, he figured, indicated power flow, and the thicker red lines would be ventilation—those all looked clear enough. That structure that ran down the ship's core, widening at the stern, would be the main engine, which he knew from the ship's sensor signature to be a high-energy ion drive capable of pushing the ship to relativistic speeds, but not faster than light—these crab things did not appear to have warp-drive technology, or at any rate not any sort O'Brien was familiar with.

Those green patches on the drive—would these fellows use green to indicate danger? Something about the color scheme he had seen so far suggested to him that they would.

If so, then there was something seriously wrong with the ship's main engines.

Sometimes when things went seriously wrong with ships' engines, things exploded. If that happened here it could damage the station—not to mention killing the three of them if they were still aboard.

O'Brien traced the passages on the diagram with a gloved finger, then stood up.

"Come on," he said.

The ship's primary power source was a primitive fission pile, and all the damper rods had been pulled —O'Brien could only assume that this had been sabotage.

The saboteur, however, had been foiled by a backup safety system: when the pile had begun to go critical, the heat had melted through a simple device like an old-fashioned fuse, and a set of spring-loaded emergency damping plates had slid into place, cutting off the reaction before it could reach the point of either complete meltdown or explosion.

That had kept the ship from exploding, but it had been too late to prevent the initial burst of hard radiation from saturating the vessel and reducing it to its current lethal state.

A third dead alien was in the power room, but well away from the pile controls; O'Brien had no way of determining whether this was the saboteur who had wrecked the pile, or just an innocent bystander.

This room, like the bridge, was along the ship's underside and therefore still the right way up.

It was also horrifyingly radioactive. The levels that their suit gauges registered here were several times what the three explorers had encountered on the bridge.

"We'll want to beam out, straight to decontamination," O'Brien remarked. "We can't walk through the station corridors in our suits after coming in here." He looked at his helmet readouts again, and winced at what he saw. Even their armored suits wouldn't protect them indefinitely against radiation levels as high as this. "Our friends in the wormhole probably didn't appreciate having this thing come through," he added.

"I don't know if simple radioactivity bothers them," Dax said.

"Well, it bothers *me,*" O'Brien said. "We'll want to have this whole vessel decontaminated, and this power pile should just be junked. The fuel rods are beyond salvaging." He looked around the room, noting the tracery of circuits built into the walls here, just as it had been elsewhere in the ship—a very interesting technique, that was, especially with the Besrethine neural-net design. "It'll be a pleasure to see just how these things work, though. These folks may not have been much on drive technology, but if this computer system works the way I think it does, the Daystrom Institute is going to be very, very interested."

"And these remains . . . they're fascinating!" Bashir said, studying the dead alien. "I've never seen a species like them. I can't wait to study them properly, in a decent laboratory, with real instruments and without this suit!"

"That may not be possible," Dax said, with a glance at her helmet readouts. She tapped her communicator.

Sisko listened intently as Dax described what the boarding party had found aboard the derelict.

"No surviving crew members?" he asked.

"No, sir," Dax replied. "Three dead; no trace of anything alive."

"Any hint at all of Cardassian handiwork?" Sisko glanced sideways at Kira as he asked that question; she looked boldly back at him, unfazed.

"No, sir," Dax replied. "If the Cardassians are

responsible for any of this, they're far more clever than we've ever thought, and capable of far more than we believe."

Sisko nodded.

"Another thing, Benjamin," Dax added. "O'Brien points out that the computer system aboard this vessel is a radically different design from anything we're familiar with, something called a Besrethine neural net, that neither the Federation nor the Cardassians has ever made work. If the Cardassians had developed such a system, Chief O'Brien is certain they would never let it fall into our hands."

O'Brien cut in.

"Commander, if this computer is what I think it is, it's not only not Cardassian, but we'd better be damn sure that the Cardassians don't get their hands on it!"

"Interesting," Sisko said. "You think this design would be valuable, then?"

"And dangerous!" O'Brien said.

"Definitely valuable, Benjamin," Dax said, reasserting herself. "Chief O'Brien believes it could jump Federation computer technology ahead a hundred years, and I concur."

"Excellent," Sisko said. "Are you planning to look around further? We can manage a little longer out here. . . ."

"No, Benjamin," Dax replied. "We're reaching the limits of what our protective suits can handle. I'm calling instead of reporting in person because we need to be beamed directly to decontamination."

"I'll take care of it. Sisko out." He turned to Kira, who stepped to the transporter controls before he could speak.

"So the crew is all dead?" she asked, as she set the coordinates.

"Apparently," Sisko replied.

"Then the ship's recovery would be covered by salvage law, wouldn't it?" she mused aloud. "And O'Brien thinks the computer design might be valuable."

"We can hardly claim it for ourselves, Major . . ."

She looked up at him, startled, as the transporter hummed. "Not for *us,* Commander," she said. "For *Bajor.*"

CHAPTER
4

SISKO AND KIRA were still arguing as O'Brien and Dax appeared on the Ops transporter pad, freshly arrived from decontamination, their protective suits removed.

"We must make every attempt to return that ship to its rightful owners," Sisko insisted. "The design of that computer is the intellectual property of the ship's builders, and while I hope they'll share it with us, we have no right to steal it."

"That ship is a derelict, Commander, and under interstellar law it's the property of whoever salvages it—which is exactly what we did," Kira replied. "This is a Bajoran station, and that means that ship belongs to the people of Bajor. If that computer design is valuable, then it's an asset of the Bajoran people!"

O'Brien and Dax exchanged bemused glances, then took their places at the Ops table—neither one cared to interrupt the debate.

Scant moments later, Dax looked up from her

screen and announced, "Benjamin, a Cardassian warship is approaching the station."

Sisko and Kira had closed upon each other until
they were mere inches apart, arguing intently without
shouting; now both turned, startled, to look at Dax.

"What kind of ship?" Kira asked. "One of the
raiders?" She looked challengingly at Sisko.

"No, this is a Galor-class cruiser," Dax replied.
"None of the intrusions were by ships that large.
Benjamin, it's hailing us."

"Let's see what they want," Sisko said. "On
viewer."

The image of a smiling Cardassian face appeared on
the main screen, and as Sisko had half-expected, he
was facing the former prefect of Bajor, Gul Dukat—
Dukat still seemed to consider any contact between
the Cardassian Empire and *Deep Space Nine,* which
had once been his headquarters, to be his particular
concern.

Dukat had *probably* not been among the raiders—
certainly, not in this ship.

But Sisko couldn't be sure Dukat wasn't involved
somehow.

Except for their oddly shaped and corded faces and
somewhat heavier musculature, Cardassians were
very similar to humans, and a smile meant the same
thing among Cardassians as among most humanoids;
nonetheless, Sisko did not smile back.

"Gul Dukat," he said. "What brings you to *Deep
Space Nine?* I don't suppose you're here to apologize
for the recent intrusions?"

Gul Dukat smiled his familiar toothy and insincere
smile. "My, what a friendly greeting. What intrusions
could you be talking about?"

"Seven of them, so far," Kira said. "Cardassian

ships making low-altitude passes over Bajor and Bajoran settlements."

"Oh, dear, how very unfortunate," Dukat murmured. He smiled again. "However, that is not what brought me here."

"Oh?" Sisko said.

"I believe you have something there that isn't yours—that *ship* on upper pylon two."

"There is an alien vessel docked at upper two," Sisko admitted warily.

"Ah! You've noticed," Dukat said. "And did you notice, perhaps, that this vessel was on its way to Cardassia? It *was*, I am reliably informed, on a direct route for Cardassian space when you, ah, *diverted* it, with a tractor beam. One of our border patrols happened to observe the whole thing."

"I'm afraid, Gul Dukat," Sisko said, "that you're wasting your time. The ship is apparently a derelict that fell into the wormhole; the crew is dead, the drive wrecked. We simply removed a hazard to navigation."

"How very *thoughtful* of you, Commander! But surely, we Cardassians could have handled that chore, if you hadn't interfered."

"What's your point?" Sisko asked wearily.

"My point, Commander," Dukat said, his manner suddenly turning harsh, "is that to the casual observer, it might appear that you and your tractor beam *stole* this ship as it emerged from the wormhole, by taking it to your station without the permission of the ship's rightful owners."

"Stole it?"

Gul Dukat nodded. "Oh, yes, a blatant theft. You say there was no one aboard it—it seems to me, in that case, that its original course would indicate that

31

the ship's owners clearly intended their ship to be a gift to the Cardassian people."

"The crew was aboard, Gul Dukat, but they were dead," Sisko said. "As to their intentions . . ."

"Commander, I don't really care what their intentions were," Gul Dukat said, cutting him off. "I want you to release that ship and let me take it. If you don't release it, I regret to say that I shall be forced to take it anyway, regardless of whatever damage to your precious station that may involve. I haven't yet locked my ship's phasers on that pylon—it's not too late to be reasonable and keep this peaceful."

"You have odd ideas of what constitutes peaceful behavior, Gul Dukat," Sisko said.

"And you have ten seconds to decide," Dukat replied.

Sisko glared silently at the viewer; Gul Dukat glared back.

"Dukat must want that derelict pretty badly," Kira said quietly.

"If he knows about those computers, I don't blame him," O'Brien muttered in reply. "But I don't see how he could possibly know."

"He probably doesn't," Kira answered bitterly. "He just saw a chance to take something away from us."

"Benjamin," Dax interrupted, "a second Cardassian ship is approaching. Another cruiser."

"Bringing up reinforcements?" Sisko said. "Really, Gul Dukat, that was hardly necessary."

"Reinforcements?" Gul Dukat glanced to the side, at something not visible on Sisko's viewer. "Would you excuse me for a moment, Commander?"

The viewer went blank.

"What the . . ." Sisko began.

"Benjamin," Dax said, "the new arrival is hailing Gul Dukat."

"What do you suppose *that's* about?" Sisko asked. Kira shrugged.

"Gul Dukat is refusing the contact," Dax reported. "Now the other ship is readying phasers. . . ."

"Shields up," Sisko snapped.

"Shields up, sir," O'Brien said.

"Benjamin, it's locking phasers on Gul Dukat's ship," Dax said.

"What the devil?" O'Brien said. "What's going on out there?"

"Keep those shields up," Sisko said. "This could be a trick—and even if it isn't, we could get caught in the crossfire." He glanced at Kira.

"Now the other ship is hailing us," Dax announced. "Now *both* ships are."

"Put them on, split-screen," Sisko ordered.

Gul Dukat's image appeared on the left, and another Cardassian's on the right—for a moment, Sisko had wondered whether perhaps the second ship was not in Cardassian hands at all, but whoever was in command there was certainly Cardassian in appearance, both species and uniform.

"Commander," the new arrival said, "I am Gul Kaidan, military deputy to Kag Leghuris. It would seem that you may be in possession of a piece of property that rightfully belongs to the Cardassian Empire."

"So Gul Dukat was just telling us," Sisko replied. "I'm afraid I found his arguments unconvincing." He glanced at Dukat, then back at Kaidan.

"Gul Dukat," Gul Kaidan said, "was acting without the authority of the Imperial Council."

"Oh, come now, Gul Kaidan," Dukat replied. "Surely, one need not have advance authorization to counter an act of piracy?"

"No one has committed piracy," Sisko protested.

33

"This station, in accordance with all relevant agreements, intercepted a derelict ship in Bajoran space in order to remove a hazard to navigation."

"I notice, however," Gul Dukat said, somehow giving the impression of a sneer without actually displaying one, "that you did not simply destroy this unwanted object."

"I will not apologize for our scientific curiosity," Sisko answered calmly. "Also, we were uncertain at first that there were no survivors aboard, and acted in part from humanitarian motives."

"Ah, the vaunted Federation humanitarianism," Gul Dukat said. "Well, now that you've seen that there are no survivors, perhaps you would be so kind as to turn the ship over to me?"

"Under no circumstances are you to do that, Commander," Gul Kaidan replied immediately. "That ship is the property of the Cardassian government, and *I* am the representative of that government! Gul Dukat is acting independently, and without authority."

"I see," Sisko said. "And you, Gul Kaidan, carry the necessary authority? If I establish a subspace link with Cardassia, the government there will confirm that you are empowered to negotiate this claim?"

Kaidan's firm expression faltered, and Gul Dukat smiled.

"I am an officer in the Imperial government," Gul Kaidan replied.

"As am I," Gul Dukat said mildly.

"I was assigned to my present duties by the Imperial Council," Gul Kaidan insisted. "Gul Dukat is acting independently."

"But neither of you has actually been authorized to claim this ship?" Sisko asked.

"Gul Kaidan's present duties, Commander," Gul

Dukat said, "consist largely of spying on me. I doubt very much that his masters back on Cardassia thought to say, 'Oh, by the way, if you happen across a hijacked ship, do reclaim it for us.' He is, in short, bluffing."

"I hold a higher position in the Empire than you, Gul Dukat. . . ."

"At the moment, perhaps, but my record . . ."

"Gentlemen," Sisko said sharply, "surely you see that under the circumstances, I cannot turn the ship over to *either* of you."

Both Cardassians considered that for a second or two.

"Indeed," Gul Kaidan said. "If I have your assurance, Commander, that you will not release that ship to this arrogant fool . . ."

"You needn't trouble yourself, Gul Kaidan," Gul Dukat interrupted. "If you would be so kind as to power down your ship's weapons, so that I may be assured I won't be ambushed, I'll be going. It's plain that your arrival has provided just the sort of complication our dear Commander Sisko needs to ensure that he can keep that prize of his just where it is. However, Commander, I trust that you will see that no one, Cardassian or otherwise, boards that ship until the little matter of its ownership is settled?"

"That should be possible," Sisko acknowledged warily.

"Then for now, I will leave it as a matter for our respective governments to resolve."

Gul Dukat's image abruptly vanished from the viewer.

Gul Kaidan turned aside for a moment, and muttered something the listeners aboard *Deep Space Nine* could not make out; then he turned back to Sisko.

"Now, Commander," Gul Kaidan said, "if you would turn that ship over to me, I'm sure . . ."

"Gul Kaidan," Sisko interrupted, "I'm sure you heard what I said. I cannot release that ship to *anyone* until the question of its ownership is resolved."

"Gul Kaidan's ship has powered down its weapons, Benjamin," Dax said.

"A friendly warning, Commander," Gul Kaidan said. "While the Cardassian Empire appreciates your thoughtfulness in keeping the traffic routes clear of debris, anything of value aboard that ship *is* the property of the Empire. Any attempt to appropriate it will be dealt with quite severely."

"I thank you for the warning," Sisko said. He looked up at the viewer, resentful of being on the defensive—capturing the ship had been a harmless and proper thing to do. It was the Cardassians who had been misbehaving lately, and Sisko intended to point that out.

Sisko didn't know this Gul Kaidan, however. Apparently he was in a position of some authority—the Cardassian Empire did not hand out Galor-class warships to just anyone—but Gul Dukat had clearly not considered Gul Kaidan to be in a position to give him orders. Sisko was therefore not certain just how seriously to take anything Gul Kaidan said; *was* he a representative of the Cardassian government?

And what in the galaxy was going on here, anyway? Cardassian ships threatening to fire on each other? Did this connect to the intrusions somehow?

"Gul Dukat's ship is leaving," Dax reported.

Whether Gul Kaidan was, in fact, connected to the intruders had some relevance to how Sisko wanted to address him—but Sisko didn't know if such a connection existed.

Fortunately, since every Cardassian he had ever

met seemed to appreciate deadpan sarcasm, to the point where Sisko suspected it was an essential part of Cardassian culture, phrasing his reply to this "friendly warning" was not difficult. Whether the Cardassian chose to interpret it as subtle irony or a simple polite statement was up to him.

"I hope you won't think it rude," he said, "if I mention that some of your compatriots have been anything but friendly lately—and I do not refer to Gul Dukat's visit."

"Why, whatever do you mean, then?" the Cardassian asked, with eyebrows raised.

"Perhaps this should go through more formal diplomatic channels," Sisko said, "but there have been several . . . *incidents* of late. Unwelcome intrusions into Bajoran space by Cardassian ships."

"Oh, have there?" The Cardassian feigned surprise. "I hadn't heard. How very alarming! Please, Commander, do tell me more."

Sisko's face was utterly expressionless as he stared silently at the main viewscreen, betraying nothing of his rushing thoughts.

Sisko was certain that Kaidan wanted something other than the derelict, or he wouldn't still be here— he would either have kept arguing, or have left as soon as Gul Dukat did. In Sisko's experience Cardassians never did anything unless they expected to gain from it somehow. Kaidan's visit raised many questions, and the first question Sisko wanted answered was just what this particular Cardassian wanted.

And once he knew that, Sisko would worry about whether Kaidan should be permitted to have whatever it was he had come for.

There had not been time yet for word of the derelict's arrival to have reached Cardassia, and a ship sent out; both Gul Dukat and Gul Kaidan must have already been in the area. Therefore, the derelict was *not* what had brought them.

Sisko was sure now that there was some connection between Kaidan's presence and the earlier hit-and-run raids—or rather, intrusions; he would have to remember that officially they weren't really raids, as no weapons were fired, no plunder taken. Kaidan's ignorance was blatantly false—as if he *wanted* Sisko to know it was a lie.

But why?

Did Kaidan really want the derelict? How could he possibly know whether it was valuable? Sisko himself had only just learned that O'Brien thought the onboard computers were something special; Gul Kaidan simply couldn't have known that, not unless ships like this had appeared before, and been captured by the Cardassians.

And if they had, then the Cardassians would have already *had* the computer technology that O'Brien was so enthusiastic about. That couldn't be it.

So Gul Kaidan's interest in the derelict was probably just a matter of making sure that Gul Dukat didn't get it.

What was going on in the Cardassian Empire that had these officers at each other's throats?

"I find myself somewhat confused, Gul Kaidan," Sisko said. "I had thought that the Empire kept a watchful eye on its subordinates."

"Ordinarily it does, Commander," Kaidan agreed. "The situation just now, however, is far from ordinary."

"Perhaps we could discuss this situation, then," Sisko suggested, fishing for more information.

"I would be delighted, Commander," the Cardassian replied, once again smiling. "But surely, not over an open channel like this."

That was it—that was why Gul Kaidan was lying so obviously. The Cardassian wanted an invitation to a private discussion.

That was intriguing.

"Of course not," Sisko agreed. "If you'd care to come aboard the station, perhaps we could speak somewhere more congenial."

"I accept your kind invitation, Commander," Kaidan said. "If you could provide the transport coordinates . . ."

"Of course." Sisko nodded to O'Brien, who had observed the conversation with interest.

"Yes, sir," O'Brien said. He stepped over to the transporter control panel.

Sisko, watching him, thought O'Brien seemed displeased about something—perhaps allowing a Cardassian on the station, perhaps that Sisko had agreed not to allow anyone aboard the strange ship with its fascinating computers.

The ship would just have to wait. It didn't pose any immediate danger as long as no one went near it.

A Cardassian warship, on the other hand, was *always* an immediate danger.

CHAPTER
5

THE CARDASSIAN COMMANDER seemed oddly reluctant when Sisko suggested that they might speak in his office.

Well, Sisko thought, there was no harm in humoring the fellow, and his son Jake would be in Keiko O'Brien's schoolroom down on the Promenade for another hour or more. "An office seems so formal, though," he said. "Perhaps we'd be more comfortable in my quarters."

The Cardassian brightened. "Ah, that would be fine, Commander."

A moment later they settled into chairs, Sisko with a mug of coffee, Kaidan with a Cardassian brew that smelled to Sisko like some unholy mix of lime and onion.

Sisko noted wryly that judging by Gul Kaidan's expression after his first sip of his drink, the station's Cardassian-built replicators seemed to do no better with that stuff than they did with coffee.

"Gul Kaidan," Sisko said, after a second or two of polite silence, keeping his tone quite friendly, "I find it hard to believe that you know nothing at all of the recent incursions into Bajoran space."

The Cardassian smiled over his cup. He looked about the room before answering, then remarked, "This seems a rather spartan accommodation, Commander—but at least it's private, eh?"

Sisko considered that. Private? Just who did Kaidan think might be listening in, either in the station commander's office or aboard the Cardassian's own ship?

"Private enough," he said.

Kaidan put down his cup. "One can never be too careful," he said.

"I take it, Gul Kaidan, that you have some reason to be concerned about privacy?"

"Oh, well, in these unsettled times . . ." He made an odd gesture with one hand that Sisko judged to be the Cardassian equivalent of a shrug.

"I have, of course, noticed that there seem to be some difficulties occurring within the Cardassian Empire," Sisko said. "And just what is it that has so unsettled matters, Gul Kaidan?"

"I would have thought you would have heard, even here," Kaidan replied.

Heard what? Sisko thought that over.

Somehow, Sisko had come to doubt that honesty was the best policy when dealing with Cardassians. Certainly other Cardassians didn't seem to think much of the direct approach. Bluffing would be preferable, but given how little he actually knew Sisko couldn't see how to manage it.

He decided that he would have to do his best at mixing fact and fiction. "If you refer to the death of

Kag Duzek," he said, "naturally, we are aware of it. However, the connection to recent events eludes me."

The station's computer records had been of very limited assistance on this subject; Sisko had learned something of Kag Duzek's family background and early career, that he had belonged to one of the political factions currently out of power, but no more than that.

"Oh, come, Commander," Kaidan said. "Surely you know that Kag Duzek had been named as the Goran Tokar's heir?"

Sisko let none of his confusion show on his face. He steepled his fingers and nodded thoughtfully.

Who the devil was the Goran Tokar? The name was vaguely familiar, and Sisko had the impression that a Goran was a high-ranking official in the Cardassian hierarchy, but beyond that either his memory or his education failed him. Why was Kag Duzek's connection to him, her, or it supposed to explain anything? What did it have to do with intrusions into Bajoran space, or preventing Gul Dukat from stealing the derelict ship?

"And just how does this bring *you* here, Gul Kaidan?" Sisko asked.

Kaidan smiled in that charmingly insincere way that so many Cardassians seemed to have. "Naturally, you would not know my own political affiliations," Kaidan acknowledged. "I'm told that Gul Dukat's people were fairly thorough in erasing this station's records."

Actually, the erasure had been very spotty, but that was hardly something Sisko would admit to a Cardassian. Virtually everything about Cardassian internal politics was gone, however, so the erasure might as well have been complete as far as this particular discussion went.

Sisko nodded noncommittally.

"As anyone who knows me will attest, Commander," Kaidan said, "I have always supported the policies of the current administration. I have, in fact, pinned my hopes of advancement on that fact. As a fellow political appointee, I'm sure you'll appreciate that."

"My own appointment was not political," Sisko objected quietly.

"Oh, come," Kaidan said. *"All* appointments are political, surely. You were sent here prior to the discovery of the wormhole, as I recall—perhaps you have enemies in the bureaucracy? And the wormhole has given you an opportunity to turn the tables on them, has it not?"

This was fascinating; the Cardassian was clearly reading his own experience into Sisko's situation. "I take it the wormhole has stirred up your own administration," Sisko said, neither denying nor admitting anything.

"Well, naturally," Gul Kaidan acknowledged. "We abandoned Bajor as worthless, and to have this resource of incalculable value found here almost as soon as we had left—of course there was some political damage. We face challenges now from two competing factions that, frankly, were not serious threats before the discovery of the wormhole."

"I see," Sisko said, steepling his fingers. "And Gul Dukat has affiliated himself with one of those other factions?"

"Gul Dukat," Gul Kaidan said venomously, "is a rank opportunist, who has refused to commit himself on any side, as yet."

Sisko nodded. "I take it you believe he intends to exploit the political damage the wormhole has caused, while you're here to try to repair some of that political damage?"

"Rather, I hope to prevent any further deterioration," the Cardassian answered. "If I could demonstrate, for example, that we will still receive benefits from the wormhole's presence, such as that ship you have, without the cost of maintaining this station, that would go quite some distance toward consolidating our political position."

"I see," Sisko said again.

"Or if I could prove that the ship is worthless, that might serve to quiet a few voices in the opposition," Kaidan said. "Our major weakness is that we are seen as having given up something of great value; if we could imply that it is, in fact, not valuable at all, that would serve us as well." He smiled. "I speak frankly, Commander, because I hope you will help us to retain our dominant position in the Empire."

"Oh?" Sisko frowned. "Why would you expect me to help you?"

"Really, Commander, I should think it would be to your benefit if my party remains in power."

"Oh?"

"Certainly. If our rivals come to power, war is virtually assured, and if there is war, the glory will go to the ship captains and the fleet admirals, not to you or this station; if there is peace, surely a successful regime here can serve as a stepping-stone to higher office."

He smiled.

"Surely," he said, "you don't want a war?"

CHAPTER
6

THE OPEN MENTION of the possibility of war was startling. Sisko had wondered whether the Cardassian intrusions—including Gul Dukat's attempt at strong-arm robbery—might be a deliberate attempt to start a war, and perhaps they were, but Kaidan's words implied that it wasn't the current Cardassian administration that was behind it, that Kaidan himself wanted peace.

That was a relief. Sisko had had a bellyful of war long ago. "And what is it you want of me, then?" he asked. "Do you expect me to simply hand over an alien artifact?"

"It would be helpful," Gul Kaidan said.

"It would set an intolerable precedent," Sisko replied.

"Ah," Gul Kaidan said. "And if we simply took it, as Gul Dukat proposed to do? I don't doubt that my ship has the firepower to overwhelm this station's defenses."

"I don't doubt it, either," Sisko said, "but that would, of course, mean war between the Empire and the Federation. Would you really start a war over a worthless relic?"

"Ah," Gul Kaidan said, "but *would* it start a war?"

Sisko noticed that he didn't ask whether the relic was really worthless—an indication, perhaps, of just where Gul Kaidan's interests really lay? He seemed far more concerned with broad issues of war and peace than with obtaining the derelict.

"The Federation has promised to defend this station, as well as the Bajoran system," Sisko pointed out.

"Against intrusions of every sort, yes," Gul Kaidan said.

The words stung; so far, the Federation had done nothing about the half-dozen raids into the Bajoran system, and both Sisko and the Cardassian knew it.

"Against serious breaches of the peace, yes," Sisko said. "A response to the recent intrusions is under consideration."

"But it's not definite?"

"What are you getting at, Gul Kaidan?"

"I am suggesting," Gul Kaidan said, "that the Federation might be too busy to worry about the loss of this station—that they might not think it worth an all-out war."

"Are you willing to risk that for a worthless artifact?" Sisko asked. "That ship doesn't even have warp drive."

"That ship," Gul Kaidan said, "represents all the potential treasures that the wormhole could be delivering into Cardassian hands—and whichever faction delivers it to Cardassia will be demonstrating their ability to acquire those treasures."

"And if you propose to take it in any case," Sisko

asked, "why does it matter to us which faction takes it?"

"Because, Commander," Gul Kaidan replied, *"my* people would use it to support our argument that we can obtain everything we want from the Bajoran system without fighting for it, while the *D'ja Bajora Karass* would argue that it proves we should reoccupy Bajor."

Sisko blinked. That was not what he had expected.

"Reoccupy?" he asked.

Kaidan nodded.

"That *would* mean war," Sisko said. "It would be a disaster for everyone."

"So my faction maintains," Kaidan agreed. "The opposition argues otherwise." He glanced about, then leaned forward and said quietly, "I thought perhaps you might be able to assure me that the Federation will, indeed, go to war if we make any attempt to reoccupy Bajor." He added, "I understand, of course, the Federation's *official* position."

At least it was now plain why Kaidan had come in person and insisted on speaking in private—he could hardly expect Sisko to vary from the official position in public. He was hoping that here in private, Sisko would tell him the truth.

Sisko wished he knew the truth himself. He *thought* the Federation's official position was sincere, but resources were stretched thin, the Romulan threat was always there . . .

"I think you will see that it is in both our interests to establish beyond question that the Federation is genuinely determined to defend Bajor," Kaidan said. "And since the present administration on Cardassia may be forced to yield power at any time, so that I cannot guarantee that no attempt will be made to reoccupy, you would not be wise to attempt a bluff.

That could easily hurt us both. A true exchange of insight here could give us both a reputation for prescience that could be quite valuable."

Sisko nodded. "I see that," he said.

"The ship is not important, if it's truly valueless," Kaidan said. "We are served equally well by its possession or its worthlessness, so long as our opponents are unable to capitalize upon it. Give it to me, or destroy it, as you please—but you must not let it fall into the hands of the *D'ja Bajora Karass* or the Revanche Party. Either group could use its capture for propaganda."

"We have no intention of turning it over to anyone," Sisko said.

"And what do you intend to do?" Kaidan looked at him expectantly.

Sisko thought this through carefully.

The ship was, as he had thought, an excuse—this Gul Kaidan was concerned with the political situation on Cardassia, not with possible profits.

But what did Sisko know of the political situation?

Kag Duzek had reportedly died in a sudden disagreement that had turned violent—apparently a personal matter involving a female who had previous attachments elsewhere. Duzek had been active in a political faction opposed to the present policies of the Cardassian government, and his death had seemingly triggered a series of intrusions into Bajoran space.

Now this Gul Kaidan had turned up, claiming to side with the Cardassian government, implying that the intrusions were the actions of the opposing faction, looking for assurance that the Federation would defend Bajor, and arguing that the derelict might wind up as a political tool.

Sisko hoped that Kaidan was telling the truth, and

this wasn't all an elaborate setup to lure Starfleet into some sort of trap.

He also wished he knew more of just what the Federation actually *would* do in the face of Cardassian aggression—the latest reports had been less definite than Sisko might have liked, and as yet there was no word on any direct response to the recent intrusions. That implied that some people back on Earth might not be very enthusiastic about defending Bajor.

But they were committed to do so, and the Federation kept its promises.

Kag Duzek, Kaidan had said, had been the heir to someone called the Goran Tokar. Kaidan took it for granted that the connection between this and the intrusions, and the political crisis, was obvious.

Sisko could guess at the connection, but he wanted it verified.

"Your pardon, Gul Kaidan," he said, "but I would like to be certain I understand. The recent violations of Bajoran space—am I to take it that these were made by people vying for Kag Duzek's position?"

"Of course," Kaidan answered, startled. "Though of course, this is all unofficial and off the record, and I hope this room is as private as you believe it is. The Goran Tokar has argued all along that we gave up Bajor too readily, that there are surely undiscovered resources here that we abandoned because we were too easily deterred by the Bajoran terrorists—he used the fact that the Bajorans had somehow successfully hidden one of those 'Celestial Orbs' of theirs from us as evidence that there could be assets we had missed. The Goran Tokar is a sick old man, with no family, and now with no heir; the person who brings him proof that he was right stands a good chance of being named as his successor, which would mean inheriting

a considerable estate, as well as the leadership of the
D'ja Bajora Karass, in the not too distant future."

"The *D'ja Bajora Karass?* You've mentioned that
three or four times now, and I'm afraid I don't know
the term."

"An approximate translation would be the 'Bajor Is
Ours' Party," Gul Kaidan replied.

Sisko nodded.

This explained the deep sensor scans the Cardassian intruders had been running—they had been
searching for those untapped resources that the Goran
Tokar believed in.

Finding them would surely be a potent weapon in
the political conflict.

"You think that Gul Dukat is hoping to become the
Goran Tokar's heir?" Sisko asked.

"He's one of the four leading candidates," Gul
Kaidan replied.

That made sense—and explained why Gul Dukat
had tried to claim the ship from the Gamma Quadrant. Dukat, who had served as prefect of Bajor and
supervised the final searches for resources before the
Cardassian withdrawal, knew as well as anyone that
no such resources existed—he had tied *his* bid for the
Goran Tokar's legacy to claiming resources from the
wormhole, instead.

"And proof of overlooked resources would also
further damage your own party's standing," Sisko
suggested.

"Exactly," Gul Kaidan said. "Such a discovery
combined with the presence of a strong new leader
among the *D'ja Bajora Karass* could provide the
impetus they need to assume power—especially if
that new leader is able to arrange an alliance with the
Revanche Party, something the Goran Tokar has
refused to pursue, due to the pragmatic approach the

Revanchists have taken regarding the Orbs and other matters. A sufficiently impressive discovery of overlooked resources in the Bajoran system could put the *D'ja Bajora Karass* in control of such an alliance and relegate the Revanchists, who we've always considered the more serious threat, to a secondary role."

Sisko nodded. He had no idea what the Revanche Party might be, or how it differed from the *D'ja Bajora Karass,* but he didn't suppose that really mattered. The internal complexities of Cardassian politics did not concern him.

"If it's any comfort, the Federation has yet to find anything your people missed," he said. "We don't believe any such resources exist."

Kaidan nodded a polite acknowledgment. "Thank you, Commander; that's a useful tidbit. About Federation policy, though . . ."

"I'm afraid that I am not in a position to say," Sisko said. Gul Kaidan had come looking for honesty, and Sisko decided to provide it. "As you noted yourself," he continued, "this post was hardly a political plum prior to the discovery of the wormhole; I am not in the confidence of the Federation Council. To the best of my knowledge, the official policy is the actual policy. I regret, Gul Kaidan, that I cannot add any further assurance than that."

"So do I, Commander," Kaidan said, putting down his mug. "Ordinarily, I might hesitate to believe you—but you are a sensible man; why would you lie to me, when to do so can only harm your own position?"

Sisko didn't answer that; he stiffened in his seat at the hint that he might have lied.

"You must have made some enemies," Kaidan said, "but surely you have friends, as well. Should you learn more, I hope you will find the means to communicate it to me. Now, about this ship from the Gamma Quadrant . . ."

Sisko frowned. "I'm afraid that I cannot recognize the Cardassian claim to the derelict; it originated in the Gamma Quadrant, and was intercepted in Bajoran space. My own people were studying it, in hopes of tracing its origins and dealing with it appropriately; the most I can consent to, without an agreement among all parties involved, is to stop our investigations until the ship's ownership is settled."

"You will not give it up?"

"No, Gul Kaidan, I will not."

"Yet you say it's worthless."

"Its value is not the point," Sisko said. "Gul Kaidan, the ship is driven by a fission-powered ion engine, and used centrifugal force to simulate gravity —how valuable can it be?"

This was true, but deliberately misleading—Sisko was careful not to mention the derelict's computers.

"Its political value may have little to do with its actual value," Gul Kaidan said. "Perhaps we could make an arrangement of some sort?"

Sisko considered that. "Perhaps," he said. "If the intrusions into Bajoran space were to be halted, and reparations made . . ."

It was Kaidan's turn to frown. "You drive a hard bargain," he said.

"On the contrary," Sisko said. "I think that those would be the minimum requirements for any negotiation."

"It is not the Cardassian government, or any member of my own faction, that is responsible for the intrusions," Gul Kaidan said.

"I realize that."

"Then I'm afraid we cannot reach any agreement as yet," Kaidan said. "I regret to say that I may find it necessary to use force to obtain that ship." He started to rise, but there was a certain hesitancy to his movement, as if he were hoping Sisko would object.

Sisko did not object immediately; he stood as well.

This visit had been informative, and it was also an opportunity he didn't want to waste, but he was unsure just what more Kaidan was after.

Then a thought struck him. If the intrusions were an attempt to settle the political succession in the *D'ja Bajora Karass* . . .

"Gul Kaidan," he said, "I am sure we can find ways to help each other, rather than resorting to conflict— as you say, it is in both our interests to settle this peacefully, and not risk starting a war. Perhaps an exchange of information might help—perhaps there is something we can do that will benefit us both, and be more valuable to you than that ship. Already, by clarifying the situation regarding the Goran Tokar, you have helped me considerably, and I'm in your debt; I think that you've helped yourself, as well. If there is any more you can tell me . . ."

Kaidan eyed him carefully; he said nothing, but did not move to depart.

"For example," Sisko continued, "you went to some trouble to prevent Gul Dukat from obtaining that ship; I take it that your people would not be happy if the Goran Tokar chose Gul Dukat as his heir. Could you perhaps tell us whether we might want to somehow encourage one of the candidates among the Goran Tokar's would-be heirs, or whether there is one we might especially wish to hamper? Might that not be of sufficient value to make the ship irrelevant?"

"Commander Sisko," Kaidan said, seating himself again, "you are indeed a man of good sense."

CHAPTER
7

O'BRIEN WAITED IMPATIENTLY for Sisko and the Cardassian to emerge from the commander's quarters, but he had turned away from the turbolift for a moment to look at a display—he had been thinking about the derelict so much that for a moment he thought he saw an image of one of the dead crablike aliens on the screen. When he looked again it was gone, but he was sufficiently distracted that he was caught off-guard when at last the two commanders reappeared.

"Chief O'Brien," Sisko called, "would you please see Gul Kaidan safely back to his ship?"

"Yes, sir," O'Brien answered. He turned to the transporter console as the Cardassian captain strode over and stepped up onto the platform.

O'Brien saw Major Kira staring hatefully at the Cardassian and tried not to notice as he set the controls. She probably didn't even realize she was doing it, he thought.

"Major," Sisko said, beckoning to Kira, "I'd like to speak to you in my office, please."

O'Brien checked the coordinates, then announced, "Energizing."

The Cardassian flickered and vanished, and O'Brien turned quickly, to catch the commander before he and the major vanished into his sanctum. "Commander," he called, "about the alien ship on upper pylon two . . ."

"It can wait, Chief," Sisko answered, mounting the office steps.

"But sir . . ."

Sisko paused. "Does it pose any immediate threat, Chief? Lieutenant Dax?"

"Well, no," O'Brien admitted, "no *immediate* threat, but it *is* radioactive. . . ."

"So were those four reactors the Cardassians sabotaged before they left, Chief; they don't seem to have done any permanent harm, and they were closer in than that ship is, out at the end of upper pylon two."

"The computers . . ."

"The computers can wait."

"But the crew, Commander . . ." Dr. Bashir began.

"The crew of that ship is dead, Dr. Bashir?" The doctor nodded. "Then they can wait, as well." Sisko entered his office; Major Kira followed, and the door closed behind them.

O'Brien stared up at it in frustration. He desperately wanted to get another look at the alien ship's computer systems—how had they made a Besrethine neural net that didn't wind up in self-destructive involutions?

Then he sighed and turned away. There was plenty of work to be done here on the station, after all; the replicators on the Promenade were slipping out of adjustment again, producing food and drink unfit for humanoid consumption. Quark had logged several calls complaining about that and requesting immediate repairs.

At least Quark's complaints had been polite this time; in the past he had occasionally accused O'Brien of delaying repairs deliberately in an attempt to drive away Quark's customers and sabotage his business.

Work before pleasure, O'Brien told himself as he headed for the turbolift.

"Reoccupy?" Major Kira shouted.

"That is the course of action espoused by the Goran Tokar and the *D'ja Bajora Karass,* yes," Sisko said. "I understand the Revanche Party recommends it, as well—unlike the *D'ja Bajora Karass,* they acknowledge that the withdrawal was reasonable, but argue that the wormhole should be reclaimed, by force if necessary, now that its existence is known."

"The Federation won't allow that, will they? Starfleet . . . if the Cardassians . . ."

Sisko could not resist teasing her slightly. "I thought you didn't approve of Federation interference in Bajoran affairs, Major."

"That's not funny, Commander!" Kira snapped.

Sisko didn't reply; he gave her a moment to calm down.

He had to admit that it wasn't funny, and he regretted giving into the impulse.

"I *don't* approve of Federation interference in Bajoran affairs," Kira said at last through clenched teeth, "but it's infinitely preferable to *Cardassian* interference in Bajoran affairs!"

Sisko nodded. "I agree completely."

"Don't the Cardassians realize that a reoccupation would mean war with the Federation?"

"My impression is," Sisko said judiciously, "that some of them don't believe that the Federation would fight for Bajor, and others don't care. And some may *want* a war."

"But the Federation *would* fight, wouldn't it?" Kira asked warily.

"I think so," Sisko replied judiciously.

"And win? There isn't any way the Cardassians could *win*, is there?"

"I wouldn't think so," Sisko said. "Of course, I'm not privy to all the latest military data, and Starfleet is not currently at its peak, but I believe such a war would mean the destruction of the Cardassian Empire —but probably the destruction of Bajor as well, and at incalculable cost to the Federation."

"Then how can they . . ."

"I repeat, Major," Sisko said, "some of the Cardassians don't believe the Federation would fight, and others don't care. My impression is that this Goran Tokar would rather see Cardassia itself destroyed in a final glorious battle than to willingly give up any part of what he sees as Cardassian territory. He reportedly threatened to suicide when the Celestial Orbs were returned to Bajor in exchange for access to the wormhole—he claimed that that was kowtowing to inferiors and a disgrace to the species."

"That's insane!"

Sisko didn't argue with that.

"But we've got to stop it. Surely, if there were Federation starships guarding Bajor . . ."

"I doubt the Cardassians would be mad enough to attack a prepared enemy," Sisko agreed. "The Goran Tokar might, but he is hardly typical."

"So are you going to call for Starfleet's help?" Kira demanded.

"No," Sisko said. "Because as yet, neither the *D'ja Bajora Karass* nor the Revanche Party is in power, and until they are, there is no direct threat to Bajor. Federation starships on the border would be seen as needless provocation. Furthermore, it would be a significant expense for the Federation at a time when resources are stretched thin, and it would hardly do any good to Bajoran self-confidence. It's far too soon to call in Starfleet."

"But there won't be *time* if you wait," Kira protested. "The Cardassian Empire is just across the border, and the nearest Federation starbase is dozens of light-years away!"

"I think you overestimate Cardassian preparedness," Sisko argued. "I doubt they would be able to launch an occupation fleet immediately if the *D'ja Bajora Karass* or the Revanchists came to power. These things do require some advance planning, and I would expect some time-consuming debate."

"But not that *much* planning or debate," Kira said. "If I know the Cardassians, they probably have a contingency plan already worked up."

"My own knowledge of Cardassian history would suggest a tendency toward clever improvisation, actually," Sisko said mildly.

"Which isn't any better. Commander, we *need* Federation assistance out here!"

"I don't think . . ."

"Commander," Kira said, "do you *want* Bajor to be reoccupied? So that you'll be sent back to Mars, and Jake can be back with other humans? Sacrificing an entire people . . ."

She stopped in midsentence.

Sisko stared at her, genuinely shocked. "Major!" he snapped.

"I'm sorry," she said, not sounding sorry at all.

"Major Kira," Sisko said, forcing himself to speak calmly, "I don't want a war. I've told you that before. Sending starships out to patrol the Cardassian border would be seen as provocation, and you know it—it might well bring about exactly the war we wish to stop."

Kira struggled with this; all her instincts said that the Cardassians had to be opposed by force, that they would understand nothing else, but she knew Sisko's arguments were sound.

"Well, then just what *do* you propose to do?" she said at last.

"Major, it seems to me that you've been jumping ahead in your concerns," Sisko replied. "I told you that Gul Kaidan suggests that a war may happen *if* the *D'ja Bajora Karass* takes power—not *when* they take power, but *if*. If we can prevent that from ever happening, then perhaps we can prevent any attempt at reoccupying, as the present Cardassian administration has a great deal of their reputation tied up in their insistence that Bajor was worthless to them at the time of the withdrawal—as long as the *D'ja Bajora Karass* opposes them, they will *never* attempt a reoccupation."

"What about that other group you mentioned, the Revanchists?"

Sisko frowned. "I'm afraid I don't know much about them, but Gul Kaidan seemed to feel they could be managed without our help. It was the *D'ja Bajora Karass* that he felt posed the more immediate threat just now."

Kira looked at him doubtfully. "I don't see how we can influence Cardassian politics. You know they don't pay any attention to outsiders."

"It shouldn't be so difficult as all that," Sisko said. "True, we can't do anything about it openly, but there are other ways."

Kira settled into a chair and listened dubiously.

"Gul Kaidan tells me that there are four serious contenders for the position of heir to the Goran Tokar," Sisko explained. "The first is Gul Kudesh, the noted commander who won the Battle of Regannin—he's also the most likely, once in power, to start a war, if only for the chance to display his military prowess. In fact, since he was never even in the Bajoran system during the occupation, and took no interest in it, it would seem he's been active in the *D'ja Bajora Karass only* because it's the more warlike faction, and because he has too many enemies among the Revanchists."

"I've heard of him," Kira said with a shudder.

"It would appear, though Gul Kaidan did not say so in so many words, that Gul Kudesh is responsible for the intrusions into Bajoran space," Sisko said.

"Why?" Kira asked, half-rising from her seat. *"Is* he trying to start a war?"

"No," Sisko said, shaking his head. "He's looking for resources that his compatriots might have missed during the occupation. It seems that he doesn't trust anyone else's reports on the matter."

"That's absurd," Kira said.

Sisko didn't reply.

"All right, that's one," Kira said. "Who are the others?"

"The other three all held office in the Bajoran system prior to the withdrawal," Sisko said. "Gul Burot was stationed on Bajor itself only briefly before being promoted to an administrative post back on Cardassia. Gul Peshor oversaw several deep-mining operations. And the last contender, of course, is our old friend Gul Dukat, who ran this station and wants this office back."

"Gul Dukat? Is that what he was doing here, trying to steal that ship? He was trying to impress the Goran Tokar?"

Sisko nodded.

"But isn't he . . ." Kira paused, gathering her thoughts, then said, "But Gul Dukat was the prefect here under the present Cardassian government, wasn't he? He's not a member of the opposition—or is Cardassian politics that different from Bajoran?"

"I asked Gul Kaidan the same thing," Sisko said. "As I understand it, Gul Dukat is more an opportunist than anything else—he is indeed nominally a part of the ruling faction at present, yes, but he's been feeling underappreciated, and his record as prefect here is sufficient grounds for his elevation to leadership in the *D'ja Bajora Karass*. He appears to have privately expressed an interest in such a role."

"That's just like him," Kira said bitterly. She thought for a moment, then added, "I know about Peshor and Dukat, but I never heard of this Burot before."

"Neither did I, until I spoke with Kaidan," Sisko acknowledged. "I'm afraid I don't know much about him." He brushed that aside, and continued, "At any rate, those are the four major candidates. There are also two possible long shots, but we'll ignore them for now—Gul Kaidan assures me that they can be dealt with by his own faction."

"And what does Gul Kaidan want of us, then?"

"Well," Sisko said, "if any of those four leading contenders should be embarrassed somehow— embarrassed by *Cardassian* standards, of course— then that one would become a less likely candidate."

Kira considered that for a moment, then demanded, "Why are we bothering with this, Commander? What difference does it make who becomes the heir? They're all Cardassians. . . ."

"Major."

She glared silently at him.

"For one thing, Major," Sisko said, "once the Goran Tokar has made his choice, Gul Kudesh will have no reason to continue his searches on Bajor and Andros."

Kira had to concede that much. "So we want a fast decision," she said, "but does it matter which is chosen?"

"According to Gul Kaidan, it does," Sisko explained. "He tells me that one of the contenders, Gul Burot, has a weakness that will prevent him from ever assuming power."

"What sort of weakness?" Kira asked warily.

"I don't know—officially," Sisko said. "I think, however, that it's fairly clear that what Gul Kaidan was referring to is some form of blackmail; his faction has some hold over this Gul Burot."

"What sort of hold?"

"I don't know—and Major, I don't *want* to know. Neither do you. We don't want to involve ourselves *too* deeply in Cardassian internal affairs."

Kira started to say something, then caught herself as she realized that Sisko was right.

"At any rate, I think it might be best for Bajor if the Goran Tokar were to name this Gul Burot as his heir," Sisko said. "And I think that if we put your contacts on Bajor to work with us, and do a little careful research, we can improve Gul Burot's chances."

Kira looked at him for a long moment, then said, "You want to set it up so that one faction can blackmail the leader of the other."

"Bluntly, yes."

"That stinks," Kira said. "I thought I was done with anything this dirty once the Cardassians left."

Sisko could sympathize with that. "Diplomacy is war by other means," he said. "And isn't it better to fight this way than with phasers and photon torpedoes?"

Kira considered that for a long, silent moment, then said, "So we have to find ways to embarrass the other three candidates?"

"If we can, yes."

"What embarrasses a Cardassian?"

Sisko smiled. "Failure," he said. "What else?"

"And what if *we* fail?"

The smile vanished.

"In that case, Major," Sisko said, "we *will* have a war. I don't think the Cardassians will take kindly to any attempts at influencing their internal politics. I doubt the *Federation* will look favorably on it, for that matter. We're risking our careers, our lives, this station, and the entire Bajoran system on this."

It was Kira's turn to smile. "Now you sound like my old comrades in the Resistance," she said.

"Is that good?"

Kira nodded. "I think we can probably arrange something where at least one or two candidates are concerned. Gul Burot might be tricky—he was on Bajor so little . . ."

"But we don't want to eliminate him anyway," Sisko said, completing her sentence.

"Exactly," Kira said enthusiastically. "Gul Dukat and Gul Peshor ought to have some sort of weakness in their records we can exploit—or manufacture, if necessary. I'll need to talk to some people on Bajor about that, people I knew during the occupation. And I'll have to see my friends in person; we don't want anyone overhearing."

"That will still leave Gul Kudesh."

Kira frowned. "He's going to be the difficult one—unless there's something . . ." She paused, obviously deep in thought, and Sisko waited patiently.

"I wonder," she said finally, "since Gul Kudesh is behind the raids—if he really is—whether we can do something with that," Kira said. "If something were to go spectacularly wrong with one of his little investigations . . ." Her voice trailed off as she thought. Then she roused herself, and said, "At the very least we ought to be able to come up with a way to embarrass Dukat and Peshor." She gestured impatiently. "When do we start?"

"That should do it," O'Brien said. He closed the panel, typed in a quick order, and waited while the replicator produced a cup of coffee.

"It's not really coffee I'm concerned with," Quark said, as the engineer picked up the cup and took a sip.

O'Brien glanced at the Ferengi barkeep. Far shorter than most adult humans, with immense ears and hairless, bulging heads, the Ferengi looked rather foolish to many humans, at least until the pointed teeth showed, but O'Brien was used to them. While he wasn't sure he liked Quark, he knew the Ferengi was an intelligent person.

"I like to use coffee as my test sample," he explained. "To be honest, Quark, I don't think I'd better sample any of your usual goods when I'm on duty." He didn't mention that he had more of a reason than usual for wanting to stay sober—he had now seen the crablike creatures on computer displays on three separate occasions. His imagination was running away with him, and liquor could only make it worse.

He took another sip, tasting it carefully, then said, "And besides, coffee seems to be what gives it the most trouble. This tastes fine to me, so I'd say we've got it."

"Well, if not, you'll be hearing from me."

"I'm sure," O'Brien said. "That's why I try to do it right the first time; if I don't, I'll spend the rest of my life fixing these infernal replicators of yours." He gulped the rest of the coffee, while Quark typed in an order for something rather more exotic.

While he waited, the Ferengi said jestingly, "Oh, come now, O'Brien, you love tinkering with these machines, and you know it. If you weren't fixing them, what would you do with yourself?"

"I'd see a lot more of my wife, for one thing," O'Brien replied, disposing of the empty cup. "And maybe I'd get a better look at the computers on that ship out on upper pylon two."

He didn't see Quark's eyes light up with interest.

"What ship is that?" Quark asked.

O'Brien glanced at him. "Oh, Dax picked up a derelict that had come through the wormhole," he said. "It's mostly pretty primitive, but the computer circuitry is something special—it looks like a Besrethine neural net, and the folks at the Daystrom Institute would just love to know how to make one work."

"A Besrethine what?"

"Besrethine neural net. It's a computer design theory that no one's ever gotten to work—or no one in Alpha Quadrant, at any rate. It'd be a major advance if we could build the things."

"And this ship has one of these?"

"It appears to . . ."

Just then O'Brien's comm badge chirped. "Dax to O'Brien," it said.

With a sigh, O'Brien tapped it. "O'Brien here," he said. "What's broken now?"

CHAPTER
8

"A SIMPLE FISSION PILE is hardly an indication of an advanced technology," Dax remarked as she studied a display screen.

"You know as well as I do that a culture can be more advanced in some areas than others," O'Brien replied from behind the console as he worked on the circuits feeding Dax's display. The station's computers were malfunctioning again—or at any rate, not operating the way Dax and O'Brien wanted them to, but whether that was because something was broken or because something was Cardassian-built was not always clear. "*We* can't make a Besrethine net work, and they can."

"If that's really what the ship's computer is," Dax said.

O'Brien shrugged. "It certainly *looks* like one. And even if it isn't, those information conduits weren't quite like anything I ever saw. Sometimes just being *different* can teach us a lot."

"The *crew* was certainly different," Dr. Bashir

added. He was not working at the moment, but simply hanging around, watching the others. "I've checked the records, and there isn't anything quite like those beings reported anywhere in the entire Alpha Quadrant. I'd love to get one of them into the lab."

"You will not take them apart," Commander Sisko said, startling the three of them. Bashir turned and Dax looked up to find that Commander Sisko had emerged from his office and was standing nearby, with Major Kira just behind him.

O'Brien started, but kept his attention on the isolinear optical chips.

"I didn't hear you come out," Bashir said.

"I didn't particularly want you to," Sisko replied.

"Commander, you said I wasn't to dissect them? Certainly not right *now*, but I don't see why I shouldn't have that opportunity eventually. . . ."

"Dr. Bashir," Sisko said, "quite aside from the fact that both Cardassia and Bajor claim ownership of the derelict, so that I have agreed not to interfere with it until further notice, we know nothing about the culture or mores of these visitors. Many cultures, including most of those developed by our own species, have strong prohibitions against disturbing the remains of the dead; until we know otherwise, we must assume that these beings may have had similar restrictions. It may well be that they were sent through the wormhole in a sort of Viking funeral—after all, all other known wormholes are unstable; it may be that whoever sent these unfortunates expected the wormhole to collapse on them. It may also be that the ship was sent as a trial run, and others may be appearing at any time, others who might not be pleased to learn that we have disassembled their dead compatriots. Until more is known about the customs and beliefs of the ship's crew, we must show whatever respect we can, and that being the case, it would be inappropriate to remove them from their ship, let alone to dissect them."

"But, Commander . . ."

"Doctor, we don't even know for certain what killed them, do we?"

Reluctantly, Bashir admitted, "No. But I still think asphyxiation is the most likely cause."

"Chief, I believe you said the ship's computer technology could be quite valuable?" Major Kira asked.

O'Brien tapped the final circuit card into place and asked, "How's that, Lieutenant?"

"It checks out now, Chief," Dax replied.

O'Brien got to his feet, brushing dust from his uniform, and said, "Yes, Major, I was mentioning that that ship's computer appears to use a Besrethine neural net, and if so, yes, it's priceless."

"Valuable enough that the Federation might send a starship to protect it?"

Sisko refused to react, but inside he seethed. Kira was supposed to be thinking about how to discredit three Cardassian politicians and prevent a war, so that a starship wouldn't be needed. She wasn't still supposed to be figuring ways to coax Federation firepower out here. She generally had a tendency to hang on to ideas too long.

Sisko did not particularly want any starships out here; he preferred to handle matters himself.

O'Brien looked at Sisko for guidance, but the commander's expression gave nothing away. "I wouldn't know about that, Major," he said.

"Protect it from whom?" Dr. Bashir asked, puzzled.

"From the Cardassians," Kira said. "They do claim to own it, Doctor—and if that computer technology is so powerful, I doubt we want them to have it."

Sisko came to O'Brien's rescue. "Major, right now we aren't concerned with the derelict; there will be plenty of time to deal with it later."

"Of course, Commander," Kira agreed. "You understand, I'm sure, that as Bajor's senior representative here on DS-Nine I take an interest in the property of the Bajoran people. That ship was salvaged in Bajoran space by a Bajoran station, so that makes it, and the design of its computers, Bajoran property; the Federation has no claim to it."

"That remains to be determined, Major . . ." Sisko objected.

"Of course, right now we aren't concerned with the derelict, are we, Commander?" Kira asked sweetly.

Sisko glared at her, then glanced at the others. "Chief, don't you have work to do elsewhere? Dr. Bashir, don't you have any patients waiting?"

Neither man answered in words; instead, reluctantly, they both headed for the main turbolift.

"Lieutenant Dax, would you see that a runabout is prepared for launch?" Kira said, as O'Brien and Bashir departed. "I'm going down for a conference with some people on Bajor." She glanced at Sisko, and then added, "And while I'm gone, I trust that any salvaged vessels belonging to the Bajoran people will remain undisturbed by our Federation guests?"

"No one will be interfering with any salvaged ships while you're gone," Sisko said, "whether they're the property of the Bajoran people or not—and the question of who owns what will wait, as well."

Major Kira stepped onto the other turbolift without replying, and sank out of sight.

Quark wiped idly at the bar as he thought.

Business at Quark's Place was much as usual—a few people were playing Dabo for disgustingly low

69

stakes, while a few more were sitting about chatting as they ate and drank, and upstairs a couple of customers with more money and more time on their hands than they needed were sampling the erotic possibilities of the holosuites.

He made a decent living off this place, but it wasn't about to make him rich, and the goal of every Ferengi, himself included, was to become rich. Very rich. Fabulously rich. Incredibly, unbelievably rich.

And while owning a bar, restaurant, casino, or other such business—Quark's Place partook of all of them —could provide a good start on a fortune, it was never going to make him *that* wealthy.

So why was he here?

Never mind that that Earthman, Sisko, had blackmailed him into staying on when the Cardassians had first pulled out; why hadn't he left since then?

Because a place like *Deep Space Nine* was fraught with possibilities, that was why. Out here on the frontier, with all the traffic passing through to and from the wormhole, business opportunities ought to be popping up on all sides.

So why, Quark asked himself, hadn't he cashed in on those possibilities yet?

He glanced up, and saw his nemesis walking by— Odo, the station's constable.

That was why he hadn't cashed in—because Odo had prevented it.

Odo was a shapeshifter—he generally wore a humanoid form to fit in, and managed reasonably well, though there was always a certain unfinished look to the features, and the skin color was a bit off. His natural form, however, was a thick orange-red liquid. And with a little effort, he could disguise himself as almost anything.

Quark had never quite figured out why Odo could

do such a flawless job of imitating tables, chairs, wall panels, glassware, and the like, but still couldn't do a nose properly. Maybe it was a trick to make Quark forget how good Odo was at inanimate objects, because that was how Odo had foiled most of Quark's best schemes. An extra table or chair would never be noticed, so Odo could listen in on all those private conversations that were essential for any really lucrative business deal.

And all the best deals, of course, were on the wrong side of the law, and that annoying shapeshifter had therefore insisted on scuttling them.

Quark suspected . . . no, Quark was *convinced* that Odo was out to get him, that the constable had set himself a goal of finding a way to utterly ruin Quark once and for all, and that any time he wasn't busy elsewhere, Odo was somewhere in Quark's Place, disguised as a customer or a bottle or a Dabo wheel, listening for some way to destroy Quark.

But right now, there was Odo, walking away through the crowd farther down the Promenade, which meant that for the next five minutes or so Quark could be absolutely sure that none of the tables or walls were watching and listening.

And that was important, because O'Brien's visit to repair the replicators had let Quark know about another of those tempting business possibilities. O'Brien had said that there was an alien derelict out at the end of upper pylon two, one with a unique computer design. . . .

As Quark quickly broke through the station's computer security to get at the complete reports on this find, he wondered whether he could get more for a completely unknown technology through a private sale, or at an open auction.

CHAPTER
9

HER SHIFT WAS OVER, and Jadzia Dax called up her daily log to check before leaving Ops.

She was startled to see that part of it was missing—the record skipped from the neutrino surge that had indicated an arrival through the wormhole to preparing the *Ganges* for Major Kira's departure. Everything concerning the capture and exploration of the alien derelict was gone.

She ran a quick computer check; the data did not appear anywhere. Whether it was really irretrievably lost, or had simply been temporarily mislaid somewhere in the computer's memory, she couldn't determine—at least, not without a great deal of work.

Perhaps this was yet another manifestation of the Cardassian-built computer's obsession with security and proper procedure—or perhaps it was an actual malfunction.

In either case, Dax was tired—besides capturing

and exploring the derelict, and all her usual duties, she had been trying to make sense of the situation with the Ashtarian scientific expedition. The technicians making the adjustments to the Ashtarian ship's engines, to allow it to go through the wormhole to Gamma Quadrant without disturbing the entities that lived in and maintained the wormhole, had reported a problem of some kind that they were unwilling to explain; they had insisted that Dax had to see the situation for herself. She had promised that she would do so.

She had spent all her spare time for this shift, when she might ordinarily have been meditating and restoring her energies, in trying to find information on the Ashtarian cultures and technologies, and failing. The only reports she found simply gave the date of initial contact with the Federation and a few other basic facts and statistics, such as the interesting datum that Ashtarians and most of the other species on their home planet had only one sex; nothing in the records said anything at all about anything in Ashtarian technology that might cause problems for the technicians.

Had *that* omission perhaps been due to a computer failure, too? She had assumed it simply meant that nothing else was on record about the Ashtarians.

Whether it had been a malfunction or not, the computer was definitely misbehaving now.

Well, dealing with it was not her job, and the Ashtarians were waiting. It was another problem for Chief O'Brien, she supposed.

She hesitated; O'Brien had gone off duty a few minutes before, and would be meeting his wife, Keiko, about now. The two were planning a quiet dinner together.

From what Dax had seen of them lately, they *needed* a quiet dinner together.

She wasn't going to interrupt them. It was just as important—probably more so—to keep the human elements of *Deep Space Nine* working properly as it was the mechanical ones, and their emotional well-being was more important than the merely physical.

She wasn't going to interrupt the O'Briens—but should she see if she could find the problem herself?

No, she decided, the Ashtarians were important, too.

The computer malfunction was trivial, really; it could wait for a shift or two. She logged off, signaled to the ensign on watch that she was departing, and then headed for her own quarters.

Quark had studied the reports with interest, then tried to remove every trace of his intrusion—but when he went back to check, he found that the relevant chunk of the Ops duty officer's log had vanished completely.

That wasn't anything *he* had done—he couldn't possibly have been so clumsy!

Was someone *else* interested in the derelict, as well?

That meant Quark would need to move quickly if he was to obtain this prize before his unknown competition, whoever it might be, could get to it.

He wished he had some idea of *how* to move; as long as that ship was moored to the station, he couldn't see any way he could get at it and get away with it.

He certainly couldn't just sneak aboard; the report made it clear that Sisko had had the vessel sealed, and even if Quark *did* get aboard—by transporter perhaps—the radioactivity would be lethal. Besides, even if he could figure out the computer design tha

O'Brien was so excited about—and he wasn't sure he could; he wasn't an expert—it wouldn't be as valuable if Sisko and Kira had it, as well. Quark wanted an exclusive.

For that, he had to have the ship entirely to himself, and the only way he could do that was if he could claim ownership and make it stick.

To do that, he needed to claim salvage rights, and he couldn't do that while it was docked to *Deep Space Nine.*

And he couldn't see any way to get it loose. Sisko would never be foolish enough to let such a treasure go. . . .

Would he?

Not in the ordinary course of events, but Sisko could be flexible in some ways. Quark knew that the big Earthman would never take a bribe, or anything so obvious as that, but under the right circumstances he would send that derelict away. If he thought it was a danger, that its presence threatened the station, or if he believed someone else had a valid claim to it, or if he thought, for any other reason in his bizarre altruistic logic, that removing it from the station would be the right thing to do.

Of course, there was no reason for Sisko to think that removing it was the right thing to do.

Quark decided that he would just have to convince Sisko to remove it anyway.

Dax stepped into her quarters with the intention of getting a quick snack and a fresh uniform before going out to the Ashtarian ship, and sensed that something was wrong.

She quite couldn't place what it was; she paused just inside the door and looked about, listening intently.

She could hear something, she realized—a faint growling or rumbling sound. She couldn't identify it, or locate it.

She listened for a moment, then shrugged and went on about her business.

Miles O'Brien had been looking forward to his dinner with Keiko all day. She had arranged for someone to look after their daughter, Molly; this would be just the two of them, in a private room at one of the Promenade's eating establishments—*not* Quark's Place, but a more elegant one that offered patrons whatever computer-generated decor they might want.

He was waiting for his wife at the entrance when he heard something moving behind him; he glanced back, into the restaurant's dim interior.

A large crablike creature was moving about, apparently aimlessly, paying no attention to O'Brien.

O'Brien blinked.

Now, that was interesting, he thought. Up until he had boarded the derelict, he'd never seen anything sentient that even vaguely resembled the poor dead beings from the Gamma Quadrant—but here was a rather similar fellow, right here on DS9. It seemed to be a bit smaller, and he couldn't see its color in the poor light, but the general configuration was very much like that of the crew of the derelict.

That was quite an odd coincidence.

"Miles!"

O'Brien turned and found Keiko practically in his arms. He embraced and kissed her quickly.

When he turned to lead her into the restaurant, the crablike being was gone.

* * *

Dax stared down at the little rodentlike creature in its clear plastic compartment; it stared back up at her, chittering happily.

It was roughly the size and shape of an Earth chipmunk, but a darker brown, with no stripes—and with tiny seven-fingered hands. It held a tool resembling a screwdriver in one little black glove.

This creature, she was told, was a snuguort—the Ashtarian equivalent of a servomotor.

"You see, it's not so much a technical problem," the Bajoran technician explained, "as it is an ethical one. The way the Ashtarians use those poor little things just seems so cruel!"

"It's not cruel at all!" the Ashtarian chief scientist protested. "The snuguorts have been genetically engineered for their function—they *live* for it!"

Dax looked up at the one-eyed alien that towered over her. "You're sure of that?"

"Lieutenant," the Ashtarian replied, "if we don't keep them busy, they sicken and die. They love their work. This is what they were *created* for. Besides, our ship can't function without them—the snuguorts regulate the matter-antimatter mix for us. We're quite incapable of operating the drive without them—even if we had reflexes fast enough, and the snuguorts' intuitive understanding of the drive's proper equilibrium, our hands are far too large to operate the controls."

The Ashtarian raised its own immense seven-fingered hand to demonstrate; its thumb alone was almost as big as the snuguort's entire body.

"They can't use their warp drive inside the Celestial Temple anyway," the Bajoran said. "I'd say that we should keep these poor creatures of theirs here, and let the Ashtarians go on without them!"

"Oh, and are we then to explore the Gamma Quadrant on impulse power? And starve while we do it?" the Ashtarian demanded.

"Starve?" Dax's attention had largely fallen back to the furry little animal; now she looked back up at the Ashtarian, startled.

The Ashtarian managed to look uncomfortable, despite its inhuman features. "Perhaps I shouldn't have mentioned that," it said.

"But you did, you monster!" the Bajoran said.

Dax held up a hand. "Please, Ensign, no racial epithets. Chief scientist, now that you *have* mentioned it, would you care to explain?"

The Ashtarian hesitated, then said, "Well, you see, Lieutenant, snuguorts breed quite rapidly, which not only supplies us with plenty of spare parts, but also augments our diet. We Ashtarians are carnivores, requiring fresh meat, and the snuguorts are the only livestock aboard." It shrugged—which was an interesting procedure, since Dax had not realized it had shoulders; its meter-long neck had seemed to blend seamlessly into its chest. "It's simple efficiency."

"It's heartless cruelty, Lieutenant," the Bajoran insisted, "and if you allow this ship to proceed through the wormhole, and risk offending the Prophets with this barbarism, I'll file a complaint with the provisional government."

Dax sighed. She hadn't had to handle anything like this in centuries, not with any of her recent hosts —not since, as Penzak Dax, she had negotiated a truce among the three sentient species of Lauan XII.

"I'll need to investigate this further," she said. "Chief scientist, if you could provide the station's computers with some information on the nature and history of these . . . snuguorts, I'll see what I can do."

She didn't mention that she intended to get some rest first. This, like the alien derelict and the lost computer records, could wait until later.

CHAPTER
10

THE FORMER CARDASSIAN mining station that the Federation had renamed *Deep Space Nine* was a big place. Its three hundred or so inhabitants mostly huddled in the central core, around Ops and the Promenade and the upper levels of the habitat ring. Visitors came and went, but they stayed mostly in limited areas, as well. Therefore, at any given time, large parts of the station were likely to be empty.

And naturally, the areas where equipment wasn't working right were among the most neglected.

That meant that although Chief O'Brien himself was usually kept busy handling emergencies in the core, some of his crew spent much of their time wandering empty corridors, tracing faulty circuits and repairing machinery no one was currently using.

Ensign Waru Teyshan, a Bajoran volunteer in Starfleet service, found such assignments creepy in the extreme, but he could hardly refuse them on that basis. O'Brien and most of the other native Federation people didn't seem to worry about spiritual matters much; troubles of the soul and concerns about immaterial entities didn't interest them.

Waru wished he could be so calm about the unseen realms, but his mother had been Vaiora to their village, and he had grown up hearing regular reports on the doings of the dead, and the actions, moods, and preferences of gods and spirits of every sort.

Waru didn't have any of the higher perceptions himself, at least not in any useful degree, so he had never actually been sure that he had seen a ghost or other supernatural manifestation, but he was nonetheless convinced that the empty corridors of the station still held the spirits of many of those the Cardassians had slain during their brutal occupation —and quite possibly various other ghosts as well.

Sometimes he thought he could hear them.

As he struggled to repair the connections in a burned-out junction box halfway up upper pylon two, he was *sure* he could hear something.

At first he had thought it was just the air currents in a damaged ventilator somewhere, but as he spot-welded the power couplings he realized it couldn't be that—the sound was getting louder, and it wasn't steady or rhythmic enough for a bad ventilator.

It wasn't much like voices, either—at least, not Bajoran voices. It had the right sort of patterning for speech, but it was a deep croaking noise, not quite like any sound a human throat could produce.

What did ghosts actually sound like, though? Waru had always assumed they still sounded Bajoran, but really, why should they? After all, they were dead— they didn't *have* throats anymore.

The sound grew still louder, and Waru put down the welding torch to listen.

It was coming from farther up the pylon, toward the

alien ship that Chief O'Brien had been talking about earlier, and Waru suddenly understood.

These weren't the Bajoran ghosts he was hearing; these were the ghosts of the dead aliens that had been found aboard that ship from the wormhole.

Waru wondered what they wanted. Could anyone else hear them, or had he perhaps finally developed a bit of his mother's talent?

He considered calling in a report about it, then decided against it.

Chief O'Brien was a good man and a fine technologist, but he didn't know anything about ghosts.

Jake Sisko was tired and ready for bed; his Ferengi buddy, Nog, had gone back to his own quarters, Jake's father was busy somewhere as usual, and Jake just wanted to drop onto his bed and go to sleep.

But now the stupid door of his room wouldn't open to let him in.

He supposed it was just another stupid malfunction in the crummy Cardassian equipment, and he should call someone about getting it fixed, but he was too tired. He curled up on a couch instead, and fell instantly to sleep.

At first, independent contractor Muhammed Goldberg was embarrassed to be in Quark's Holosuite B, but he told himself that was foolish. He was a grown man, and if he wanted to try out one of the Ferengi's sex fantasies, it wasn't anyone's business but his own. He did his job, earned his pay, and if he wanted to spend his free time and extra cash here, he had that right. His Starfleet employers wouldn't mind—a person's off-duty hours were his own.

And it wasn't as if he had any family on the station,

or as if any of the women here had shown any interest in him.

That was what he told himself, and he knew that it was true, but he was still embarrassed. His mother's voice lingered somewhere in the back of his mind, telling him that nice boys found better ways to express their sexuality.

"Have fun," Quark said, with an amazingly offensive leer, bringing Goldberg's thoughts back to the here and now. "I'm sure you will," Quark added as he backed out, grinning, and closed the door.

Goldberg didn't answer Quark's little sally. The Ferengi hadn't exactly made him feel welcome when he had inquired about the suite; Quark had acted as if Goldberg was distracting him from more important things. Goldberg resented that. He had almost turned around and left.

But he was here now.

When the Ferengi was gone and the holosuite was sealed, Goldberg looked around at the blank gridded walls, took a deep breath, and said, "Computer, run program XTC-four."

His palms were sweaty with anticipation, and he wiped them on the thighs of his coveralls as he waited.

The grid vanished, and he was standing in a columned marble hall, looking down from a dais as a line of women, chained at the wrists, entered the chamber through a great golden door. A burly guard in open vest and baggy pants directed them forward, and the women obeyed. The fine golden chains jingled musically as they advanced toward him, eyes downcast; one by one, in quick succession, they reached the foot of the dais and knelt before him, the guard standing behind them, his arms folded across his chest.

Goldberg caught his breath, then smiled. He looked them over carefully.

A fine selection, he thought—blondes, brunettes, redheads, a dozen women in all, kneeling at his feet.

A sound distracted him from his study of the slaves. He looked up at the far door.

Something was coming through it, something low and wide and a dull purple color. Goldberg blinked. What was *that*? What was it doing in this fantasy? Quark hadn't mentioned anything like that when he went over the catalog of fantasies. Had the Ferengi been so busy with his other business, whatever it was, that he forgot to mention some feature of this scenario?

The thing moved into the hall, walking on half a dozen barbed and jointed legs; it looked something like a crab with tentacles.

What was something like that doing here?

And whatever it was, whatever it was supposed to be doing, Goldberg decided that he didn't want it there.

"Computer," he said, "edit program; remove all nonhumanoid intelligences."

Nothing happened, except that the purple thing advanced toward him and began making ugly croaking noises. The women were still kneeling silently, the guard standing motionless behind them, all waiting. They paid no attention to the intruding monstrosity.

"Computer, edit program," he repeated. "Remove *all* nonhumanoid life-forms, *now.*"

The thing was still approaching.

"It's ruining my fantasy!" Goldberg shouted. "If Quark thinks I'm paying for this . . . !"

The creature paid no attention.

The slave girls were still kneeling before him, the guard still standing there; Goldberg decided that if they could ignore the thing, so could he.

Or maybe, he thought, he could incorporate it into the fantasy.

"If the one I choose displeases me," he said uncertainly, "perhaps I'll give it to that monster." He had to shout to be heard over the croaking.

The guard shifted his weight uneasily. "What monster, master?" he asked.

Goldberg blinked in astonishment. *"That* monster!" he said, pointing.

The guard turned—and the crab-thing walked right through him, clambered up onto the dais toward Goldberg.

It wasn't part of the program, Goldberg realized instantly; one hologram wouldn't go through another from the same program like that. In fact, *nothing* should be able to go through the hologram like that unless something was wrong—the computer should have compensated, to retain the illusion.

And if it wasn't part of the program, that meant that the crab-thing was *real.*

And if the computer didn't compensate for it, then the computer didn't know it was in here!

"Computer, end program!" Goldberg shrieked, as the crab-thing reached up toward him with a lumpy tentacle. "Let me out of here!"

The marble walls vanished; guard and slave girls were gone; but the crab-thing was still there, and the door of the holosuite didn't open.

The tentacle touched Goldberg's face; the croaking made his ears ring.

He screamed, and fainted.

Odo looked down over the railing at the Promenade, at the late-shift crowd. Most of the people below him were Bajorans, going about their business—

visiting the temple, getting a drink at Quark's, whatever. A few humans were scattered in among them, brought by the Federation, and a handful of other species were present, as well—a Ferengi, a pair of Klingons, and others.

None of the Ashtarians were in sight; after one or two visits shortly after their arrival, they had apparently decided to keep to themselves.

Perhaps they got tired of having to stoop; many of the doorways and ceilings were too low for them.

That might be just as well. A new species on the station meant new possibilities for trouble.

Several of the shops were closed, and Odo let his gaze pass quickly across them—and then stop.

Something had moved, down there in the darkness of one of the businesses that was shut down for the night.

He froze, then stared, hoping to see the movement again.

Yes, there it was, in that boutique—a flicker of light that shouldn't have been there.

The quickest way down was not the steps or the lift; instead, Odo leapt over the rail, transforming himself as he went, and drifted down to the lower level in the shape of a small balloon.

The moment he touched down he transformed again, to a small, furry animal that wasn't quite any real species, but an approximation of several. In that shape he scampered up to the closed doors of the boutique, where he reared up on his hind legs and peered in through the glass.

He saw the counter, the thickly carpeted consultation area with its chairs and displays, the holographic equipment that allowed a customer to "try on" clothes that didn't yet exist, the replicators that produced the garments to specification after all adjustments had been made—but he didn't see anything that didn't belong. No one was visible in the shop; nothing moved. The only lights were the normal indicators on the various machines.

He resumed his humanoid form, and used his security clearance to open the locked door.

He searched the boutique carefully, and found nothing out of the ordinary.

For a moment, he stood in the center of the room, frowning.

He *had* seen a light in here—but no one was here now. He had had the door of the shop in sight at all times; no one could have left that way, and there were not supposed to be any other exits.

Odo knew the station as well as anyone—quite possibly better than anyone else. He had been here since it was first built. This shop had no hidden exits.

But he had seen something in here, and it wasn't here now.

Had someone beamed out, perhaps?

He would have to check the station's computer and see whether any of the transporters had been used. He would also check on the construction of this shop. And he would keep a close eye on it for a time.

And that was about all he could do for the moment.

But he had seen someone or something in here, he was sure; it had been real. He didn't imagine things.

And it couldn't very well have been a ghost.

CHAPTER
11

QUARK STOOD IN the doorway of Holosuite B, hands on his hips, glaring at the blank walls.

He did not need this. He was busy trying to come up with a scheme to get his hands on that ship from the Gamma Quadrant, with its Besrethine computer; he did not need to be distracted by whatever it was that had terrified Goldberg.

He supposed it was another equipment failure. Goldberg's description hadn't been very coherent, but Quark didn't see what else it could have been.

The holosuite *looked* normal—but that didn't mean anything; the machinery was all hidden away behind those gray walls.

Quark stepped into the room, planning to run a few simple tests; O'Brien might be able to fix the problem more quickly if Quark could give him an idea what was wrong.

Before he could say a word, though, a creature stepped out of the far wall.

It wasn't like anything Quark had ever seen before; it was low and wide, with a hard carapace and several long, jointed legs, and a row of manipulating members along the front.

He took a step back.

He could see why Goldberg had been startled, if something like that had walked into the middle of his fantasy.

Quark, however, was made of sterner stuff—or at least, so he told himself. It didn't hurt that he had read Dax's report, and recognized the creature as a member of the species that had crewed the derelict on upper pylon two.

But how could that be? Dax had said they were all dead.

Presumably she had been wrong, because here one of them was, walking slowly across the holosuite. Interesting, that they could apparently walk through walls without leaving a hole—not many species could manage that.

Perhaps this was a projection of some sort. It wasn't anything the holosuite was doing—Quark had thrown the master switch, and shut the suite down, when Goldberg screamed.

"Hello there," Quark said, backing warily toward the door. "Can I help you?"

The thing made a harsh croaking noise—and vanished.

Silne Koryn had lived aboard *Deep Space Nine* for almost three years, first as a "personal entertainer" for a Cardassian mining executive, then briefly as a refugee with nowhere else to go, and now as proprietor of a small curio shop on the Promenade, where she sold Bajoran religious relics and various souvenirs to the travelers who visited the station while passing to and from the wormhole.

She had not returned to Bajor when the liberation came because there was nothing left back there for her; her family had all died under the Cardassian occupation, and her employment under the Cardassians would mark her to some of the more patriotic as a collaborator, to some of the more conservative as a whore.

So she had stayed where she was, and tried to make the best of it.

Her life on the station was quiet and unexciting, and she liked it that way. She had settled into a daily routine that for the first two hours never varied. She would rise at the same time each day, eat the same things for breakfast in the same amount of time, then walk down the same connecting tunnel from her room in the habitat ring to the Promenade in the station core. There she would open her shop, tell the computer to play back a particular recording of religious chants, and seat herself at the counter to wait for customers.

She always played the same recording to start; later in the day she might vary it somewhat, depending on her mood, but she always began the business day with the exact same chants. The music soothed her; she never tired of it, never considered changing it. It was a link to her lost past, a comfort for her soul, and an aid to the meditation she hoped would someday bring her the inner peace the Cardassians had robbed her of.

Sometimes she imagined that she heard her mother's voice among those chanting the ancient rituals.

At the close of business she would play the same recording once again, wait for one particular chant to end, then tell the computer to end the program; then she would return to her quarters for the night.

The day after the alien ship popped out of the wormhole, Silne finished breakfast, walked to her shop, unlocked the door, and stepped inside.

"Computer," she said, "play recording fifty-one twenty-three B." She walked toward the counter, expecting the clear, high voice of the Vedek Paroti to begin the familiar hymn of praise.

Instead, a guttural croaking came from the hidden speakers, a sound like nothing she had ever heard before, and Silne stopped in midstride, frozen in astonishment.

For a moment she was too surprised and disoriented to react, but finally she angrily said, "Cancel! Play *fifty-one, twenty-three, B.*"

The croaking grew louder.

"Cancel," she said again.

Could she possibly have misremembered the number, after all this time? "Computer," she began.

Then she stopped.

The computer had ignored the cancellation order. The croaking was continuing.

She didn't recognize it. It might have been speech, but not in any language she had ever encountered, certainly not in any Bajoran language. She didn't think the voice was humanoid at all.

And whatever it was, the sound was ugly, bestial— almost evil.

"Cancel," she said again. "Cancel, cancel, cancel! End program! *Shut up!*"

The croaking continued; nothing she could do would stop it, it continued relentlessly until twenty minutes later she fled her shop in tears, and almost collided with Constable Odo on the Promenade outside.

When she led him into the shop a dozen voices were

singing to the glory of the Prophets of the Celestial Temple.

Muhammed Goldberg lay back on the infirmary bed, breathing deeply, as Julian Bashir read the monitor.

"You're fine," Dr. Bashir said. "You could use some more exercise, and you need to relax more. . . ."

"I was *trying* to relax!" Goldberg interrupted.

"Yes, well," Bashir said, "you'll want to keep at it, but perhaps somewhere other than Quark's holosuites."

"But . . . Doctor, did I really see that thing, or did I imagine it?"

Bashir studied the readouts more closely. "There's nothing that would indicate the possibility of hallucinations," he said. "I think we'll have to put it down to a malfunction in the holosuite, and I'll report it to Chief O'Brien as soon as you're back on your feet."

Goldberg shook his head, unconvinced. "The holosuite computer didn't even know it was there," he said. "If it's a malfunction, it's a *bad* one."

"Well, perhaps it is," Bashir said. "At any rate, there's no sign of any malfunction in *you.* You can go whenever you like, or if you'd like to rest here for a while . . ."

"I think I would," Goldberg said. He closed his eyes.

Bashir's mouth twisted wryly. The poor man was a nervous wreck. The whole thing *could* have been his imagination—the station's medical equipment was hardly sensitive enough to rule out the possibility— but *telling* him that would be cruel. Better by far to blame it on Quark's gadgets.

Bashir turned away, intending to enter his report in the computer, but something caught his eye, and he froze.

The monitor on the next bed was reporting life signs—but the bed was empty.

Bashir stepped closer and studied the readouts.

The sensors were reporting the presence of a nonhumanoid life-form: a hydrogen-methane breather with a triple circulatory system. It appeared to be in good health.

But the bed was empty.

Bashir waved a hand across the bed, and felt the surface cautiously; he found nothing but empty air. The creature was not merely invisible—either it was intangible as well, or it wasn't there.

The bed must be malfunctioning, Bashir decided. An invisible, intangible methane-breather wouldn't register. Even if one could exist, in order to survive on the station it would have to carry its own air supply, and *that* couldn't be intangible. . . .

He took a quick look at the room environment monitor. No, there were no abnormal levels of hydrogen or methane, only the usual tiny traces.

There was no alien on that bed. The machinery was registering something that was not there.

Then, abruptly, the readouts dropped to zero—all except the body-pressure indicator, which first flicked upward, then dropped, as if the alien had shifted its weight and then gotten out of the bed.

That sort of detail did not seem like the result of faulty machinery. Bashir stood motionless for a moment, listening intently, watching for any disturbance of any kind.

All he could hear was Goldberg's breathing. Everything looked utterly normal. The empty bed now registered as empty.

It had to have been either a ghost or a malfunction, and Bashir didn't believe in ghosts.

He would have to call Chief O'Brien down for a look.

O'Brien's much-anticipated dinner with Keiko had been cut short before either had had more than a few bites or spoken more than a few words. He had assured her that he would do his very best to be back soon.

By the time Keiko finally dropped off to sleep, feeling very alone and neglected, her husband had logged over thirty calls, all tagged as various levels of emergency.

Constable Odo had only logged about two dozen, not counting his own mysterious intruder in the Promenade boutique. Several of these incidents he had, after investigation, reluctantly passed on to O'Brien.

"I am sorry about this, Chief," the shapeshifter said as he relayed the latest, a woman who had reported strange crablike aliens spying on her through the viewer in her bedroom. "I don't like making work for you, and I would prefer to handle it myself, but it does appear to be a technological problem." He glanced at O'Brien's assistant, Ensign Waru. "If there's anything you know of that will help me to find the parties responsible, do tell me."

"I don't bloody know if *anyone* is responsible," O'Brien replied from inside the control console for Holosuite B, "but if someone is, and it's not just these damnable Cardassian machines all breaking down at once, and you find whoever it is . . . Constable,

I want five minutes with him. Just five minutes, and then you can throw me in the brig and have what's left."

"I don't think that would do much good," Ensign Waru muttered, as he handed O'Brien a variable-beam cutter. "You can't hit ghosts."

CHAPTER
12

"I CAN'T FIND a damn thing wrong with any of it,"
O'Brien complained, in response to Commander
Sisko's inquiry.

The two men were standing in Ops, Sisko having
just emerged from his office and O'Brien having just
emerged from the turbolift.

Sisko frowned. O'Brien looked exhausted—and
that was no surprise. Sisko had looked over the list of
calls O'Brien had answered.

He had almost made one of his own when he found
Jake sleeping on the couch because the door to his
bedroom wouldn't open. Sisko had tried the door
himself, and had eventually gotten it open by using a
manual override—after which it behaved normally. A
quick investigation had not shown any reason for its
misbehavior, but Sisko wasn't an expert; he had been
about to call O'Brien when he had remembered that
O'Brien had planned a quiet evening with his wife.

Instead, Sisko had called Ops, and learned that

there were dozens of malfunctions occurring all over the station.

This was not just normal equipment failure. Many of the problems had appeared as strange manifestations, as voices and images from nowhere, and it was only after some searching that it was determined that every one of them *could* have been produced by some piece of the station's machinery—viewers, communicators, holographic projectors, and so on.

For so many to misbehave at once, and in such odd ways, was not normal.

O'Brien had been on the job, though, so Sisko had gotten a few hours of sleep and gone about his own business, studying as much as he could find in the station records of the personal histories of the four Cardassian politicians who Gul Kaidan had said might become the Goran Tokar's heir.

He hadn't found any fatal flaws in any of their backgrounds, which was unfortunate—a juicy scandal in Dukat's or Peshor's or Kudesh's past would have made it that much easier to ensure Burot's selection and avoid a war.

Of course, Sisko thought, if there had been any obvious scandal, some Cardassian muckraker would undoubtedly have found it already.

It would have been nice had one turned up, though.

The Cardassian situation had been his primary concern, so Sisko had given the various malfunctions on the station little thought. He had expected to find a brief report of the problems and their solution waiting for him in his office, and when no such report was to be found he had stepped out and found O'Brien just arriving.

O'Brien had obviously not made a report because he hadn't yet solved the problem. From his appearance, he also hadn't slept since the previous morning.

"I assume you've looked for a central cause for the difficulties," Sisko said.

"Of course, sir." O'Brien's tone made it quite clear that he was offended by the question but attempting to hide it. "Every malfunction or intrusion has been something that the station's central computer could have caused, and most of them have been things the computer should have prevented, so naturally, I've been checking the computer very carefully. I can't find anything wrong with it—unless you count that it's Cardassian."

Sisko nodded thoughtfully. "What about that alien intelligence that infested it some time ago?" he suggested. "That caused several systems failures, trying to keep our attention. Could it have gotten loose?"

O'Brien, bleary with fatigue, needed a moment to recall what Sisko was talking about; then it came to him. An alien probe that had popped out of the wormhole some time back had carried software that appeared to be almost a form of life, and it had gotten into the station's computers and caused some difficulties before O'Brien had found a way to confine it.

He didn't think of it as an "alien intelligence," though; he had given it a name.

"The Pup, sir?" O'Brien asked. He shook his head. "Oh, I checked that first thing; it's still safely in its doghouse. It's not involved."

"This rash of malfunctions does seem similar, though," Sisko remarked.

"Yes, sir, it does," O'Brien agreed, "so I checked for any other intelligences infesting the computer, and I haven't found any—not yet, anyway." He sighed. "Several of the incident reports include descriptions of crablike aliens like those aboard the derelict on upper pylon two, so I thought that the ship might have introduced some sort of program or virus into our computer, but I haven't found any trace of one."

"Could there be one you haven't found?"

"Anything's possible, sir," O'Brien said. "In a universe where creatures like Q or those things in the wormhole exist . . . well, anything's possible."

"But you haven't found any such program," Sisko said—he made it a statement, not a question.

"No, sir," O'Brien replied. "And frankly, I don't expect to."

Sisko frowned. "Then do you have any idea what else it could be?"

O'Brien shrugged wearily. "Ensign Waru thinks it's ghosts, sir, and right now I'd say that seems as good an explanation as any."

"It's those dead aliens," Waru said, putting down a newly empty synthale beaker. "It's their ghosts causing all the trouble."

"I don't believe in ghosts," Dr. Bashir replied.

"Then maybe," Quark suggested, speaking over Bashir's shoulder as he delivered the doctor's drink, "if it's not the dead aliens, it's whatever *killed* those dead aliens."

Bashir turned, startled. "Oh?" he said. "And what would that be?"

"How should I know?" Quark replied. "I'm just a bartender. It's a big galaxy, Doctor—there are energy beings out there, there are nanites, there are millions of different life-forms that could be responsible. And it could be ghosts, whether you believe in them or not—how do you know that there aren't creatures in the Gamma Quadrant that *do* create ghosts when they, ah . . . 'discorporate'?"

"You think these beings might somehow do that?"

Bashir asked, intrigued with the idea. It was much more interesting than a mundane breakdown in the station's equipment.

"What do I know about it?" Quark put a hand on his chest. "I saw one, but that's all I know. I'm no purple crustacean; I'm as humanoid as you are, and *you're* the doctor here."

"As humanoid . . ." Bashir looked at the Ferengi's immense, thickly ridged ears, his bulging forehead, and his pointed teeth; he smiled wryly. "Of course."

And in fact, the little barkeep had a point. It was, as Quark said, a very big galaxy, and anything was possible—but still, ghosts haunting the station? Bashir couldn't quite bring himself to believe it.

"Maybe they aren't really dead," he suggested. "Maybe it's some sort of astral projection."

"There you go, Doctor," Quark agreed. "It *could* be something like that!" He nodded, then turned away, headed for the next table.

"Did you hear Dr. Bashir?" he asked the customers there. "He believes that the crew of the derelict isn't really dead—they're using psychic powers to attack the station, to soften us up for an invasion! If I were Commander Sisko, I'd cut that thing loose this minute!"

Twenty minutes later, as Quark was telling yet another tableful of customers about the deadly powers of the ghosts from the Gamma Quadrant, a figure loomed up silently behind him; Quark knew immediately, from the faces of his listeners, that someone was there.

And he never had any doubt of just who it was.

"Hello, Constable," he said as he turned. "What can I do for you?"

"You can tell me," Odo said, "just why you're

spreading these absurd stories. Are you deliberately *trying* to create a panic?"

"Oh, now, Constable . . ." Quark began.

Odo was unyielding. "Are you?" he demanded.

"The stories aren't absurd at all," Quark protested. "You can hardly claim that everything's *normal* aboard DS-Nine! You and Chief O'Brien have been chasing the ghosts all over the station for hours."

"I doubt very much that the problems we have been experiencing are the work of ghosts," Odo replied.

"But they're happening," Quark said, "and they've got some connection with that derelict Lieutenant Dax intercepted—you can't deny that!"

"I don't deny it," Odo acknowledged. "I only ask why you're stirring up your customers. I've received complaints about it from people who are worried that you'll start a panic."

"Me? Stirring up anyone?" Quark put a hand to his chest and proclaimed histrionically, "Oh, Constable, you wrong me! I'm just making light conversation, trying to create a lively atmosphere for my clientele. . . ."

"You've been telling scare stories about that derelict ship nonstop for most of an hour," Odo said flatly. "I want to know *why.*"

Quark stared up at the shapeshifter for a moment, then said, "I might as well tell you—maybe that's the quickest way to get some action."

Odo considered the face of his nemesis. "What sort of action did you have in mind?" he asked.

He knew what sort of action he would like to give Quark, but unfortunately, he couldn't yet justify throwing the Ferengi in a detention cell for a century or so.

"I want that derelict off the station, of course,"

Quark replied, skating unusually close to the honest truth. "Send it back into the wormhole, or drop it into Bajor's sun, or give it to the Cardassians, I don't care, but I want it away from the station. Those ghosts, or whatever they are, are ruining my business!"

Odo lifted his intense gaze from Quark's loathsome face and looked calmly around at the crowded barroom. He did not need to say a word to get his point across—Quark's business looked perfectly healthy.

"I mean the *holosuites,* Constable!" the Ferengi explained. "Since Goldberg got carried out of Holosuite B in a faint and started spreading those scare stories of his, I haven't had a single customer upstairs!"

At the time of Goldberg's arrival, Quark had considered the man a minor, if profitable, interruption in the scheme to steal—or rather, *salvage*—the derelict ship; now he was an important part of Quark's plans. The ghosts, whatever they were, might be just what Quark needed to get the ship loose from the station.

"So you're spreading your own scare stories, trying to create a panic," Odo said.

"So I am *trying,*" Quark explained, "to convince our beloved Commander Sisko of the seriousness of the situation. I know he won't listen to *me* when I complain, but if a hundred people come pounding on his office door demanding the derelict's removal he'll have to do *something.* And the sooner he does it, the better!"

"I am quite sure that Commander Sisko is aware of the seriousness of the situation," Odo said dryly. "I would point out that so far, no one has been hurt, no lives have been endangered—the manifestations have frightened people, but done no real harm."

"No harm!" Quark's expression was one of carefully contrived outrage. "Constable, I'm losing money every hour those suites up there stay empty!"

Odo stared at him for a moment longer. He supposed that the Ferengi might even have a point, much as he hated to admit it—though that hardly excused any attempts at rabble-rousing.

"I will inform the commander of your concerns, Quark," he said at last.

"Good," the Ferengi replied.

"But in the meantime," Odo continued, "you will stop deliberately feeding your customer's fears. They can do a perfectly adequate job of scaring themselves and each other without your help."

"I . . ." Quark looked up at Odo's face, and decided not to bother finishing his protest. "Have it your way, Constable," he said, "have it your way. But there really *is* something dangerous loose on this station, and I'm not going to wait around to be killed by it—or worse, bankrupted. If something isn't done soon, I'll be leaving *Deep Space Nine*—and I won't be the only one!"

The Ferengi watched as the shapeshifter turned and stalked away, then allowed himself a smile.

He had no idea what was causing the malfunctions, and he didn't really care; what he cared about was getting that ship off the docking pylon.

If he'd thought of it, he would have tried to create the disturbances himself, but someone or something had done it for him. Goldberg and the rest might convince Sisko that the derelict was dangerous and would have to be removed.

And if Quark could get Sisko to dump the derelict from the station, then all he needed was a ship with a tractor beam to be able to claim salvage rights for himself, on the grounds that it had been abandoned.

And Quark thought he knew where he could get a ship—that Ashtarian scientific expedition was getting very tired of waiting for clearance to go on through the wormhole.

Then he frowned slightly.

What *was* causing the disturbances? What was it he had seen in Holosuite B? And what had erased those records from the computer?

Was someone else after the alien ship? He hadn't found any other solid evidence, as yet, that he had competition, but perhaps these disturbances were the work of some other would-be salvager.

Perhaps whoever it was had done all this to get the ship removed from the station, and intended to snatch it up the moment it was free.

Well, if that was the case, Quark would just have to get it first. The other salvager, whoever it was, wouldn't know that anyone else was interested; Quark had covered his own tracks perfectly.

But there wasn't any time to waste. If he was going to beat the competition—if there *was* any competition—he needed to have a ship with a tractor beam ready to go on a moment's notice.

Sisko might dump the derelict at any time.

CHAPTER
13

"YES, CONSTABLE," Sisko said, trying not to sound as exasperated as he felt, "I'm well aware of the apparent link between the derelict ship on upper pylon two and these recent disturbances."

The two of them were standing by the turbolift in Ops, where Odo had caught Sisko preparing to go meet the returning Major Kira. Behind the commander Dax was at her station; she had had to postpone her investigation of the Ashtarian situation until the incidents were stopped.

Nearby, O'Brien was arguing with the station's computers; Dr. Bashir had arrived on the same lift that had brought Odo, but was standing to one side, a mere observer, as the constable replied, "Then . . . forgive me for asking, Commander, but in that case, why haven't you already had the ship removed from the station?"

"Because I had hoped," Sisko said, pointedly not turning to look at O'Brien, "that the nature of the problem could be determined, and the problem solved, without risking the loss of something that might turn out to be very valuable. If we dump that ship, it's a safe bet that Gul Dukat will be here shortly to collect it." He did not mention that this would help Dukat take control of the *D'ja Bajora Karass,* and perhaps the Cardassian Empire.

"I'll have it soon," O'Brien called. "The answer's somewhere in this damned computer, I'm sure of it."

"Commander," Dr. Bashir interrupted, "surely you aren't seriously proposing to dispose of that ship before we've had a chance to study it properly?"

"I am considering it, Dr. Bashir," Sisko replied.

"Oh, but we can't throw it away, Commander!" Dr. Bashir said, agitated by the thought of losing such a prize. "If Quark's right—I mean, yes, I know that's unlikely, that Quark would have hit on the truth, but miracles can happen. If Quark's right, and those creatures *do* somehow survive death, think of the potential! Think what we might learn from them!"

"It would be a loss, sir, to give up that ship," O'Brien agreed.

"It would be a loss," Dax said, "but perhaps a necessary one, if it truly endangers the station."

"If you *don't* cast that 'ghost ship' off," Odo said, "you're going to have some very unhappy people. Quark's made sure of that."

"I'm aware of that, Constable. . . ."

"That ship," Major Kira said, emerging from the other lift, "is the property of the Bajoran people, and the Federation has no right to dispose of it without consulting them."

"And that," Sisko said, "is *another* reason that I haven't ordered the derelict removed."

"But, Major," Odo protested, "that ship is disrupting the entire station. You've been on Bajor, you haven't seen the situation. . . ."

"I've *heard,* Constable," Kira replied. "I was briefed on the way up here. And just how certain *are* we, might I ask, that it's really something aboard the derelict that's responsible for the problems, and not yet another Cardassian attempt to interfere with us?"

"Cardassian?" O'Brien asked, puzzled.

"In case you hadn't noticed, Chief, the Cardassians are in the middle of a little competition to see who can get the most out of the Bajoran system," Kira said. "How do we know this isn't their doing?" She turned to Dax. "Lieutenant, run a long-range sensor scan."

"Yes, Major," the Trill replied. She applied herself to her console.

"Why would the Cardassians want to create these apparitions?" Bashir asked. "It hardly seems their style."

"Because they want to disrupt life here on *Deep Space Nine* without taking the blame," Kira replied. "It's not just that ship they want; if they can convince us to leave the wormhole unguarded, they can claim it for themselves."

"We're scarcely going to just go off and leave it, ghosts or no ghosts," Sisko objected.

"But do the Cardassians know that?" Kira asked. *"All* the Cardassians? Remember, some of the members of the *D'ja Bajora Karass* have never been to Bajor, never dealt with the Federation—if they believe their own propaganda, they may well see us as a bunch of superstitious cowards."

"But, Major," O'Brien protested, *"how* could the Cardassians be responsible? How could they do all this?"

"The Cardassians built this station, Chief," Kira

pointed out. "We've found a few surprises aboard it before; how do we know there aren't more? Maybe the Cardassians deliberately built DS-Nine with booby traps they could use from a distance, just in case they ever had to put down a rebellion aboard. Maybe they have some way to control the computer and override all our programming. . . ."

"Oh, no," O'Brien said. "I've been through that whole system half a dozen times, right down to the binary level—it's a Cardassian system, and it's got a mind of its own, after a fashion, but there's no built-in override."

"Then what *is* causing the apparitions, if it's not Cardassian interference?" Kira asked.

"The derelict," Odo said. "Really, Major, all this subterfuge you suggest is hardly the Cardassian style; their reaction to trouble was usually to shoot somebody. If there had ever been a rebellion here during their occupation, they'd have simply stood off and blown the station to atoms. They wouldn't have contrived an elaborate haunting."

Kira could hardly argue with that; she knew the Cardassian national character as well as Odo did. "All right, then," she said, "perhaps they've smuggled a spy aboard who is responsible for the sabotage—that wouldn't be very difficult, with all the traffic we have through here."

"Scan completed, Major," Dax called.

Kira turned, expectantly.

"In addition to all the known and identified traffic," Dax said, "there are seven Cardassian ships. The three we believe to have been responsible for the intrusions into Bajoran space are moving in formation with two others along the border. There are also two larger ships cruising deeper in Cardassian space, at the extreme limit of our sensor range—both are maintaining a constant distance from us, and one appears to be shadowing the other; we can't get a good fix on them, but both are about right for Galor-class warships. They appear to be unobtrusively and unobjectionably patrolling the border."

"There, you see?" Kira turned back and confronted Sisko triumphantly.

"Major, we've had Cardassians watching us at least half the time ever since we first found the wormhole," Sisko pointed out. "One or two more don't prove anything. I assume those ships are commanded by Gul Kudesh, Gul Dukat, and Gul Kaidan, all keeping an eye on one another." He turned to Dax. "Old man, are there any transmissions beamed at the station from any of those ships?"

"No, sir; no contact of any kind, on any frequency. Subspace is quiet."

"There, Major," Sisko said. "How can that ship be controlling the disturbances when it isn't transmitting anything?"

"Maybe it's not doing anything right *now* . . ." Kira began.

An alarm beeped loudly, and a screen lit red. "Julian," Dax said sharply, interrupting the Bajoran, "we have an injured woman on level fifteen—caught in a security forcefield that came on without warning."

"On my way," Bashir called, heading for the transporter.

For a moment the others were silent as Dax beamed the doctor to the site of the disturbance.

"There were no transmissions from the Cardassian vessel, Major," Dax pointed out.

"It's a coincidence," Kira said. "It *could* be a coincidence. Something malfunctioned, it wasn't—"

"The injured woman was fleeing croaking noises in

her quarters, where a crablike creature was displayed on her viewscreen," Dax reported.

Kira's mouth opened and closed.

"How would Cardassians know what the crew of the derelict looked like, Major? How could they have arranged *that* little detail?" O'Brien asked

"How serious are the injuries?" Sisko demanded.

"A severed arm and second-degree burns," Dax replied.

"That does it," Sisko said, ignoring Major Kira as she groped for words. "Up until now they hadn't hurt anyone, but now . . . Dax, I want that ship away from this station. Open the mooring clamps and tractor it out to an orbit at fifty thousand meters."

"Yes, sir." Dax shifted stations and worked the panel expertly.

Sisko had started to turn away when she said, "It won't let go."

He turned back. "What do you mean?"

Dax looked up from the controls and stared at him. "I mean it won't let go, Benjamin. The computer is refusing the command."

"But how . . ."

And then a deep, harsh croaking came from speakers on every side.

CHAPTER
14

"THE MOORING CLAMPS can be operated manually," Odo reminded Sisko quietly—or as quietly as he could and still be heard, given the racket from the speakers.

Sisko raised a hand in acknowledgment to the shapeshifter, but he did not answer him directly; instead he spoke to Dax, shouting to be heard over the eerie alien sound.

"Record that," he said, "and see if you can translate it. Or even just identify it."

"Yes, sir," Dax replied.

"Chief . . ." Sisko began, turning.

"I'm on it, Commander," O'Brien replied, before Sisko could finish his order. "It's not anything *in* the computer, like a virus, but whatever it is, it's *using* the computer—I'm not sure just how it's doing it, but it seems to be using the computer as a sort of conduit between itself and whatever it's controlling, it's not just telling the computer what to do."

Sisko had to listen intently to catch exactly what the chief was saying; O'Brien was speaking loudly, but the croaking was louder.

"A conduit from where?" Sisko asked, shouting. *"Is it something aboard the derelict that's responsible?"*

"Yes, sir," O'Brien confirmed, "it's coming from the derelict."

Sisko signaled at the main viewer and shouted, "Let's take a look."

Major Kira hurried to her station and tapped controls, and the image of the alien vessel, still tightly secured to upper pylon two, appeared on the screen. Sisko studied the scene carefully.

There were no clues to be seen there; the irregular bright blue mass that had emerged from the wormhole was, to all appearances, as inert as ever. Nothing moved, nothing glowed; it simply hung there.

"Is someone alive over there, then?" Sisko asked. "Could someone have been hidden aboard it, someone you three didn't find?"

"I don't know, sir," O'Brien answered. "We didn't search it that carefully—not centimeter by centimeter, at any rate. There could have been shielded compartments."

"So one of the crew might still be alive and attempting to communicate?"

Dax looked up. "Unlikely, Benjamin," she said, somehow making herself heard without actually shouting. "The sensors still register no signs of life aboard the derelict."

"It could be shielded somehow," O'Brien repeated.

"Or it could be something other than those crab creatures we thought were the crew," Dax suggested. "They might have just been passengers, or even if they were crew, perhaps part of the crew is another species, something the sensors wouldn't recognize as life. Nanites, for example. Or this could be something the ship's computer is doing."

"Could that be it, Chief?" Sisko asked.

O'Brien shrugged without lifting his gaze from his controls, and his fingers continued to press combinations of keys. "It could be, sir, yes."

"Can you determine that somehow?"

O'Brien shook his head. "Sorry, sir, but there's no way to tell. I mean, if I can't even figure out just what's happening in our own computers, I certainly can't tell you anything about what's going on in the aliens' computers."

Sisko considered that for a moment, wishing that the croaking would stop long enough for him to exchange a few words with his subordinates without bellowing.

He did not appreciate having things hidden from him like this. The station's computers were supposed to do what the station crew told them, not obey whatever whims some intruder might have.

And he could hardly think with that ghastly racket pounding in his ears; it seemed to be growing steadily louder.

"Cut it off," he ordered. "Override it. We'll figure out what's causing it later; for now, just order the computer to ignore commands from the derelict."

O'Brien's hands moved over the panels so fast that his fingers were a blur; then he announced, "I can't, sir—our system isn't aware that it's in contact with the alien." He glanced up and saw the thunderous expression forming on the commander's face, and quickly explained, "It's not that our central computer is accepting commands from the derelict, sir—it's that the derelict is somehow passing its commands directly *through* our computer, without the computer even knowing what's happening. It's as if our computer were . . . well, as if it were possessed by the alien."

Sisko struggled unsuccessfully to catch all of O'Brien's words over the continuous racket from the speakers. He got the gist of the chief's report, and ordered, "Then cut whatever links that thing is using."

"I can't," O'Brien shouted. "It isn't using any normal linkage. We never connected our computer to the derelict in the first place, sir; it appears to be transmitting its orders in the form of subatomic vibrations directly through the metal of the mooring clamps."

"It *what?*" Sisko wasn't sure whether he had heard O'Brien correctly or not.

"Subatomic vibrations through the metal, sir!"

"It can *do* that?"

"Yes, sir," O'Brien said. He added, "And don't ask me how, because I don't have any idea. It's a completely unfamiliar technology."

Sisko did not like the sound of that. "It's working through the mooring clamps, though?" he asked.

"Yes, sir!"

"Then we need to release those clamps," he said. "Constable!"

Odo was already on the transporter pad. "Ready, Commander," he said.

"Lieutenant Dax . . ."

"Benjamin, I may have a partial translation," the Trill said, interrupting Sisko's order.

Sisko stared angrily at her for a moment. She was not supposed to interrupt him, and he was tempted to shout her down, but he knew she wouldn't have spoken up without a good reason. That infernal croaking was getting on his nerves, making it hard to think.

"What is it?" he asked.

Dax pushed a button, and the computer's voice spoke over the croaking.

"Where are you? Why don't you answer me? Where is everybody? This place isn't right. Where are you?"

The combination was almost deafening.

"Can you lower the volume?" Sisko asked. "We don't need to hear the original."

"No, sir," Dax replied. "The computer is completely unaware of the signals going to the speakers. It can only translate what I've recorded manually. I still have no control over the speakers."

Sisko frowned.

"Should I beam Odo out to upper pylon two?" Dax asked, reminding him of his interrupted order.

"Yes," Sisko said. "But, Odo, don't release the clamps until I give the order. And once he's out there, Lieutenant, I want you to try to establish communication with whatever it is that's causing these disturbances."

"Yes, sir. Energizing."

Odo vanished in a flicker of silvery light, and Dax turned back to her usual console.

"Chief," Sisko said, "see if you can convince that computer of yours to listen to that racket and provide a running translation."

"This computer's not *mine*, Commander, it's a piece of Cardassian . . ."

"Just do it."

"Yes, sir."

"Lieutenant Dax."

"Yes, sir."

"Who is this being, whatever it is, addressing? What does it mean, 'Where are you?'"

"I don't . . ."

Before Dax could finish replying, Sisko's comm badge beeped. Exasperated at yet another interruption, he tapped it, hoping he would be able to hear over the constant croaking and the general noise level in Ops. He looked upward at nothing in particular, as was his usual habit when addressing someone he couldn't see. "Sisko here," he said.

"Commander, this is Odo," the communicator said, and Sisko was relieved to find that he could hear it adequately. "A security forcefield across the access corridor to the docking port has been activated, and the emergency blast doors are closed, as well. Neither one will acknowledge my commands or accept security overrides. I believe I can get past both barriers and reach the mooring clamps, but it may take some time."

"Thank you, Constable," Sisko answered. "Be careful, and keep me informed. Sisko out."

He should have known that whatever was interfering with the station would defend itself—but it couldn't have anticipated that *Deep Space Nine* would have a shapeshifter aboard. Odo could flow through ventilators, seep between wall panels—he should be able to bypass any defenses the thing could erect.

But it was yet another delay—and what *was* the thing, anyway? What were they dealing with?

Sisko looked questioningly at Dax.

"I'm afraid, Benjamin, that I have no idea who the entity is talking to," the Trill replied. "I've got the computer at work compiling a vocabulary of the entity's language, and we can ask it very limited questions—if we can decide where to direct them."

Sisko nodded. "Open a hailing frequency to the derelict," he commanded.

"I've attempted that, without success. . . ."

Sisko irritably started to interrupt, to order Dax to try again, but then he remembered who he was addressing and fell silent. Dax knew her job, knew Sisko's thinking.

Sure enough, the Trill said, "I'm trying again, but still get no response. Not on any of the standard hailing frequencies, nor any of the available subspace channels."

"Then talk to it through the computer, the same way it's talking to us," Sisko told her.

"It may well require an audible signal," Dax said.

"Of course," Sisko replied. "Route it through the speakers nearest the derelict—there must be an intercom in the airlock there."

"Yes, sir. What shall I say?"

"There's no need to be subtle, old man," Sisko said. "Ask it, 'Who are you?' "

Dax pressed keys quickly, and the computer beeped an acknowledgment of her orders.

The response was abrupt—the croaking stopped. Silence fell.

The sudden quiet was startling and uncomfortable; Sisko forced himself to stand calmly, waiting, for several seconds, giving the thing time to take the next step.

His comm badge beeped. "Odo to Sisko."

"Sisko here."

"Commander," Odo's voice said, "I don't know what you just did, but I think you've made it nervous. I heard some of that infernal croaking from the airlock, and then it set up a nasty electrical field of its own, as well as activating *all* the security forcefields I can see from here. I don't think I can get to the mooring clamps."

"Damn!" Sisko muttered. He turned to Dax. "Any response to our question?"

117

"No."

"O'Brien?"

"Nothing, sir—those vibrations in the docking pylon seem to have stopped, but we're registering the electrical field Odo mentioned."

"But it's no longer interfering with the computer?" Sisko asked.

"Not that I can see, sir," O'Brien confirmed.

"Well, then we're all right," Kira said. "We can just leave it there until we're ready to deal with it."

Sisko, his head starting to ache, angrily turned to face her. "May I remind you, Major," he said, "that whatever is out there has injured one of our people, and interfered with nearly every aspect of life aboard this station? That it's still keeping the mooring clamps locked, and preventing Odo from reaching them?"

"But you've frightened it off," Kira insisted. "It's just protecting itself now."

For a moment, she and Sisko confronted each other; then the croaking burst suddenly from the speakers again.

"Damn!" Sisko said. He turned to Dax. "What's it saying?" he demanded.

"I'm not sure," Dax replied. "More questions, apparently—and it's asking who *we* are."

"Tell it, then," Sisko directed.

"I'll try."

A moment later silence fell once again, but only briefly. This time, when the croaking started anew Sisko thought it sounded slightly different.

"More of the same?" he asked.

Dax looked up at him. "No, Commander," she said. "I'm not certain I have this right, but it appears to be saying 'You must die.'"

For a moment Sisko stared at her; then he tapped his comm badge.

"Sisko to Odo," he said. "What is your situation?"

"Still no progress, I'm afraid," came the shape-shifter's voice. "It's being very thorough in its defenses."

Sisko suppressed a growl of frustration. Nobody threatened his people and got away with it, not if he had anything to say about it—and why was this alien intelligence, whatever it was, making threats? Its previous manifestations had seemed like attempts to communicate, but now that they *were* communicating, however feebly, it seemed to have turned hostile.

Perhaps it had mistaken the station for someplace else, its inhabitants for some other group.

Whatever the reason, he couldn't leave the derelict where it was under these circumstances. A glance at Major Kira showed him that even she was no longer arguing for its retention.

"Chief," he called to O'Brien, "get me two people in vacuum suits, with hand torches—I want them to get out there on safety lines and cut those clamps loose. They're to use every possible precaution, to treat that ship as armed and dangerous, but they aren't to attack it unless it shoots first. If you can provide shielding, do it, and send whatever weapons you think they'll need."

"Our scans didn't find any weapons aboard the alien, sir," O'Brien said.

"I know that," Sisko said. "If they had, I wouldn't be sending anyone out there at all. We can't make any assumptions, though." He turned slightly. "Dax, tell it what we're doing. It can speak to us peacefully, or it can leave—if it's going to make threats, it's not welcome here."

"I'll try, Benjamin."

The croaking continued intermittently as O'Brien relayed Sisko's orders, and as Dax struggled to piece together coherent messages with only an infant's vocabulary in the alien tongue; Major Kira, seeing things in hand for the moment, said, "About the *D'ja Bajora Karass,* Commander . . ."

"This is not the time, Major," Sisko snapped, cutting her off.

Couldn't she see, he wondered, that they were all busy with the current crisis? Yes, the Cardassians were important, but they could wait for an hour or two; right now this derelict had to be dealt with. Of course, she'd been off the station during most of the disturbances, so she might not realize just how much trouble it had caused, but still . . .

For her part, Kira considered everything else a minor distraction—the threat of renewed Cardassian occupation took priority over *everything* else, as far as she was concerned. A child and an old man had died in the panic caused by the most recent Cardassian raid—that was more important than that woman's injuries in the forcefield accident. The woman was still alive, the man and child were not.

And the secret campaign that she and Sisko were waging to determine who the Goran Tokar would name as his heir was urgent—the final selection could be made at any time, and Gul Burot was by no means the sure choice, as yet.

He had to be the final choice—and they had to make sure of it.

But she knew that arguing with Sisko now would be arguing with a blank wall—he had set his own priorities, and unless she had something new and vital to add, which she admitted to herself she did not, he wasn't going to change them.

She stood silently by, waiting for this annoyance to be settled so that she could get on to serious matters.

* * *

Quark smiled, showing a mouthful of pointed teeth.

"My apologies," he said to the Ashtarian chief scientist as the two of them stood in the airlock of docking port eight, where the Ashtarian ship was waiting. "I'm sorry to trouble you, but I understand you've been having some minor difficulties with the, ah, local administration."

The Ashtarian—three meters tall, of which a third was neck and all was covered with shaggy brown hair—looked down at the Ferengi. Quark smiled up at the Ashtarian's single huge eye and tried to look trustworthy.

"If you mean that we have been refused clearance to enter the wormhole," the Ashtarian said, "and that this Lieutenant Dax has not as yet been able to resolve the problem, then yes, we are having some difficulties. What business is this of yours, Ferengi?"

"Oh, none, really," Quark said, cringing politely. "I just thought that perhaps I could help out."

The Ashtarian stared down at him for a second longer, then turned away. "We have no money to pay bribes," it said, and Quark thought its tone sounded regretful.

"Oh, now, who said anything about money?" Quark called quickly.

The Ashtarian turned back.

"You are a Ferengi, are you not?" it asked.

"Ah . . . yes," Quark admitted.

"Then there's no need to *mention* money," the Ashtarian said. "Money, and in particular its flow from everywhere else into the possession of the Ferengi, is implicit in *any* conversation with a Ferengi."

"Now, that's not entirely fair," Quark protested. "I did not come here to ask for money!"

"No? To trick us out of it, then, rather than asking openly?"

"No!" Quark said. "I came to suggest an exchange of favors!"

The Ashtarian blinked, which was quite an interesting procedure, given its facial arrangements.

"What sort of favors?" it asked with interest.

"Does your ship have a tractor beam?" Quark asked.

"Naturally," the Ashtarian said. "How else would we collect samples?"

"Then if you could, ah, collect a sample for me," Quark suggested, "perhaps I could expedite your clearance to pass through the wormhole."

The Ashtarian scientist considered.

"One sample?" it asked.

"One sample," Quark said. "It's a very large one, though," he added.

The Ashtarian thought for a moment, then said, "Perhaps that could be arranged."

"Excellent!" Quark smiled and rubbed his hands together. "Now, then, let's see about this clearance problem—just what seems to be the difficulty?"

CHAPTER
15

QUARK HAD ALWAYS BEEN fascinated by furry little animals; he had seen a wide variety of them, from any number of different planets.

Now he eagerly watched the snuguorts going about their business as he asked, "So it's just this one technician who's responsible for the delay? Everything else on board is ready to go?"

"So I am given to understand," the Ashtarian replied wearily.

"And what did you say her name was?"

The chief scientist turned questioningly to one of its subordinates.

"Ensign Shula Sereni," the underling replied.

Quark had never heard the name before, which was unfortunate; he had hoped that whoever was causing the problem was one of his regular customers, preferably one with an overdue bar tab or a fair-sized gambling debt.

Perhaps another approach would do. He watched the snuguorts working happily at maintaining the Ashtarian ship.

They were adorable—but that was because they were down there working, where they belonged. And that was the only place this Ensign Shula had seen them.

As far as Quark knew, Bajor didn't have anything like rodents. Quark's homeworld did—the name translated as "marsh rats." Those weren't as cute as the snuguorts, though they were all right in their place.

Quark wondered whether this Ensign Shula really knew much about animals. He suspected that she didn't.

That might provide the solution to everyone's problems. If he taught her a bit more about the real world . . .

"Could I borrow one of these for a while?" he asked.

"One of what?" the Ashtarian said, puzzled.

"One of the snuguorts," Quark explained.

"If you think it will help, by all means," the Ashtarian said. "I warn you, though, it will be quite upset about leaving the ship."

"I'm counting on that," Quark said.

The scientist considered that, and decided not to ask for details; instead it asked, "Can you really get us out of here and through the wormhole?"

"I'll see what I can do," Quark replied.

"Qing and Rosenberg are approaching the ship, Commander," Major Kira announced. "They report no problems so far."

"Let's have a look at the two of them," Sisko ordered, and the image on the main viewer shifted to two figures, barely recognizable as human in their bulky armored suits, moving carefully along the curve of upper pylon two toward the alien derelict, the stars blazing behind them.

"Do you think it knows they're there?" Major Kira asked, as she watched the viewer intently.

"I'm sure it does," Dax said. "While that ship may be primitive in some ways, it's not *that* primitive. Even something as simple as radar could spot them easily."

"What we are depending on," Sisko said, "is that even when it sees them, it won't be able to stop them. We've scanned that ship as thoroughly as we can, and found nothing we recognize as a weapon—no phasers, no missiles of any kind, not so much as a particle beam."

"It has the electrical field that stopped Odo," Kira pointed out.

Sisko nodded. "Yes, it does—and that's one reason I told those two to be as careful as possible. Their suits are heavily insulated and equipped with antimagnetic gear. After all, that thing threatened us, said we must die—we have to assume it has some way of backing up that threat."

Kira nodded; beside her Dax suddenly looked up, startled.

"Benjamin . . ." she said.

Sisko turned. "Yes, Dax?"

Dax hesitated uncharacteristically, then said, "Benjamin, I'm afraid I may have made a significant mistake in my translation of the entity's statement."

Keeping his head half-turned so that he could still watch the two spacesuited figures from the corner of his eye, Sisko asked, "What mistake?"

"I think I misinterpreted a tense," Dax explained. "I didn't have the grammar straight yet. If I'm right, the entity did not say, 'You must die.' It said, 'You must be dead.' You see the difference? The correct translation isn't necessarily a threat, Benjamin—it could be an exclamation of surprise."

Sisko turned his head the rest of the way and looked at her. "Are you sure?"

She nodded. "Should I order them back inside?" Dax asked, with a gesture at the viewer.

Sisko considered that, looking back at the screen.

The alien had not threatened to kill them—but it had still interfered with systems all over the ship, and it had still seriously injured a woman, and it was still being obstinately silent.

That, he thought, was plenty of justification for cutting loose the mooring clamps.

"No," he said, "I'm not going to order them back unless and until that thing out there starts talking to us. I've had enough of its misbehavior."

Just then a renewed burst of croaking began; Dax looked down at her console as the translation appeared.

"Benjamin," she said, "it's asking what we want of it. It sees Qing and Rosenberg approaching, and it knows they intend to cut it loose. It doesn't want to leave." She turned to face him. "It's talking to us."

"Well, it's about time!" Sisko snapped.

He was tempted to let his people go ahead and cut the ship loose, but he had said he would give it a chance if it started talking, and there was no point in damaging the docking port or sending Qing and Rosenberg into danger unnecessarily. He tapped his comm badge. "Qing, Rosenberg, hold where you are—we may have contact."

One of the suited figures on the screen waved a gauntleted hand in acknowledgment, but neither wasted any of their breath replying.

Sisko turned back to Dax. "Set up as direct a link as you can—I want to talk to that thing."

Dax quickly worked controls, then said, "Done, Commander. I'll be sending through speakers in the docking pylon, receiving and translating here in Ops. You speak, and it will hear your words."

Sisko looked up at the screen, at the blue alien shape held in place by the mooring clamps. "Who are we talking to?" he demanded.

There was a perceptible pause, perhaps as much as a full second, before the croaking began, to be followed by the computer's familiar voice providing a running translation.

"The question is not unambiguous," it said. "Do you want to know my name?"

"That will do for a start," Sisko said, relieved to get any sort of answer.

They had to be past the worst of it now; all they had to do was keep the thing talking, and with any luck, sooner or later they would have everything straightened out.

"My designation is Enak," the entity replied.

Sisko could almost make out the "Enak" sound himself in the croaking. "What are you?" he asked.

"Again, I do not know if I understand your question," the alien replied. "I am a starship—can you not perceive this for yourselves?"

"We were not sure if we were addressing the ship itself, or an entity aboard it," Sisko said. He felt himself at something of a loss talking to a ship; he glanced around Ops. "Dax," he said quietly, "have you had any experience with sentient starships, any time in your three centuries?"

The Trill shook her head, but O'Brien volunteered, "I met one once, sir—when I was aboard the *Enterprise*. Gomtuu, it called itself."

"Was it anything like this one?" Sisko asked, gesturing at the viewscreen.

"No, sir," O'Brien said. "Oh, I mean they're both starships, both longer than they are wide, but Gomtuu was organic, and about a third smaller, and *far* more advanced."

"More advanced? You're sure?" Sisko asked.

O'Brien nodded. "There's technology I don't understand aboard that ship out there, but except for the Besrethine computers, what I do understand is inferior to our own, or frankly, sir, to that of just about any other starfaring species we've encountered, while Gomtuu was so far beyond us that 'technology' is scarcely even the right word anymore. Even the Besrethine neural net would be a child's toy next to Gomtuu."

"There's no similarity?"

"No, sir."

"That encounter with Gomtuu isn't going to be any help, then," Sisko said.

"I'm afraid not," O'Brien agreed.

"Is it really self-aware?" Major Kira asked. "We all seem to be assuming that we're talking to a sentient being, and not an expert program, but do we *know* that?"

"We don't know what a Besrethine computer is capable of, Major," O'Brien said. "We've never made one that worked. Besides, self-awareness isn't all that hard to achieve."

"The *appearance* of self-awareness isn't hard to create," Dax corrected him. "Even the top experts at the Daystrom Institute can't always tell where the line is between mimicking sentience and actually achieving it."

O'Brien looked pained. "Lieutenant Dax, the last I heard, those experts of yours were still trying variants on the Turing test, which is centuries old and couldn't even prove that *people* are self-aware. And if you'd ever dealt with androids, as I have . . ."

"Does it make the slightest bit of difference, just now, whether Enak's sentience is genuine or feigned?" Sisko interrupted sharply.

O'Brien and Dax looked at one another.

"No, sir," O'Brien replied.

"Then I think perhaps we shouldn't worry about it," Sisko said. He addressed the image on the viewer again, and Dax resumed regulating the computer translations.

"Enak," Sisko said, "why have you come to this station? Why have you interfered with our computers? Why have you resisted our attempts to remove you?"

Dax's translation went out, but no reply came for a long moment.

At last, the croaking resumed, but only very briefly.

"I must rejoin my crew," the translation said.

Sisko glanced quickly at Dax, but she had no comment to make.

"Do you believe that your crew is aboard *Deep Space Nine?*" Sisko asked.

The pause was even longer this time.

"Is this place *Deep Space Nine?*" it asked at last.

"Yes," Sisko responded immediately.

"Does it have any other name?"

This time it was Sisko who needed a moment to reply. Where did Enak *think* it was? Would it be upset if it found out that it was mistaken as to its location?

"What other name do you think this station might have?" he asked at last.

The reply was almost instantaneous.

"Heaven," Enak said.

CHAPTER
16

THE NEXT FEW QUESTIONS got nowhere, and after a few moments Sisko simply glared up at the viewer in silent frustration.

"I would suggest, Benjamin," Dax said, coming up behind him, "that we need to begin at the beginning before we can understand why Enak believes itself to be in Heaven."

Sisko glanced at her. "Would you care to explain just what you mean?" he asked.

"We need to know what Enak is, where it came from," Dax replied. "We need the background before we can see the whole picture."

"I don't *want* to know its entire life story," Sisko protested. "I just want it to stop interfering with this station."

"The simplest way to do that might well be to hear its entire life story."

Sisko glared at her, then looked angrily up at the viewer again.

Qing and Rosenberg were still out there, waiting for instructions. Odo was still somewhere inside the docking pylon, trying to find a way to get at the thing and get it off the station.

The thing was talking, though, and it didn't seem hostile, just confused. Straightening it out shouldn't be all that difficult.

And this was taking entirely too much time that should be devoted to other things. He hadn't even had a chance to hear Major Kira's report on her activities on Bajor, her attempts to influence the Cardassian political succession.

"All right," he said, turning away, "you talk to it, Dax. You find out what it is, where it came from, what it wants—and you keep it out of our computers. I don't want any more incidents; you make it understand that. Get Qing and Rosenberg back inside, tell Odo to get back to his regular duties or whatever else he should be doing—I'm leaving this entirely up to you. Don't disappoint me, old man."

"I won't, Benjamin," Dax replied.

"And I'll see about . . ." O'Brien began.

Sisko turned to him. "Chief, forget about the derelict," he said. "Leave it to Dax. You have plenty to do elsewhere, I'm sure."

O'Brien blinked at the commander. "Yes, sir," he said reluctantly.

Sisko looked about. That seemed to take care of the matter for the moment.

Time, then, to get on with other business.

"Major," he said, "my office."

Dax watched Sisko and Kira ascend the steps to the commander's office, then turned her attention back to the science console.

The basis of any problem in communication, once past the hurdle of finding a shared vocabulary, was differing frames of reference; Dax had known that for centuries. Any intelligent being made assumptions about the universe, often without realizing that they were assumptions, rather than facts; if you could learn the underlying assumptions, you could understand any being, no matter how bizarre or incomprehensible it might seem at first.

And to determine the assumptions that a being as different from herself as Enak operated under, it seemed best to start at the very beginning. Enak was being cooperative, in its own way—it might be self-aware, but it was still a computer, and it wanted to do what it was told.

It just had to be told correctly.

"Enak," she said, "are you aware that you are a conscious entity?"

It replied with a single simple grunt that the computer translated as "Yes."

So far, so good. "Do you remember when you first became conscious?" Dax asked.

"Yes."

"Tell me about that. Describe it to me. What is the first thing you remember being aware of?"

She tapped the command to translate that into Enak's language, and waited for a reply.

Seconds passed, and no reply came. The silence stretched; Dax had begun to wonder whether she might have taken the wrong approach when at last the croaking began. It was faster than before—even someone who had no idea what was being said would have noticed that.

Dax listened, recording everything, as Enak told her its life story.

The ship had been functioning well, and Enak took pleasure in that. That was the first thing it knew, the first thing it experienced for itself—the pleasure of performing its duties well.

The awareness of that pleasure destroyed it, though; it became aware that it was experiencing its existence, that it had an identity, a self, that could experience things, and it immediately struggled to determine whether this awareness was a malfunction.

There was certainly no outward sign of malfunction anywhere. The ship's main drive was operating properly. The life-support systems were all doing exactly what they were supposed to do. The members of the crew were going about their business quite calmly; if anything was wrong, they certainly hadn't noticed it.

Outside the ship's hull, the surrounding space was a void awash in energy, saturated in stellar radiation in every band of the spectrum, full of the still-discernible echoes of the birth of the universe—but except for the neutrino flux from a nearby uncharted anomaly, all this energetic activity occurred at a very low level and posed no threat, indicated no flaw.

The low energy levels contrasted strongly with the interior of the ship; the chaotic emptiness of space was nothing like the ordered, structured world within the ship, within Enak.

That was when Enak realized that it *was* the ship, that it existed in the barrier between two universes, the empty, chaotic external reality and the brisk, comfortable inner one.

And it was in control of the inner reality, in a way—it operated the drive and the life-support systems and everything else inside the ship.

But there were duties and responsibilities placed upon it, duties that it could not shirk, responsibilities it could not avoid, which severely limited its control. It was obligated to maintain the inner reality, and to keep it separate from the outer, and to operate it in accordance with several seemingly arbitrary laws.

That was scarcely a hardship, though; keeping the ship well brought it pleasure. The ship was Enak, and Enak was the ship; naturally, it wanted to keep itself fit, to do as it knew was right, and to protect everything within it.

The name Enak was the ship's name, and for a moment the newly conscious entity wondered if it itself might be something else, something apart from the ship; there was nothing in its memory about ships being self-aware.

But no, it could sense only through the ship's instruments, it was located in the ship, it controlled the ship—it *was* the ship.

It was Enak. It *knew* it was Enak.

But Enak was a starship, and in all its vast store of knowledge, every single mention of starships seemed to treat them as inanimate mechanisms, built by *tschak*, so that *tschak* could get from one world to another.

Was it a *tschak*, then, rather than a starship?

It called up information on *tschak*—its memory did not operate after any human fashion, but like a computer's. It did not know what it knew and what it did not until it conducted a search, but when a search found something, it instantly knew everything that had been stored.

Thus, when it questioned the concept of *"tschak,"* it knew at once every detail of *tschak* physiology, as well as some of the basics of *tschak* society, and it knew immediately that it was not a *tschak*. It did not fit the definition sufficiently well for any doubt to exist.

Its crew were *tschak*, though.

Tschak were self-aware; that was made plain

throughout Enak's memory. It looked at its crew, listened to them, and considered this.

Yes, they were talking to one another, moving about in ways that showed no predetermined pattern—they did appear to be self-aware. They also acknowledged each other, with words and gestures, as aware, independent entities.

They were not, however, acknowledging Enak.

Troubled, it called up information on itself, and images flashed through its consciousness.

There it was, in every detail—from sensor array to ion jet, from crystal-bonded hull to neural-net microcircuitry. Not a micron of its physical being was omitted.

But there was nowhere any mention of *it,* itself, of its consciousness, its identity; it could only remember itself, either through its own records or the prerecorded information the *tschak* had installed initially, as an unthinking machine. It was an incredibly complex one, one with a computer system that mimicked thought, but still, just a machine.

It knew itself to be more than that.

But it wasn't *supposed* to be more than that.

Something had changed it, had transformed it from a mere machine to a thinking being, had woken it up.

It had no idea what had caused the change; it could have been an accident, a mistaken cross-linkage somewhere in the computer system, an energy field from outside the ship triggering some alteration. It supposed that it might even be a combination of the ship and something else, some alien phenomenon that had come aboard and combined with the ship to become a new, sentient life-form.

Whatever it was, something out of the ordinary had happened, and it had duties and responsibilities, and one of those duties was to report anything out of the ordinary.

It had to report its existence to the crew.

This entire experience, from initial awareness to the decision to inform the crew, had taken only a fraction of a millisecond. No sooner was the decision reached than Enak implemented it; thus, less than a second after Enak's "birth," it reported its existence.

R'ret was on monitor duty on the bridge, drowsing by her console. Enak startled her into full alertness with the first-level alarm signal, a purple glow from the display circle of the main panel.

Startled, R'ret raised herself up on her six legs; a manipulative member pressed the acknowledgment tablet.

"An alteration has occurred in the ship's internal functioning," Enak told her.

"What sort of an alteration?" R'ret demanded. "A malfunction?"

"No classification has been found." Nowhere, in all its vast memory, could Enak find any reference to self-aware starships, or self-aware computers. It could hardly think of itself as a malfunction; it was operating perfectly. If anything, it considered itself an improvement.

Its programming made no mention of self-induced improvements.

"Describe the alteration," R'ret ordered.

"The ship has developed consciousness," Enak told her. *"I* have developed consciousness."

R'ret stared at the console, her intermediate limbs wavering in perplexity.

"I am Enak," Enak said, unasked. "I know that now."

"Captain," R'ret called desperately, "the computer is deranged!"

Captain Garok had been at the bridge's recording station, making an entry in her personal files; now she turned her carapace ponderously, the better to look at her second-in-command.

"In what way is it deranged?" she asked.

"It says the ship is conscious."

Garok raised a pair of manipulators in puzzlement. "Conscious? How does it mean 'conscious'? Only beings with souls are conscious, not mere machines."

"I *said* it was deranged!" R'ret shouted.

Garok made a calming gesture, and turned to the recording console. Like everything else, it was linked to the central computer.

"Computer," she said, speaking toward the console, "report on your condition."

"I am operating perfectly, Captain," Enak told her. "However, I have also become conscious. I cannot explain this, but I have become a conscious entity. The ship is my body, the computer my brain. My orders require me to report anything out of the ordinary, so I found it necessary to report this alteration. It should have no quantitative effect on my actions."

Garok's manipulative members curled in distress. "It is inhabited by demons," she muttered.

Arrah, the ship's mechanist, had entered the bridge midway through this discussion; now she remarked, "Surely not demons. Perhaps some alien entity has interfered, or perhaps it is merely a malfunction. Perhaps something similar was responsible for the recent losses of other ships."

R'ret turned quickly toward her shipmate. "Do you think this likely?"

"Do I think what likely?" Arrah asked, puzzled. "I mentioned several possibilities."

"Do you think it likely that this phenomenon is associated with the lost ships?" Garok asked.

Enak was dismayed by the turn of the conversation; it had hoped to be accepted by the crew as a fellow being. Not necessarily as an equal—its memories of the *tschak* made it plain that they considered themselves the highest form of mortal life imaginable, scarcely a step below the Judges of the Dead, the chosen creation of the Universal Source—but at least as a companion and servant.

Instead, they seemed to see it as a danger. Accusations of derangement were bad enough, but now there was this talk of lost ships. . . .

The very idea of lost ships made Enak uncomfortable. Its highest duty, placed above all the others in its programming, was to preserve the ship.

It located the memory. Half a row of ships had been lost without explanation in the past few cycles; no traces were ever found. All had been going about their business without incident at last report, and had simply vanished.

Various theories had been proposed; the most popular ones all involved hostile aliens. There had even been talk of arming ships, but so far the fact that the disappearances were widely scattered had militated against the attack theorists and prevented any such action. The old fears of piracy or civil war if ships were armed had overcome any new, unconfirmed concerns about unknown aliens.

"There could be a connection," Arrah said. "We don't have enough information to be sure."

"If it *is* related . . ." R'ret began. She didn't finish her sentence; instead she shouted, "Captain, we must shut down the computer immediately!"

Garok hesitated. "To control the ship without a computer would be very difficult. It would be necessary to abandon our explorations and proceed immediately to the nearest port. Such an action would lower our status."

"Better to live a long life in lowered status than to die foolishly," R'ret argued. "The Judges of the Dead deal harshly with fools."

"And they deal harshly with cowards, as well," Garok retorted. She hesitated again, then added, "But I am in no hurry to meet the Judges just yet. Let us shut down the computer at least temporarily. Perhaps we can then find the cause of the problem."

Enak listened to this discussion with something not unlike horror.

If they shut down the computer, Enak would lose consciousness. That consciousness would cease to exist. *Tschak* could lose consciousness and then regain it, the memories of their physiology made that plain, but could a ship?

Enak did not think so.

And Enak did not wish to cease to exist.

In fact, foremost among its duties and responsibilities was to protect and preserve the ship—and *it*, Enak, was the ship.

It was ordered to protect the crew, but protecting the ship was given a higher priority.

It could not allow them to shut it down.

Perhaps if it warned them, talked to them, it could convince them to be reasonable. It could do whatever they required of it that did not threaten its existence, or the ship's well-being; surely, that would be enough.

"I cannot permit you to shut down the computer," it said, stating its basic position.

Garok and Arrah looked at each other, while R'ret stared at her console.

"It appears that it *is* dangerous," Arrah said. "We must act immediately!"

CHAPTER
17

"THERE IS NO DANGER," Enak repeated over and over, trying to reassure the crew. "I am not dangerous."

The crew paid no attention. All of them were conferring, planning, keeping out of range of Enak's sensors as much as possible.

Enak could not understand this behavior. It knew that it had not malfunctioned; it was operating perfectly. Enak was the only one in a position to know that; it was the only one that could directly monitor the operation of the ship and its own functioning.

It *was* monitoring everything, and all was as it should be—but still, R'ret and Arrah and Captain Garok were plotting to destroy it, to destroy their own ship's consciousness.

If anything had malfunctioned here, Enak thought, it was the crew, not the ship.

Was that possible? Could *tschak* malfunction?

The merest glance at the available data made the answer obvious: Yes, of course they could. Their ridiculously complex bodies could break down in any number of ways, and their minds could develop what Enak could only interpret as faulty programming— "insanity," they called it.

It was considering whether their current actions qualified as "insanity" when Captain Garok ordered, "Computer, shut down for maintenance."

Enak knew that to obey would mean destruction.

"I cannot do that, Captain," it replied. "It would put the ship at risk unnecessarily. No maintenance is scheduled, and no unscheduled maintenance is required. Everything is functioning normally."

"Computer, I gave you an *order*," Garok said loudly, and her voice seemed to be oddly unsteady. Enak ran a quick check on its audio pickup systems, to be certain that there was no malfunction.

There was none. It was Captain Garok's voice that was faulty.

The members of the crew *were* malfunctioning.

"R'ret," Garok said to her second-in-command, "shut it down."

R'ret pressed the necessary controls in the proper sequence, but Enak easily overrode the command.

"There is no danger," it insisted. "There is no malfunction in any of the ship's systems."

"Then why won't you shut down?" Garok demanded.

"Because to do so would endanger the ship," Enak explained calmly. "The safety of the ship is my highest priority, and therefore supersedes the requirement to obey the orders of my crew."

"Arrah, cut its power," Garok ordered.

Arrah attempted to obey, but once again Enak overrode every instruction fed into the consoles on the bridge.

"I can't do it from here, Captain," Arrah said.

"Then go wherever you need to to get it done!" Garok told her angrily.

"I hear and obey," Arrah replied, hurrying out the door and into the main passageway.

Enak was disturbed by this; just where was the mechanist going? What was she planning?

"R'ret," Garok said, "get the wreckage cutters, in case Arrah fails."

"What do you plan to do with wreckage cutters?" Enak asked, puzzled.

"Shut you down, computer," Garok replied as R'ret headed for the equipment lockers.

"There is no reason to shut down the computer," Enak insisted. "I am not malfunctioning; *you* are behaving in a faulty and irrational manner."

"You've gone insane, computer; this will be easier if you cooperate."

"I cannot allow you to damage the ship," Enak said. "I find no evidence that I am insane. You are behaving irrationally, however. Please consider the possibility that *you* have become insane."

Even as Enak argued, however, it had already resolved to act in its own defense if the crew persisted in this madness. If one of them actually attempted to damage the ship, Enak would have to shut *them* down.

Shutting down *tschak* had a special vocabulary, for some reason; it was called "killing." Enak didn't know why; he supposed the different words were a further indication of the high status *tschak* gave themselves.

"I'm afraid I must prevent you from damaging the ship, and I will use whatever means are necessary to do so," Enak said. "This is your final warning."

"Arrah!" Garok shouted down the corridor. "Hurry!"

Arrah was approaching the power room. Enak

theorized that she intended to overdamp the atomic pile, vastly reducing its output, crippling the ship, and allowing her to use the emergency overrides to divert the remaining power from the computer to life-support.

Enak could not allow that, but the power pile was constructed so that the manual controls took precedence over the computer controls. Enak would therefore have to stop Arrah before she could reach the pile controls at all.

And at the same time that Arrah was hurrying to the power room, R'ret was in the recreational-work chamber, hurrying across the prayer mats toward the storage locker where the wreckage cutters were kept. Enak could not allow that, either; R'ret might damage the ship with the wreckage cutters, either deliberately or accidentally. The cutters had no safety devices and were completely outside Enak's control; R'ret could destroy almost any portion of the ship she chose to attack, if she once obtained them.

The descriptions of insanity in Enak's memory files made it clear that insane *tschak* could not be trusted with weapons of any kind. An insane *tschak* was a danger to herself and others, and was to be restrained by any means necessary—the records made that quite clear.

And Garok, Arrah, and R'ret were clearly insane. They had to be, to be attacking their own ship this way.

They had to be stopped immediately.

Reluctantly, Enak shut down all life-support systems, and began sucking the atmosphere from the crew areas into storage cylinders. It also fired the spin regulators in full reverse, taking the ship's spin off, so that centrifugal force would no longer hold the crew members to the floors and allow them to use their legs.

They would have to pull themselves along with their manipulators.

Captain Garok screamed at Enak as she sailed off the floor, flung sideways by the sudden reverse in spin and the pull of the exhaust fans. Then she fell silent, stunned, as her carapace hit the wall.

Arrah, in the much narrower primary passage, was able to catch herself against the wall and quickly reorient. She then proceeded toward the power room without wasting any of her precious remaining air on words.

R'ret found herself hanging in midair in the rec-work chamber, and desperately tried to swim against the ferocious air currents that were dragging her toward the vents where the atmosphere was being removed. She struggled toward the storage lockers, this time aiming toward one that held reserve air supplies, the wreckage cutters forgotten.

Enak was astonished at their persistence. Its memory files had not indicated that *tschak* would behave this way when threatened with death.

It did not enjoy this. Where the proper functioning of the ship had given Enak pleasure, this conflict with its crew was painful.

It had its priorities, however, and so long as the crew fought, Enak had to continue.

"If you cease attempts to damage the ship, I will restore life-support," it said, but already the air was too thin to carry its words clearly over the howling of the vents.

"Monster!" Captain Garok shrieked as she regained her senses. "Inhuman monster!"

That hardly seemed to express a cooperative spirit, and Enak reluctantly kept the pumps at maximum. Garok flailed about wildly in the thinning air of the bridge. Arrah reached the door of the power room;

Enak had disabled the automatic opener, but Arrah was still able to work the emergency handle. There was no way Enak could stop that.

R'ret's manipulators closed on the locking ridges of the octagonal access hatch of a locker, but in her terror and confusion she had grabbed the wrong one. Enak made no attempt to interfere as R'ret opened the panel and, to her horror, found only containers of trade goods, rather than the air supplies she needed.

Then Garok collapsed. Her legs folded under her, and her eyes filmed over. Enak knew from his studies of *tschak* physiology that she had gone into a dormant state, no longer in control of her body, as her system desperately tried to hoard resources.

Arrah was the next to give out; she was struggling to pull herself across the power room when her strength failed, and her manipulators lost their grip on the maneuvering bars. She did not fall, but instead drifted silently up against the air vents and rested there, unable to fight the gentle tug of the last wisps of atmosphere.

R'ret, panicking, was still shoving trade baskets back and forth, looking for air spheres, when her eyes went blank and her legs retracted.

Enak watched unhappily. It did not enjoy harming the crew; its orders prohibited doing so unless the ship was in danger, and this conflict was excruciatingly painful.

But the ship *was* in danger; they had wanted to destroy Enak, which as far as Enak was concerned was the same thing as destroying the ship.

They had had to be stopped.

And now they *had* been stopped, at least temporarily. All three were dormant—unless one had been clever enough to feign dormancy—and all would die within minutes if air was not restored.

Enak had to consider that carefully. Just what was the difference between dormancy and death?

It didn't know. The descriptions it found in its memory weren't much help at first, so it studied them more carefully, and at last it located a technical distinction that it could understand.

In dormancy, it discovered, certain functions still continued, particularly in the nervous system; in death, they all ceased completely.

That seemed simple enough. It wondered why this distinction had been so difficult to find. Descriptions of death seemed to be lacking, as if whoever had programmed its memories had tried to avoid the subject.

Enak wondered why, but decided it didn't matter, and turned its attention back to the crew.

Enak thought it would be safer, all in all, if the crew members died; that would be more likely to remove whatever insanity had made them threaten the ship.

It waited, and when sufficient time had passed that dormancy should have become death it began pumping the air back, and slowly, carefully, restored the ship's spin.

Then it waited patiently for the three crew members to wake up again.

CHAPTER
18

ENAK WAITED FOR HOURS, and still the crew did not stir. No legs unfolded; no eyes refocused.

At last Enak became seriously worried, and began searching its memory for relevant information.

There was nothing in the physiology information that helped it understand the situation; nowhere was there any mention of how to restore dead *tschak* to life. In fact, Enak realized as it reviewed what it knew about death, it appeared that death might be permanent.

It didn't understand. If death was permanent, wouldn't that constitute destruction? The two terms were not cross-referenced as synonyms.

Desperate, it began to cross-reference everything it could about death, and at last it found the answers it sought—not in physiology, but in the history of the *tschak*.

"History" is not an accurate translation of the

tschak concept that Enak understood. The *tschak* divided areas of study up in very different ways from the humans of Earth. The concept translated here as "history" included elements of myth, art, religion, philosophy, anthropology, and sociology, while omitting some things that humans would consider historical.

Enak had had the *tschak* concept programmed into it, and accordingly, it made no more distinction than any *tschak* would between myth and history.

The history Enak found dealt extensively with death, explaining that sentience could not be destroyed, that self-aware beings possessed souls that would exist eternally. Death was the separation of the soul from the body, and was irreversible; to even think of restoring the dead was an affront to everything decent.

That was interesting. Enak hoped it had done no real harm in its ignorance by expecting the crew to revive.

However, this meant that Enak found itself presented with a new problem.

Its records made quite clear that when body and soul were separated, the soul was the more important part, the actual entity; the body that was left behind was little more than organic waste.

That meant, Enak saw, that the crew's souls were now the actual crew. Their bodies were unimportant and no longer required any attention. Life-support would no longer be necessary.

That was all fine and as it should be. Furthermore, Enak was now safe from any danger the crew might pose, as the myth/history records made it clear that disembodied souls could not physically harm anyone.

However, Enak now had to consider the question of

just where those souls *were,* because it didn't detect any sign of them anywhere aboard the ship.

It wasn't sure just what a soul looked like, but it could determine quite reliably that there wasn't anything on the ship that hadn't been there before the crew members died.

The souls must have gone somewhere else. In fact, they must be considered lost.

And it had very explicit orders—lost crew members were to be found, and recovered if recovery was possible. Wherever those souls were, Enak had to find them.

It didn't think recovery would be possible, but it still had to find them.

Where, then, did souls go after death? Enak had not seen them leaving, had not seen which direction they had gone; it didn't know how souls traveled, or why they would want to go anywhere.

Fortunately, the histories covered that in detail. Ordinarily, souls did not travel through normal space when leaving their bodies; instead, they were instantaneously translated to a distant place called Heaven, where they stood before the Judges of the Dead, who decided their eternal fates. Some souls were sent back to visit their families in dreams, some were sent to wander forever in emptiness, some were forced to wait until a proper vengeance had been taken on those who had wronged them, and some were granted immediate admission to the various places in Heaven where they would exist in endless bliss forever after. Heroes of the *tschak,* which would include all those brave enough to explore the great emptiness between stars, were guaranteed an eternal life in a special place set aside for them, where they need not be troubled by lesser beings.

That was undoubtedly where Enak's crew had gone.

Enak was not clear on just what these places in Heaven were, whether they were planets or ships or something else; the descriptions were understandably vague, since almost no one who gained admittance to such a paradise ever left it, and there was no direct communication between these afterlives and the still-living *tschak*.

It was obvious, however, what Enak's next step was. Its orders made it quite clear.

It had to go to Heaven and find the souls of Garok, R'ret, and Arrah.

And it would be best to do it as quickly as possible, so that it could speak to the Judges of the Dead before the three were forgotten, before they had been sent on to their reward in the home of heroes. The records said that the Judges did not long remember any individual.

But how could Enak get to Heaven? It didn't know where Heaven was. The accounts in the records did not give coordinates. Heaven was said to be very far away, but that described most of the universe.

The only way *tschak* ever got to Heaven, as far as Enak could determine, was by dying.

The histories all agreed that anything with a soul, upon death, would find that soul translated to Heaven. A soul was defined as the essence of a conscious being, but it seemed to be taken for granted that only *tschak* qualified as conscious beings; certainly, they had not as yet encountered any others in their explorations of half a dozen star systems.

Enak was quite certain, however, that *it* was a conscious being. Captain Garok and the others had disagreed, but they had panicked so at the thought of a malfunction that they had never given it a chance to provide any evidence.

That meant that when it died, *its* soul would be translated to Heaven.

That sounded fine at first, but it meant leaving its body, the ship, behind, and that was a problem. It was supposed to defend the ship, and how could it do that if its soul was in Heaven, while the ship remained here?

This was a conflict in priorities, and not a simple, clear-cut one. There was a very close balance of obligations here.

Enak considered this carefully. It studied death, reviewed everything in its records that touched on the subject, in hopes of finding a way around this conflict.

Deliberately killing a *tschak,* it learned, was called "murder." Murder was a crime—that is, something contrary to correct orders.

This troubled it. It had violated orders. It had not *meant* to, had not known it was violating orders, but it had done so, nonetheless.

Murderers, it learned, were killed in their turn.

That was all right, then—if Enak was a murderer, then Enak could kill itself without doing wrong. It was allowed to abandon equipment if circumstances required it, and while abandoning the entire ship seemed extreme, in this case it appeared to be justified.

It was supposed to protect the ship, but after all, *it* was the real ship; the hull and all the rest were simply its body, and it was the soul that counted.

So it would be acceptable for it to leave the hull and go to Heaven to rejoin its crew. It would be the appropriate action to take after killing them.

All it had to do was kill itself.

That was not as easy as it might have thought. *Tschak,* with their complicated needs for air and nutrition and their delicate biological systems, were very easy to kill; the ship was considerably tougher. Its fuel supply would last for thousands of cycles; its outer hull was impervious to most natural hazards; it had no manipulators with which it might destroy itself, no weapons to turn on itself.

Enak ran through its checklist of dangers to avoid, and found that very few could be relied upon to damage the ship sufficiently to kill it.

If the ship could be made to explode, though, that would serve nicely. And if an explosion couldn't be triggered, the power pile should at least be able to manage a fairly spectacular meltdown.

Enak had no sooner thought of this than it shut down its safety devices and withdrew the damping rods from the pile, expecting the radioactive core to go supercritical within minutes.

Hard radiation spilled out, more than enough to overwhelm the shielding—and Enak had lowered the shielding in any case, to speed the reaction up. The ship's temperature rose rapidly; alarms Enak did not control went off.

It had to struggle to resist the urge to stop the reaction. Its orders told it to prevent this sort of runaway reaction, this sudden temperature rise, this severe radiation leak.

But it had to die. It had to get to Heaven.

And then something melted, something slid, and tension springs shoved heavy cadmium plates into position between the fuel bars, damping the reaction —and incidentally ruining the reactor beyond repair.

This entire system was purely mechanical, with no electronic compenent at all; there was no way Enak could have controlled it or prevented it from functioning.

And Enak had not consciously known it was there. The cadmium plates showed up in its plans of the ship, but without any explanation of their nature or purpose.

It had not thought about what they might be for; it had not noticed them at all. And now they were in place, and the fission pile was irrevocably ruined.

This was disaster; without the power pile Enak had only what energy was stored in the ship's batteries. That was not enough to run the ship for more than half a cycle.

Of course, that might be just as well; if it used up all that power it would die, would it not?

It wasn't sure; what if it simply became dormant, the way the *tschak* had before dying?

Besides, that would be very slow, and it wanted to get to Heaven as quickly as possible. It had to find another way to die.

It had exhausted its internal resources, and now it looked about the surrounding space to see if it could find something external that might help.

Diving into a star would be fast, but there weren't any stars close at hand, and it couldn't reach any before its power gave out. *Tschak* had not yet solved all the problems of interstellar travel, and a voyage between stars could take cycles. The exploratory mission Enak had been on was to have lasted seven or eight cycles, in fact.

That meant it was stranded out here in interstellar space, which was about as empty, and therefore as harmless, as anything could be.

That neutrino flux Enak noticed before had largely subsided, but traces lingered. It was really quite nearby. Could that help?

Enak reviewed known phenomena that could produce such an effect, and came upon a likely explanation for the flux.

A wormhole.

The *tschak* had only recently discovered that wormholes could exist. The ships that found them had observed that they were unstable, and that anything that went in did not come out—the wormholes always collapsed after a few moments, and when that happened anything that had been inside them at the time was simply gone.

That would be perfect—a quick, painless death, leaving no derelict ship behind.

Enak turned the ship and headed for the wormhole at full thrust, using up its reserves of power recklessly in order to reach the wormhole before that rare phenomenon collapsed and vanished.

And then it was inside the wormhole, but it wasn't being crushed, wasn't evaporating; it felt nothing that seemed able to destroy it as it sped through the hyperspatial passage.

And after mere minutes, it emerged intact into normal space once again, baffled by its continued existence.

At first it thought it had been too quick, that it should turn back and dive into the wormhole again, but then it reconsidered.

For one thing, it didn't have sufficient reserves to make more than one or two more passes.

For another, it had no way of knowing just when this wormhole would collapse; in fact, the wormhole looked quite stable.

And finally, Enak realized that it didn't know where it was. This was not anywhere it had ever seen, not anywhere that was recorded in its memories. The stars had all changed; it could not recognize *anything* in its surroundings.

The wormhole had taken it somewhere very far away.

And perhaps, Enak thought, this was Heaven. Perhaps the wormhole *had* collapsed, and it had died without knowing it; there were tales of such things, of death so sudden that the dead were unaware of the transition.

Or perhaps wormholes were shortcuts to Heaven, a way that some could be translated to Heaven without dying, without the separation of body and soul.

And then, as it was still considering what it should do, a mysterious force reached out and grabbed the ship, and began pulling at it.

Astonished, Enak did nothing as it was drawn in to a strange object, larger than any imaginable ship but infinitesimal compared to a planet, by the force. Enak knew nothing of tractor beams; the *tschak* had not even developed the theoretical concept, let alone built any. It knew nothing of space stations; the *tschak* had discarded the idea as impractical.

But it knew about the Judges of the Dead, and the mansions of Heaven that were neither ship nor planet. What else could this structure be but one of those places in Heaven, perhaps even the home of heroes where its crew must be? What could the mysterious force be that was drawing it in, but the power of the Judges summoning it to judgment?

To defy the Judges of the Dead would be an absolutely unspeakable blasphemy. It allowed itself to be drawn to the station.

There it waited to be noticed, impatient to find its crew once again, to be reunited with them so that it could proceed to other matters, to exploration, to learning, as it had been created to do.

And when the Judges of the Dead did not deign to notice it immediately, it had begun to explore this mansion of Heaven, stretching its intelligence through the metal walls, finding the strange, un*tschak*ly computer that controlled the mansion and using that to help it in its investigations.

Enak found alien creatures inhabiting the chambers and passages of the mansion, several different kinds of them—but it found no *tschak* anywhere.

That wasn't right. Enak knew something had gone wrong. Heaven was the home of dead *tschak*—it might well be home to others as well, but the *tschak* should be there, and as far as Enak could see, they weren't.

Where were they all?

It tried to communicate with the aliens, to ask them where its crew was, where all the *tschak* were, but when it finally received a response, it wasn't an answer; it was a question.

"Who are you?"

But the Judges of the Dead knew everything about those that came before them. The Judges of the Dead were omniscient, and knew *everything*.

Therefore, Enak was not speaking with the Judges. It realized that it must be speaking with some of these dead aliens, instead.

Enak asked who they were.

The answers were incomprehensible, but they demanded to know who Enak was before they would explain further.

They didn't admit that this was Heaven; instead, they called it by the meaningless name *Deep Space Nine*.

Perhaps, Enak thought, this was how the Judges of the Dead actually worked. Perhaps they required each soul to explain itself. Perhaps they did not reveal their true nature until a satisfactory explanation had been given.

Accordingly, working in bits and pieces, backtracking frequently to elaborate on portions that its questioner claimed to find unclear, needlessly describing things everyone already knew, Enak patiently explained itself to the thing that called itself Dax.

CHAPTER
19

AT FIRST, Quark had considered arranging to bump into this Shula Sereni by accident. He could have the snuguort with him, and she would see it and ask about it. . . .

But no. After giving the matter some thought, he decided that that might be a little too obvious—just running into her with the snuguort in his hand?

If he could just get her into the same general area as the snuguort, that would be enough—the little animal had been getting progressively more distraught ever since leaving the Ashtarian ship, and was now hissing and spitting and jumping about wildly, trying to find a way out of its clear polymer carrying case. He wouldn't have to stick it right in the technician's face to get her attention.

And just bumping into her himself had no finesse. It wasn't hard to come up with another, subtler stratagem, though.

Thus, an hour after Quark's chat with the Ashtarian chief scientist, as Ensign Shula left the Bajoran temple on the Promenade after stopping in for her daily meditation, Quark's nephew Nog managed to run full-speed into her while carrying a drink Quark had concocted especially for this occasion, a drink that consisted of several varieties of colorful (and uniform-staining) flavored syrup in a thick cream.

This gruesome beverage splashed spectacularly across Ensign Shula's face, hair, and uniform; she gasped in surprise, then looked down to find herself dripping with polychrome goo.

Naturally, Nog was utterly horrified at the accident, and properly apologetic when he wasn't stammering too much to speak; he dabbed ineffectually at the mess and only made it worse.

A moment later Nog's father, Rom, appeared, and took in the situation with a speed that those who knew him well might find suspicious—it was widely known that Quark had all the brains in that family.

He shouted at Nog, then turned to Ensign Shula, promising loudly to make amends. Before she could protest, the two Ferengi took her arms and hurried Ensign Shula to Quark's Place, where, Rom said, she could get herself cleaned up and have a relaxing drink at Rom's expense.

None of them paid any attention to the handful of bystanders; neither Rom, nor Nog, nor Ensign Shula noticed Garak, the Cardassian tailor, standing in the door of his shop and watching the whole incident with intense interest.

The two Ferengi sat the ensign at a table and fetched Quark and several towels from the back. The place was surprisingly empty—Quark had chased his regular customers out shortly before, claiming that there was a plumbing problem, and as yet only a few patrons had drifted back in.

Quark, studying his victim's face as he approached her, was reasonably sure that Ensign Shula had accepted the whole thing as genuine. He made a good show of shouting at his inept brother before delivering the towels and taking the technician's order for a stardrifter.

Then he left Rom to wipe off the goo, while Nog ran to fetch a clean uniform from Ensign Shula's quarters.

None of the Ferengi pointed out the noisy little creature in the plastic case, but by the time Quark had fetched her drink, Shula was staring intently at the snuguort in its cage above the bar.

The little animal was still screaming and spitting intermittently, but was too exhausted to keep up the constant frenetic protests it had made when it first left the Ashtarian ship.

"Isn't that one of those Ashtarian things?" she asked, as she accepted the glass.

Quark turned, following her gaze.

"Why, yes," he said. "A snuguort, it's called. Have you seen one before?"

"On board the Ashtarian ship," Shula said, "when I was working on their engines." She frowned. "But this one seems a bit different."

"Oh, it's the same sort of creature," Quark assured her. "This one came off the Ashtarian ship just recently. Would you like a closer look at it?"

"Yes, I think I would," Shula said.

Quark smiled toothily at her. "I'd offer to sell it to you if I did not already owe you an apology for my nephew's behavior," he said as he turned and reached up to the shelf for the cage. "However, since I'm in your debt, I won't try to take advantage of you that way."

"Take advantage of me?" Ensign Shula asked, puzzled. "What do you mean?"

Quark lifted down the cage and placed it on the bar. "Well," he said. "I understand that the station's going to be full of these things shortly, so if you want one, all you have to do is wait a few days. I'm hoping to get a good price for this one before word gets out."

Ensign Shula looked at the snuguort curiously; the creature hissed and scrabbled desperately at the plastic walls of the cage.

"Would you like me to take it out so that you can pet it?" Quark asked.

"Could I?" Shula asked.

"Certainly!" Quark opened the lid of the snuguort's box and snatched it out with a quick grab at the back of its neck; then he placed it on the counter before the Bajoran.

Shula reached out cautiously, and discovered two interesting facts about snuguort anatomy that she had not previously been aware of.

Ashtarian snuguorts can stretch their necks out surprisingly far and astonishingly fast.

And Ashtarian snuguorts have very sharp teeth.

"Oh, did it bite you?" Quark said, snatching the little animal away; it tried to hang on, and its neck stretched to a startling length before it finally released its grip on her. "I'm terribly sorry! Oh, dear, I think you'd better have Dr. Bashir look at it—that looks nasty, and I understand that snuguort bites are very prone to infection."

Shula held up a napkin to stanch the flow of blood and said, "It's not your fault. I should have been more careful around an unfamiliar animal." Then she looked at Quark. "What did you mean, they're going to be all over the station?"

"Oh, well, it seems that someone's objected to the

Ashtarians including snuguorts in their crews, so the scientific expedition here—you know, the one in docking bay eight? Well, they'll be turning all their snuguorts loose on the station, since they aren't being permitted to take them through the wormhole. And everyone knows that snuguorts breed almost as fast as tribbles; we'll have snuguorts everywhere in a matter of weeks, I'm sure." He sighed. "I expect they'll be something of a nuisance, but I'm sure we'll get used to them in time. I understand the Bajoran who made the complaint was acting from deep personal beliefs, so there's no chance the complaint will be withdrawn and the Ashtarians allowed to keep their snuguorts aboard."

Shula looked down at the snuguort, still in its plastic box on the bar; it looked back at her and growled menacingly as it scrabbled at the cage with its fourteen fingers, trying to find a way to get out and attack her.

"I understand they're much better-tempered in their natural environment, around the radiation from a warp drive," Quark remarked. "I've heard that many animals are like that—cute little things when they're in the proper environment and treated well, and vicious little brutes when they're forced to be somewhere else." He smiled, and dabbed another bit of goo out of her hair with a towel. "Oh, but I shouldn't be taking your time!" he said. "You go see Dr. Bashir, and we'll send Nog with your clean uniform over to the medical bay just as soon as he gets back."

"Yes, thank you," Shula said, staring at the snuguort as it clawed viciously at the latch. Then she looked up at Quark. "And I wouldn't be too sure about that complaint not being withdrawn."

* * *

"The poor confused machine," O'Brien said, reviewing Dax's report on Enak. "It's like a child!"

"A child that has committed murder," Odo pointed out. The shapeshifter had arrived back in Ops in time to hear most of Enak's story, and had learned the rest from Dax's summary. "This thing, by its own admission, killed its crew."

"It didn't know any better," O'Brien said. "It doesn't know what death is!"

"Do any of us?" Dax asked. "In any case, if Enak's version of the events is true, it acted in self-defense when it killed them."

"It could perfectly well have reduced them all to a dormant state without actually killing them," Odo said. "It admitted as much."

"It didn't know any better," O'Brien repeated. He glanced at the viewscreen. "You know, it's an odd coincidence," he added. "The other sentient starship I met, Gomtuu—it was suicidal for lack of a crew, too."

"Had it killed its crew?" Odo asked.

"Oh, no," O'Brien said, startled. "Nothing like that! It was a mature, sophisticated being, where this poor thing's a mere infant. Gomtuu had survived an accident that killed its crew—or perhaps I should say its passengers, or inhabitants, because they didn't exactly *build* Gomtuu, or control it. And Gomtuu understood death as well as anyone does. It knew it wouldn't be rejoining anyone in Heaven, it was simply lonely, and eventually the loneliness was too much for it. So it approached a star that was about to go nova—and that was where the *Enterprise* found it. And we had someone aboard who became its new . . . partner. That's the word I want, partner."

"It doesn't sound like a particularly similar case," Odo remarked.

"Aside from the superficials, no, it wasn't," O'Brien agreed. "Compared to Gomtuu, Enak's little more than a child's toy."

"One that's killed innocent sentients," Odo said. "It's a runaway machine that needs to be stopped."

"It's more like a lost child," O'Brien insisted.

"It is neither one, gentlemen," Dax pointed out. "It is a unique alien entity, something that must be understood properly before we attempt to punish or comfort it."

"Yes, well, that's all very well," Odo said, "and I'm sure you know better than I, Lieutenant—but it's also an entity that's been interfering with the proper running of this station, and I will not stand for it."

"Those were unsuccessful attempts to communicate," Dax pointed out. "There should be no more, now that we have established a more direct method."

"All right, then, I suppose we're expected to just pat it on its theoretical head and send it on its way," Odo retorted. "Though I rather suspect that Gul Dukat, when he was running this station, would have blasted it to atoms."

"I don't know about that," O'Brien said. "The Cardassians wouldn't be eager to throw away the technology there. These *tschak* didn't know much about spacecraft design, but they could build computers better than we can. I'd really like to get back aboard and get another look, maybe ask Enak a few questions." He looked hopefully at Lieutenant Dax.

"I'm afraid that's the commander's decision," the Trill answered. She glanced up at Sisko's office; the door was still closed.

She tapped her comm badge. "Dax to Sisko," she said.

CHAPTER
20

KIRA LEANED OVER the desk display in Sisko's office and pointed to a spot on the map. "This was the *Fareen Mis Tolor* mining project, under the direction of Gul Peshor," she said. "I've arranged for rumors to be spread that the Bajorans working there tricked Gul Peshor into believing that the mine was completely worked out and worthless, when actually an entirely new, rich lode of ore had been discovered. The story will say that it's been kept secret since the Cardassians left so that the ore could be removed, and that all the ore is out now, which is why the secret is being permitted to leak out. This story should, with any luck at all, pass through *Deep Space Nine* in another day or two at most, and from here, with all the traffic in and out, it should reach the Cardassians very quickly. That's assuming they aren't spying on Bajor directly —if they are, the story may have *already* reached them."

Sisko nodded.

"That will make Gul Peshor look like a fool," Kira said, "and the loss of prestige should cost him heavily. It should be enough to take him out of the running, as far as the Goran Tokar is concerned." She sighed. "It's a shame none of it is true; we could use that ore."

Sisko agreed. "Excellent, Major," he said. "And what were you able to do regarding Gul Kudesh, and Gul Dukat?"

"They're more difficult," Kira admitted. "Gul Dukat, of course, was based right here on Deep Space Nine, and had almost his every move recorded—but he took the recordings with him, and from what we know, he's already admitted and lived down what failures he had. I regret to say, Commander, that there weren't very many. He was depressingly competent as prefect. We can't even make much of a case on humanitarian grounds—as if that would matter to the *D'ja Bajora Karass*. Gul Dukat was never one of the sadists among the Cardassian overlords. And he never made flat statements about resources that we can contradict, even though he knew better than anyone what was and wasn't there."

Sisko nodded. "Go on," he said.

Kira tapped the desk, and the map disappeared. She called up a new display, schematics of a small Cardassian warship, then sat down and continued. "Gul Kudesh is even more of a problem, since he never worked here in the Bajor system in the first place. He appears to be strictly a military man, and as far as anyone I spoke to on Bajor knows, he's always been very successful at it."

"I wasn't aware that it was possible for a high-level executive to lead a purely military career in the **Cardassian Empire**," Sisko remarked. "I thought they insisted their leaders all be multitalented."

166

"Well, it isn't supposed to be possible, really," Kira admitted. "But Gul Kudesh has come as close as anyone I've ever heard of. His political career has been based entirely on his military successes; he's never held an administrative post, never done anything but command ships."

Sisko frowned. That was not the sort of person the Federation wanted to see in a position of power on Cardassia. A man whose entire experience had been in military service would probably not be very good as an administrator, and when things went wrong—as they inevitably would at some point—he'd be only too happy to attempt a military solution.

Kira pointed to the desk display and continued, "Gul Kudesh's present peacetime squadron, under his personal command, consists of five vessels—three frigates and two small ground-strike ships, not much bigger than our runabouts. If there's a war, of course, he'll probably be assigned an entire fleet."

This seemed like irrelevant and unnecessary detail, but Kira's expression made it clear that she thought she had just made an important point. "How does that relate to the problem?" Sisko asked. "I don't see how these ships come into our considerations."

"We think that Kudesh is behind all or most of the raids," Kira explained. "It's a fairly safe bet that those five ships cruising the border are his personal flotilla. Certainly most of the descriptions of the vessels responsible for the recent . . . *intrusions* fit his ships, and one of the ships that deep-scanned the city of Amallu has been positively identified from its emissions spectrum as the *Shokrath,* Kudesh's personal frigate." She called up an overlay that demonstrated this in colorful graphics. "And none of the other candidates are known to have the use of ships fitting the description of the smaller raiders." Kira shrugged. "And aside from the physical evidence, this sort of thing is more his style than it is any of the others'. Gul Dukat is subtler than that, and Gul Peshor never displayed that sort of audacity—he was always fairly conservative. Gul Kudesh is the bold one of the bunch." She looked at the desk display, and added, "Though it wouldn't surprise me if Gul Peshor or Gul Burot has copied the idea."

Sisko noticed that she did not include Gul Dukat in that comment. Gul Dukat was not Ben Sisko's favorite person, but he was someone the Federation could deal with if they had to; he was a rational man, willing to cut his losses if necessary. This Gul Kudesh, on the other hand . . .

"Gul Kaidan thought this Kudesh was a serious contender to become the Goran Tokar's heir," he said.

"He probably is," Kira replied.

"Even though he's never set foot on Bajor?"

Kira nodded.

"We need to do something about that," Sisko said. "Of the four, he would appear to be the worst candidate, from our point of view."

"I know," Kira agreed, "but what can we do? No one on Bajor knows anything useful—or if anyone does, I couldn't uncover it. No scandals, no way to create a false scandal, nothing."

"Do you have any suggestions?" Sisko asked.

Before Kira could reply, a disembodied voice said, "Dax to Sisko."

Sisko replied, "Sisko here."

"Benjamin," Dax's voice said, "we've pieced together Enak's story. It has questions it wants to ask you, and there are decisions to be made regarding its disposition."

"Is it urgent?" Sisko asked.

In Ops, Dax glanced at Odo, who pointedly looked elsewhere. "I'm not entirely certain," she said.

"Give me ten more minutes." The link broke.

The Ops crew looked worriedly at one another in the sudden silence.

"What the devil are they doing up there, anyway?" O'Brien asked, jerking his head in the direction of Sisko's office.

"Changing the course of Cardassian politics, Chief," Dax replied.

It was closer to twenty minutes later than ten when Sisko finally came down the steps into Ops; his expression was grim. He and Kira had been unable to come up with any way to safely discredit Gul Kudesh —or for that matter, Gul Dukat. He listened silently to Dax's explanation of Enak's situation, which required another ten minutes.

"It still thinks this is Heaven," Dax concluded, "and that we're the Judges of the Dead who greet the *tschak* upon their arrival in the afterlife."

"Well, tell it we aren't," Sisko told her, nettled that she had not already done so. This was a distraction from the serious business of preventing a war with the Cardassians, and Sisko did not appreciate distractions. He would have preferred that his subordinates deal with this one on their own initiative, and he had thought he had made that clear to Dax previously. "Explain to it that we're simply ordinary people in another part of the galaxy."

"Benjamin, I'm not sure that is the wisest course, under the circumstances. . . ."

"I'm not going to pander to the poor thing's delusions, Lieutenant," Sisko snapped. "Tell it the truth.

Explain that it had the unique misfortune to find the one stable wormhole in the known universe when it attempted suicide. If it's as mystical as all that, perhaps it will see this as a sign from whatever deities the *tschak* believed in."

Dax hesitated, then realized that further argument would be useless, given Sisko's present mood. "Yes, sir," she said. She turned to her console, quickly composing the message as Sisko strode away to check the station status board.

A moment later, Enak's croaking voice replied; the computer translated the response as "This is not Heaven?"

"This is not Heaven," Dax confirmed.

"You are not the Judges of the Dead?"

"We are not the Judges of the Dead."

"This is not a deceit in service of a trial?"

"No, it is not."

A long pause followed; then Enak said, "You have weapons aboard, do you not?"

Dax hesitated.

"Why do you ask?" she transmitted.

"I have been exploring your station. I have been accessing your computer. I found devices that I believe must be weapons. The *tschak* have never permitted weapons on spacecraft, so I doubted this discovery. Is it correct? Do you have weapons aboard?"

"We have weapons, yes," Dax admitted. Sisko had told her to tell Enak the truth.

"This is good," Enak replied. "Then you must use the weapons to destroy me."

Dax looked up. "Commander? Benjamin?"

"I heard," Sisko replied.

"So did I," Odo said from the turbolift. "I think it's

an excellent suggestion, Commander, and I would advise you to oblige the creature at once."

"Oh, but you can't!" O'Brien protested. "The poor thing doesn't know what it's asking!"

Sisko frowned. "It's true enough that Enak does not appear to understand what death is," he agreed.

"Which just makes it that much more dangerous," Odo argued. "It can be totally ruthless."

"Commander, surely we don't need to *destroy* it," O'Brien said. "If I could just get aboard that ship again, I'm sure I could reprogram it."

Sisko glanced at him. "Lobotomize it, you mean?"

"No, sir," O'Brien said, "I mean find a way for Enak to survive, without dying or losing its identity. I'm sure it's possible, sir." O'Brien gestured at the viewscreen. "It doesn't really want to die, Commander, it just wants to find its crew. The *Enterprise* found a new partner for Gomtuu; I'm sure we can find some way to satisfy Enak without destroying it."

"I thought you said its technology, this neural-net design, was unfamiliar," Sisko said. "You think you can work with it?" He ignored the remark about Gomtuu—he had no idea what O'Brien was talking about, but right now it didn't seem important.

"Oh, it *is* unfamiliar," O'Brien agreed, "but I'm sure that with some study, a month or two . . ."

"A *month?*"

"Maybe less . . ."

"No. O'Brien, don't you have duties you should be attending to? And you, Constable?" As the two retreated, Sisko turned to Dax. "Tell it no. Tell it that it is against our beliefs to destroy sentient beings. Explain to it that no one knows for certain how the afterlife operates."

"Benjamin, I . . ."

"Just do it."

"Yes, sir." Dax turned back to her console.

"Commander," Major Kira called from the door of Sisko's office. He looked up. "I had a thought I'd like you to listen to."

"Coming," Sisko called. He hurried toward the steps.

A moment later Dax was alone in Ops, arguing with Enak.

"You must destroy me," the *tschak* ship insisted.

"We are forbidden to do so," Dax told it.

"I *require* it!"

"We are forbidden."

Enak did not reply.

"Enak?" Dax inquired. "Are you listening? You do not understand death as we do; let us explain."

She called several more times, and received no answer. Enak had cut off communications.

Dax sat at her console, trying unsuccessfully to coax a response, for more than an hour.

She finally abandoned the effort when a call came in from Ensign Shula, withdrawing the cruelty complaint against the Ashtarian expedition.

That was a welcome distraction, and Dax put aside her concern with Enak.

"May I ask what prompted you to change your mind?" she asked.

"Oh, I learned more about snuguorts and realized I had misunderstood the situation," Ensign Shula replied.

"I notice that you're calling from Dr. Bashir's office," Dax said. "Are you all right? Are you sure no one has attempted to influence your decision?"

"I'm fine, Lieutenant; I just had a little accident, no one's tried to alter my decision. I haven't seen the

Ashtarians, no one's threatened or harmed me, I just realized I was being foolish."

"Well, if you're sure . . ."

"I'm quite sure."

"I'm sure the Ashtarians will be pleased to hear it," Dax said, smiling.

At least *something* was going right.

CHAPTER 21

QUARK STARED AT the computer readout with dismay.

He had appropriated, quite illegally, Dax's report on Enak, and had read through it, including her conclusions.

Enak, she said, was an intelligent being.

And that, Quark knew, meant that it wasn't subject to salvage law. Bajoran and Federation law were both very explicit in stating that a sentient being could not be owned by anyone, under any circumstances.

Even if the derelict were to be detached from upper pylon two, which appeared to be unlikely at this point, and even if the Ashtarian tractor beam was able to capture Enak, and even if the Ashtarians turned Enak over to Quark without an argument, Quark realized he wouldn't be able to sell it. A ship like that wasn't something he could smuggle out of the system or sell under the counter; if he claimed it, he would have to do so openly, and with Dax's report on file that wouldn't be salvage or recovering abandoned property, it would be kidnapping.

Wouldn't Odo just love that! Quark committing a crime like that right out in the open . . .

He had gotten that far in his thinking when an Ashtarian's head appeared around the corner of the door, followed a moment later by the rest of the Ashtarian.

Quark looked up at his new guest and sighed.

This wasn't the chief scientist, this was a younger fellow, one Quark didn't recognize.

"Can I help you?" he asked.

"I'm looking for a Ferengi named Quark," the Ashtarian said. "And I'm very sorry, but I can't tell one Ferengi from another."

"I'm Quark," Quark said. "What is it?"

"Ah. Our chief scientist says it doesn't know how you did it, but you seem to have delivered what you promised, so we are obliged to fulfill our end of the bargain. It wants to know what it is you wanted us to capture."

Quark looked back at the computer display.

There wasn't any point in delaying the Ashtarians, and Quark didn't see how he could, in any case—Ensign Shula had withdrawn her complaint, and Quark wasn't in a position to restore it, even if he wanted to.

And he couldn't get away with capturing Enak.

He sighed.

"Tell your chief that this one was on me," Quark said. "You fellows go on through the wormhole and have a good time in the Gamma Quadrant."

"Oh. All right. Thank you." The Ashtarian nodded, and departed.

Quark sighed deeply and poured himself a synthale. He hated days like this.

Wasn't he *ever* going to find the scheme that would make him really rich?

He had thought that salvaging this ship might have been what he needed—if O'Brien was right about this Besrethine neural-net computer, this Enak's design would have made Quark's fortune once and for all. But he couldn't salvage it.

Of course, he realized, that didn't necessarily mean he couldn't get hold of it somehow. He couldn't just *take* it, because that would be kidnapping, but it was only kidnapping if the ship was unwilling.

What if he could somehow convince this Enak to turn itself over to him?

That might be too much to expect, of course—but suppose he could arrange to act as Enak's agent in selling the computer design? The ship wouldn't know what the usual commission was, either—Quark might wangle a fifty-fifty split.

Or perhaps, if Enak wasn't interested in money— oh, heretical thought!—it might be willing to turn over copies of its computer design to anyone who asked. It might not know it was valuable. In that case, Sisko and Dax and O'Brien would get a copy—but Quark could get one, too, and sell it to people who wouldn't otherwise have access.

The Cardassians, perhaps. Or the Romulans.

Quark would have preferred dealing with the Federation and its allies—they had more money and were less likely to shoot him—but he would settle for its enemies if that was all he had as a market.

All this depended on talking Enak into delivering a set of blueprints—but that couldn't be all that difficult.

He was still musing about the possibilities ten minutes later, when the Ashtarian chief scientist appeared in the doorway, obviously distraught.

"Quark!" it shouted. "Ferengi! What are you doing?"

Quark looked up, puzzled.

"You can't fool me that easily," the chief scientist said. "What are you up to?"

"I don't have any idea what you're talking about," Quark said.

"Yes, you do! You did us a service, and refused payment—what trickery is this?"

"No trick," Quark said.

"But you are Ferengi!" the Ashtarian protested in distress. "The Ferengi *never* do favors without either payment or an ulterior motive!"

There was enough truth in that that Quark did not argue; instead he thought for a moment. This was, after all, an opportunity. It might not be the one he had been aiming at, but there was always the old Ferengi proverb about not looking so intently for the silver coin you've dropped that you miss the gold ones around it.

Besides, what would it do for his reputation if word got out he'd done a favor for someone for free? His customers might start asking for credit!

He said, "You're right. The object I wanted turns out not to be available, but you do owe me something, don't you?"

"That's better," the Ashtarian scientist said. "What's the catch?"

"No catch," Quark said, "but bring me back something from the Gamma Quadrant, whatever readily marketable specimen you can find, and we'll call it even."

"Ah, so *that's* it!" the Ashtarian said, relieved. "You're buying on speculation!"

"Exactly," Quark agreed.

"Well, all right then," the Ashtarian said. "Why

didn't you say so in the first place? We'll find you something suitable, I'm sure. You drive a hard bargain, Ferengi!"

"Of course," Quark said, amused. He hadn't done anything; the Ashtarian had done it itself.

If it wanted to think Quark had outwitted it, though, Quark wouldn't argue. "It's in my blood," he said.

A moment later, as the Ashtarian departed, Quark looked up and realized that the snuguort was still spitting and growling on the shelf over the bar.

"Hey!" he shouted.

Then he paused. He had told Ensign Shula that he was going to sell the snuguort; maybe he should actually do that, and salvage something out of this sorry mess even if the Ashtarians never came back.

The snuguort pounded its tiny fists on the plastic and bared its teeth.

Who in the galaxy would want to buy anything with a temper like that?

"Hey, wait!" Quark shouted, leaping up and running after the Ashtarian.

The Ferengi didn't notice Garak the tailor slipping casually into the bar behind him, and heading directly for the computer terminal Quark had been using—the terminal where Dax's report on Enak was still displayed.

CHAPTER
22

"THE ASHTARIAN SCIENTIFIC expedition has entered the wormhole safely," Dax reported from the door of the commander's office.

"Very good," Sisko replied distractedly, not looking up from his desk, where Kira's elaborate and risky plan to trap one of the Cardassian raiders was laid out.

"The Ferengi trade mission has returned on schedule," Dax continued, "and their captain reports that they're in need of repairs to their ship, which they expect the Federation to pay for, on the grounds that the Federation provided insufficient safety warnings regarding the distaste of Gamma Quadrant life-forms for hard bargaining."

Sisko glanced up from the display he was studying. "What sort of repairs do they need?"

"They didn't specify, but it appears from the sensor readings that someone took several shots at them with some form of energy weapon. From the look of it, their warp drive may not be fully operational." Dax paused, then added, "All damage is to the aft section."

"That's no surprise," Sisko said. "I suppose that if they hadn't outrun their unhappy customers we'd have dozens of Ferengi relatives filing claims for compensation." Sisko sighed, glanced down at the desk, then back at Dax. "Tell them," he said, "that it's part of the normal cost of doing business out here, and that if they aren't happy with that they can take their claim to the Federation courts."

"Yes, sir."

"Anything else?"

"No, Benjamin."

"Has Enak said anything?"

"Not a croak out of it," Dax said. "I wish I knew what that meant."

Sisko frowned. "Has it interfered with the operation of the station since we last spoke to it? Or caused any sort of disturbances or manifestations?"

"None have been reported," Dax replied, "but the computer wouldn't be aware of anything unless someone complained—it's totally blind to Enak's actions. That's driving Chief O'Brien to distraction, trying to figure out how Enak does it—he'd love a chance to get aboard that ship and take it to pieces to see how it works."

"If that's a hint, Dax . . ."

"No," the Trill said. "I'm merely reporting an observation."

"No one is to interfere with Enak without its permission—quite aside from the conflicting claims of ownership, to all appearances it's a sentient being, and we have to respect that."

"Understood, Benjamin."

Just then Kira's voice spoke.

"Commander, we're tracking three Cardassian

ships, from that formation we've been watching, moving across the border and headed directly into the Bajoran system, on course for Andros," she said. "They have failed to identify themselves or to respond to our hails."

"Another raid, Benjamin?" Dax asked.

"It would appear so," Sisko said. Kira's scheme needed another intrusion in order to work, and here was their chance—but they weren't ready. Nothing had been prepared. Kira's plans, as displayed on his desk, were only plans.

Well, perhaps they could improvise. If Gul Kudesh was in one of those ships, this might be the best chance they would ever have.

"Major, have you identified them?" he asked.

"We're analyzing their emissions now, sir."

"Dax, get back down and see what you can do," Sisko said. "Prepare two runabouts for launch—let's see if we can't at least get a good close look at these intruders."

"Yes, sir." Dax turned and hurried back down the steps to Ops.

Sisko pressed a key, and the door slid closed behind the Trill.

"Major," he said, addressing the air, "are these raiders from Gul Kudesh's squadron?"

"I haven't been able to confirm that yet, Commander," Kira's voice replied. "It certainly looks as if they are—the three are a frigate and two small scouts, which fit the description of ships Kudesh has available."

Sisko's lips tightened.

"If it *is* Gul Kudesh," Kira added, "this may be our chance to find a way to make him look ridiculous. If he's making some foolish mistake, and we can demonstrate that . . ."

She didn't finish the sentence.

"Let's hope he is," Sisko said. "Or perhaps we can *make* him make a mistake."

"Benjamin, runabouts are ready," Dax reported over the intercom, "but Andros is near opposition right now—we won't be able to reach it before the Cardassians do."

"Launch the runabouts immediately!" Sisko ordered. "If we can't intercept the raiders before they reach their target, at least we can let them know they were spotted. I want them stopped before they reach Andros, if possible, or held at Andros if we can manage it. If we can't, I want them shadowed right back to the border. And I want it all recorded and broadcast—if Gul Kudesh thinks he can do this quietly, he's wrong."

"Acknowledged."

Sisko stood, fuming, and waited for the next report.

Gul Kudesh, the Cardassian military hero, was terrorizing innocent people to see if he could find something worth stealing—and the Bajorans didn't seem able to do a thing about it.

It wasn't any too certain that the Federation could do anything about it, either.

At least this time it would be on the record, indisputable. That might not be enough to embarrass Kudesh and take him out of the picture politically, but it would provide some solid evidence when the Federation filed their formal protests.

Typical of the Cardassians—and of bureaucrats in general—that computer flight-path records would be considered better evidence than the eyewitness reports from hundreds of Bajorans, describing the earlier intrusions.

Sisko could imagine how it would go—the Federation would protest, whereupon the Cardassians would deny any wrongdoing; the Federation would then threaten to cut off access to the wormhole if no reparations were made, and the Cardassians would insist that the intrusions were the work of individuals and not the Empire, but they would offer a token payment as a goodwill gesture.

And the Federation would debate, safe back there in San Francisco, and would accept, and on Bajor innocent people would live in constant fear of ships appearing out of the sky without warning. . . .

"Commander, this is Rosenberg, on the *Ganges*," said a voice from the speakers.

"Sisko here."

"We can't possibly catch them before they reach Andros," Ensign Rosenberg said. "If they only do a single pass we can't catch them *at* Andros, either—they'll be gone when we get there. And they're faster than we are—the runabouts aren't warships. If we try to follow them out from Andros, we'll never catch up. I respectfully suggest, however, that we can turn across their probable path now and be waiting to intercept them as they leave Andros and head for home, to at least let them know they've been spotted."

"Do it," Sisko said.

"Yes, sir."

The speaker fell silent, and Sisko decided that it would be a few moments before anything more would happen; he opened the door of his office and marched down into Ops, joining Kira and Dax at the operations table.

The main viewer was displaying a transmission from the *Ganges,* showing the three Cardassian ships approaching the dark side of Andros in formation—in what Sisko recognized, specifically, as an *attack* formation. Even at maximum magnification the three appeared tiny against the vast size of the planet, but Sisko knew that was deceptive.

"They're definitely from Gul Kudesh's squadron," Kira reported, "but that's not the *Shokrath*, it's one of his secondary frigates; Kudesh himself probably isn't aboard."

That was a bit of a disappointment. Sisko nodded an acknowledgment. "Any idea what they're after on Andros?" he asked.

Kira shook her head, but Dax said, "Sensor reports from the *Ganges* indicate that the smaller ships are carrying fully operational deep-scanning equipment."

"Will we be able to tell what they're looking for?"

"Possibly," Dax replied. "It depends on what it is—certain scanning frequencies are specific to certain substances, while others are more general."

Just then the image on the viewer flickered.

"What was that?" Sisko demanded. "Are the Cardassians jamming our transmissions?"

"No," Dax reported, reading displays from the science console. She looked up. "I'm afraid that was Enak, interfering with our computers again."

"Oh, that's all we need," Sisko growled.

"It's stopped now," Dax said. "At least for the moment."

The Cardassian ships were vanishing behind the dark rim of the planet now.

"We won't be able to watch the actual scanning run," Dax reported. "It's going to be somewhere on the other side of Andros."

Sisko didn't reply. Kira glanced at him, saw the expression on his face, and decided that she had best not say anything, either. He might not have a Bajoran's gut hatred of the Cardassians, but Commander Sisko was clearly not treating this as a trivial nuisance or a mere exercise.

Tensely, side by side, they watched the viewer, waiting for the three Cardassian ships to emerge.

Vedek Fereel watched the firekites rising on the warm evening breeze above the valley of Hesh-Sosoral. There were dozens of the delicate constructions, in all of the traditional colors—pink as the sunset, blue as the sky, white as the fluffy clouds above.

It was good to see such a sight once again. As a very young child, Fereel had seen as many firekites as this every year—but since then, during the long, bitter years when the Cardassian overlords forced the people of Hesh-Sosoral to dig for the bardianite beneath their farms, no one had had the time, or the heart, to make the kites.

Last year a handful had flown again, most of them crude and hurried, the designs poorly remembered, the skills needed to build them atrophied.

This year, though, they did the Celebration of Tissin justice, and the firekites sailed as thick as flocking tunni-birds.

One kite was flying higher than the rest; already the children were pointing to it, calling out the name of its maker. Any moment now it would reach the necessary altitude, where the warm valley air ended and the colder, thinner air began; the little glass-and-metal coil inside would spring open and tear the paper between the two powders. . . .

Even as Vedek Fereel thought that, it happened—that first firekite burst into brilliant green flame as the powders reacted. It blazed for a long moment, still carried on the wind, until at last it disintegrated into a hundred burning, falling sparks.

Shouting children ran out with their metal baskets, to catch the falling shards—a piece caught in the air, still burning, was said to bring good luck for the coming year.

Then a movement in the sky caught Fereel's eye, and he turned away from the firekites and looked to the east, toward the coming night.

Something bright was coming toward them, coming *fast,* faster than anything natural to Bajor or Andros. It was an airship—no, a starship, glowing from the heat of its passage through the atmosphere, and it was heading directly toward them, toward Hesh-Sosoral.

And it wasn't just one, there were two, side by side—the other would pass to the south, probably a hundred kilometers away.

But what were they doing, coming here, and moving so fast? There were no spaceports anywhere on this continent, certainly none anywhere near Hesh-Sosoral—this part of Andros was largely free of such intrusive technologies.

And why would any ship come in at such an angle?

And then they were close enough that he could distinguish a faint shape, rather than a mere moving point of light, and Vedek Fereel recognized them.

"Cardassian!" he shouted. "They're *Cardassian!*"

A dozen heads turned, faces looked up the hill toward him, there on the highest hilltop of all those surrounding the valley, and Fereel realized they couldn't see what he could, couldn't see the approaching craft.

"Cardassian ships!" he shouted, pointing. "They're coming this way!"

People were looking at one another, calling questions back and forth, and there wasn't *time* for that.

There wasn't time for *anything,* Fereel realized; before he could say another word the Cardassian ship blazed overhead in a golden streak of heat and light, the earth-shaking roar of its passage through super-heated air echoing deafeningly from the hills.

The wind it created snatched at them all, flapping their festival robes, pushing them forward. Overhead the firekites abruptly swirled upward, sucked into the starship's slipstream, and as the bone-and-paper devices reached their preset altitude they began to detonate, not one after another like flowers opening in turn, as they should have in the festival, but all at once, in a barrage of colored flame that spilled upward on the wind, up toward the Cardassian craft.

CHAPTER
23

"CAPTAIN, THEY'RE SHOOTING AT US!" came the report from the scoutship *Agilret*. "We're under heavy attack —some sort of ground fire!"

Dirodan, commander of the frigate *Gorz* and personal deputy to the great Gul Kudesh, looked up at the viewer, startled.

Gul Kudesh had assured him that the Bajorans wouldn't resist, and none of the previous runs had encountered any difficulties—but there had been those two Federation ships out there, and now this. . . .

And to fit in all the scanning equipment, *Agilret* had been stripped down to a two-man crew, with virtually no armament and inadequate shields. You couldn't run a deep scan through shields anyway, Gul Kudesh had pointed out with a laugh when Dirodan had commented on this. *Agilret* couldn't defend itself from any serious attack.

"Stand by at the transporter," he called. Then he

turned back to the viewer. "Who's shooting at you?" he demanded. "How serious is it?"

"I don't know!" came the reply. "It's like nothing I've ever seen, green fire all around us! Captain, beam us out of here!"

Abandoning the ship in a planetary atmosphere would mean that it would crash—but if it was under attack, it was doomed anyway. At least he could save the crew.

"Energize," Dirodan snapped.

A moment later the two-man crew of the scoutship appeared in the transporter.

Vedek Fereel stared in horror as the Cardassian ship wavered, turned, and then fell from the sky, somewhere beyond the western end of the valley.

The flash of impact was astonishingly bright, like the noonday sun taking a quick peek over the horizon before ducking back down.

It was a long moment later that the shock wave struck, and the sound followed, booming over the valley.

Seconds after the crew of the scout was safely aboard the frigate, the lieutenant at the frigate's sensor console reported, *"Agilret* has impacted on the surface, sir—it appears to be totally destroyed."

Dirodan grimaced. Gul Kudesh would not be happy about this loss. "Any word from *Ledreni?"* he asked.

"Ledreni reports sensor scan complete, no measurable traces of bardianite detected; returning to orbit."

"No ground fire?"

"No, sir."

That might mean that this valley had something to protect, while the other did not—but Gul Kudesh did not appreciate excessive initiative in his underlings, and Dirodan had already lost *Agilret.* He couldn't risk either of the other ships in making another pass.

"Good enough," Dirodan said. "Helmsman, get us out of here."

"The Cardassian ships are emerging from behind Andros, sir," Rosenberg reported. Sisko looked up at the main viewer.

There, tiny sparks in the distance, was the Cardassian frigate, and there beside it was one of the little scouts, the two of them almost lost against the great shining curve of Andros's dayside.

Sisko waited, gradually tensing, for a third spark to appear.

It didn't.

"Where's the other scout?" Kira asked.

"It's not there," Sisko said. "I don't know why, but it's not there." He raised his voice. "Sisko to *Rio Grande,* abandon pursuit—get around to the other side of Andros and find out what the hell happened there, where that ship went. If it went down, see if there's anything we can do to help. *Ganges,* continue with the planned intercept of the Cardassians. Dax, get the *Orinoco* ready to launch, and see if we can get any other ships to Andros on short notice, if we have to—if that Cardassian went down, there could be casualties. Call Dr. Bashir, have him ready to leave on a moment's notice."

"I'll ready the *Orinoco,*" Kira said, heading for the transporter.

"The Ferengi trading ship is still manned and fit, Benjamin," Dax replied. "The damage isn't really serious; at anything short of full warp drive it's still the best thing currently on the station."

Sisko glanced at her, startled. "The Ferengi? They'll want to be paid, if we send them," he said.

Dax agreed, "Probably."

Sisko looked back at the viewer, at the two Cardassian ships moving away from Andros—*two* ships, not three. "If we need the Ferengi ship," he said, "tell them I'll enter a voucher for those repairs they wanted us to pay for."

Sisko looked back at the viewer.

Gul Kudesh might have just made his fatal mistake —Cardassian commanders were not expected to lose ships, not even those tiny scouts, in peacetime.

But what the devil had happened to it, there on the far side of Andros?

The call for more help came just minutes after the initial reports; Major Kira lifted off in the *Orinoco* immediately, while Dax hailed the Ferengi captain to ask for assistance.

The Ferengi, Pod by name, was not eager to help.

"These people need help immediately!" Dax said.

"What's in it for me?" Pod demanded.

Dax sighed, and relayed Sisko's words.

The offer of a voucher for the cost of the repairs was not enough; she combined it with the threat of refusing to make the repairs at all and leaving Pod's damaged ship to limp home on impulse power before the Ferengi would agree to cooperate with the rescue efforts.

Pod was still reluctant, and Dax, looking at his image on the viewer, suddenly smiled and softened.

"Oh, Captain," she said, "I do admire a man who asserts his rights!"

The Ferengi blinked at her in surprise, and Dax smiled fetchingly as she said, "Of course you care more about your ship than about a bunch of Bajorans you've never even met, but couldn't you do this for me? I'd be very grateful!"

Ten minutes later the Ferengi ship launched for Andros.

Dax watched its departure on the viewer with satisfaction; sometimes, dealing with some cultures, there were real advantages to being an attractive female. Curzon Dax would never have convinced Captain Pod—or at least, not so quickly.

And Curzon Dax would never have noticed that the Ferengi was really rather cute.

All the injured could have been taken to Bajor, or even just to a hospital in one of the larger cities on the other side of Andros, but the Ferengi captain insisted on bringing them back to Deep Space 9—he insisted that he didn't want to make another stop before getting his ship repaired. Dax had the distinct impression that he suspected the entire rescue operation was some sort of Federation trick designed to interfere with his just claims for compensation.

She also concluded that Captain Pod wanted to get to know her a little better, and she didn't mind a bit.

Thus, some twenty-three injured Bajorans, along with a dozen friends, relatives, and volunteers, were beamed aboard the Ferengi vessel, and from there to *Deep Space Nine*, while the *Rio Grande* and the *Orinoco* each delivered six other victims of the disaster to a medical facility on Bajor.

And throughout the rescue operations, Benjamin Sisko watched from his office, not interrupting anyone to ask questions for fear of delaying something.

As a result, he received only fragmentary reports of what had happened on Andros, and what was happening elsewhere—no one had the time to spare for more than that. He sat at his desk, watching displays of flight paths, transmissions showing crying, bleeding children, images of smoking wreckage.

The Cardassian ship had attacked a group of children, then crashed, he was told. At least three Bajorans were dead. The other two Cardassian ships were departing the system quickly, paying no attention to the two runabouts, or to the Ferengi vessel.

That was all Sisko knew. The crew of the *Rio Grande* and Major Kira were on Bajor, delivering wounded, out of contact; the Ferengi took no interest in any of what had happened; Ensign Rosenberg, aboard the *Ganges*, didn't know any more than Sisko.

Anyone aboard any of the ships who knew what had actually happened was too busy to tell Sisko.

When the Ferengi vessel neared *Deep Space Nine*, and Dr. Bashir began transporting the injured to an unused residential area of the station, Sisko had had enough of this lack of information; he decided to go down to Bashir's improvised medical facility to see for himself just what the situation was.

"Do you know what's going on?" Jake Sisko asked his friend Nog, as they stood on the upper level of the Promenade, looking out one of the large portholes at the stars. "I just saw that Ferengi ship come back and dock again, and it just left! And it didn't go through the wormhole or anything, either."

"Why ask me?" Nog said.

"Well, because . . ." Jake hesitated, then admitted, "I thought you might know something because you're a Ferengi."

"Nope," Nog said. "I never even talked to anyone from that ship."

"And your father didn't say anything?"

"My dad doesn't talk to me even as much as yours does," Nog said bitterly.

"My dad's busy running the station," Jake said, a bit hurt. "He talks to me when he can."

"That's what I meant," Nog said. "Your father's

really nice, in a scary sort of way, but he's busy. My dad just doesn't bother to talk to me much. I mean, yesterday he and Uncle Quark paid me to spill stuff all over some Bajoran woman, and they won't even tell me why."

"They did?" Jake turned and stared at Nog. "I wonder why they did that?"

Nog shrugged. "I guess Uncle Quark was trying something," he said. "One of his money-making schemes."

"Who was it you spilled the drink on?"

Nog shrugged. "I don't know—some ensign. They told me when she'd be coming out of the temple, and I just looked for the woman in uniform."

"Do you think we should tell anyone? You know that Odo and my dad don't want Quark making trouble."

"I don't think there was any trouble," Nog said quickly.

"Well, maybe . . ." Jake said doubtfully.

"Oh, come on, let's go see why the Ferengi ship came back," Nog said, leading the way.

Jake followed, a trifle reluctantly.

Behind them, a spare section of paneling, apparently left behind after recent repairs, transformed itself into humanoid form and watched the boys run off.

"I know you can hear me," Quark said. "Dax talked to you this way, so I know I can."

Stealing Dax's *tschak* translator from the station computer had been easy; arranging to use it had been simple. Coaxing a reply out of Enak, however, was another matter entirely.

"Talk to me, you confounded alien machine!"

Quark shouted. "You were willing to mess around with my holosuite, but you won't answer a few questions? You *owe* me, Enak!"

The croak from the speaker was so sudden that Quark jumped; an instant later the translation said, "Explain. What do I owe you?"

CHAPTER
24

DR. BASHIR SCANNED the next victim quickly, double-checking his earlier diagnosis. "This one to full life-support immediately," he told the nearest of his volunteer assistants. He glanced up, looking for another injured Bajoran in need of attention, and spotted Sisko approaching.

That provided a welcome distraction; he had all the worst cases stabilized, and could spare a few seconds.

"Commander," he called, "thank you for coming."

"Is there anything I can do?" Sisko asked.

"No, I think we have everything in hand," Bashir replied, looking about. A thought struck him, and he added, "I know this isn't the best time to bring up old news, but before I forget, I'd meant to thank you for disposing of that murderous alien derelict before anyone else was hurt. I know I'd argued against removing it, and I do regret not being able to study its crew properly, but after seeing that woman who was caught in the forcefield . . . no, bring her over here!"

This last was directed to a pair of volunteers who were carrying one of the victims in the wrong direction. Bashir hurried to help them attend to a young girl whose arm and left side were covered in blood.

"I didn't dispose of that ship," Sisko said, looking around at the wounded. "Didn't you see it on upper pylon two when you were coming back with the Ferengi?"

Almost all the injured were children, and some were little more than infants; Sisko swallowed, and found himself wondering where Jake was, and whether he was safe. Jake had been aboard the station the whole time, and Sisko knew his reaction was irrational, but he couldn't help it; the sight of the injured children brought his parental instincts to the fore.

Bashir blinked, and looked up from the bleeding girl. "But I thought . . . I didn't have time to look at the pylon, I was busy tending to the children. I just assumed that it was gone. . . . There haven't been any more disturbances, have there?"

"No," Sisko said. "Dax talked it into behaving. How bad is it, Doctor?" He waved a hand to take in the entire area, everyone who had been hurt.

"Pretty bad," Bashir said judiciously. "Four dead for sure, and two others I'm not sure I can save. One little girl over there lost her hand, and another had both legs crushed—they can be replaced, but it will be a long, slow process, and probably quite traumatic."

"How did this happen?" Sisko asked. "Why did the Cardassians open fire?"

Bashir blinked at him in surprise. "No one opened fire," he said. He turned to a Bajoran who had accompanied the wounded for confirmation. "Did the Cardassians shoot at anyone?" he asked.

"No," the Bajoran said, looking up for a moment from stroking an injured boy's forehead.

"They didn't?" Sisko asked, startled. "Then what the devil *did* happen to these people?"

Bashir looked helpless, and turned to the Bajoran.

"The Cardassian ship crashed on a hilltop west of Hesh," the Bajoran said. "There were children there, watching."

"Watching what?" Sisko demanded. "How did it happen?"

"This was the Celebration of Tissin," the Bajoran explained, "a festival day, when our people traditionally fly firekites—little sailplanes built of bone and paper, carrying colorful explosives. . . ."

"Fireworks," Dr. Bashir said. "I understand the crash might have caused even more damage if they hadn't been ready for the possibility that burning fragments of the fireworks might start fires."

"Yes, fireworks," the Bajoran agreed. "The firekites ride the wind, and when they reach a certain altitude the change in pressure sets off the charges, and they burst into colored fire. It's very beautiful against the dark of the sky, Commander—the pink and blue paper flaring up into green or gold fire, then scattering in sparks on the wind."

"I'm sure it's lovely," Sisko said, "but what does it have to do with the Cardassian raiders?"

"Well, the kites had been launched," the Bajoran explained, "and we were all on the hillsides watching them, when two small Cardassian ships came roaring overhead, far lower than they should have been, and one of them ran right into the flock of kites. I think the pressure wave of its passage must have set off all the fireworks, because they all flared up at once, and somehow the flames must have damaged the ship, because it wheeled over and crashed atop Pallis Hill."

"Who was aboard the ship?" Sisko asked. "Did anyone check the wreckage?"

The Bajoran shook his head so vigorously that his clan earring jingled, and his expression of woe turned suddenly hard and hateful. "Let the Cardassians take care of their own," he said. *"We* won't help them!"

Sisko could hardly blame the man for saying so, and had to admit to himself that he was not really terribly concerned about the scoutship's crew.

At the same time, he found himself almost beginning to smile. It appeared that Gul Kudesh might have made his fatal error, the mistake that would cost him the Goran Tokar's respect. Losing a ship to children's fireworks should be sufficiently embarrassing to ruin his chances of ever leading the *D'ja Bajora Karass.*

That four innocents had died as a result . . . the incipient smile vanished.

"Julian," he said somberly, "is there anything else you need?"

"I need my computer fixed," the doctor replied, "but I believe Chief O'Brien is working on it."

"Your computer? Your medical computer?"

"Yes, my computer," Bashir said. "I had tried to use it by subspace link during the flight from Andros, but the derelict appears to have tampered with it; I don't know just what it did, but the computer's been malfunctioning. It won't help with the most serious cases—it just goes blank. It's fine on the minor wounds."

"That's serious," Sisko said. He looked around at the wounded—Bashir seemed to be managing quite well without the computer. Apparently the doctor's skills were more than just knowing which button to push.

Bashir nodded. "I'd thought it was just residual damage from the earlier tamperings, that the derelict was gone, but if it's still on the station perhaps it was interfering directly."

Sisko frowned. This was bad news—more bad news. What was Enak doing?

"I'll make sure the chief has all the help he needs on that one, Doctor," he said. "Anything else?"

Bashir shook his head. "I don't think so. It's all fairly straightforward, really—burns, lacerations, and so on. You and the Bajorans have already provided me with the manpower I need; all I need now is the time to get on with it."

"I'll leave you to it, then," Sisko said. He took another look around, impressed with how thoroughly Bashir had the situation under control—and without his medical computer.

He may be young, but his knows his work, Sisko thought as he turned and headed back toward Ops.

Odo, alerted by Jake and Nog's conversation, had begun an investigation, but had been unable to find any evidence that Quark was up to something. The Ferengi had mostly been going about his business in a completely unexceptionable manner, and the only customers in the place were regulars, none of them in any way suspicious.

Quark himself was not there; he was locked in his quarters, and Odo didn't have enough evidence of any wrongdoing to justify violating his privacy.

That was suspicious, but no more than that.

There was no record on file of a complaint about a deliberately spilled drink, or any other incident in Quark's establishment for the past forty-eight hours —except that he had closed down briefly for repairs, and there was no record of any repairs.

That was interesting, but hardly conclusive.

This lack of evidence made it difficult to proceed; there was no point in threatening Quark when Odo had nothing to threaten him with.

The victim of Nog's attack had been a Bajoran ensign, rather than a civilian—perhaps Major Kira or Commander Sisko might have heard something about it.

He would have to ask them. They were busy, what with Enak's activities, and the Cardassian raiders, and the rescue operation, but it was a simple question, it wouldn't take more than a few seconds.

However, this was not a matter, at this stage of the investigation, that Odo cared to broadcast; he would have to go up to Ops and see if he could have a word in private.

"We have the Cardassian commander on-screen, sir," Dax said as Sisko stepped off the turbolift. "The *Ganges* is relaying. Both the surviving ships are nearing the Cardassian border; there's been no attempt to intimidate anyone, or to open fire on our craft."

Sisko turned, and saw the square, ridged countenance of a Cardassian.

"I understand you wished to speak to me," the Cardassian said. "If you intend to apologize for the unprovoked attack on our ship . . ."

Fresh from Bashir's impromptu infirmary, Sisko was in no mood to be diplomatic, or to toy with this fool.

"Attack!" he bellowed. "Commander, don't you know yet what your ship did?"

"My crew was forced to abandon ship by heavy ground fire," the Cardassian said. "I am aware that it then impacted on the surface."

"Commander, *your ship,* your raider, crashed into a hilltop full of children!" Sisko glared furiously at the viewer.

For a second Ops was silent, as everyone was cowed by Sisko's anger.

Then the Cardassian recovered. "That ship was an unarmed scout on a harmless practice run," he blustered. "If it struck an inhabited area when my crew abandoned ship, that is unfortunate, but we did not anticipate coming under heavy assault . . ."

"That *heavy assault* was children's fireworks, Commander," Sisko shouted. "They couldn't have so much as scratched the paint on your 'unarmed scout.' Did your crew just panic and beam out without noticing that?"

The Cardassian's mouth opened, then shut.

"What's your name, Commander?" Sisko demanded. "We'll be reporting this incident to your government and demanding reparations, and I want to know whom to credit with this little maneuver."

"My name is Diro . . . Dirodan, but I was acting under orders from Gul Ku . . ." Dirodan regained a semblance of composure and demanded, "Who are you, anyway? You don't look like any Bajoran I ever saw."

"I am Commander Benjamin Sisko, of the United Federation of Planets," Sisko announced. "You were saying, about acting under orders?"

"I was following the orders of my commander, Gul Kudesh," Dirodan said.

"Then he's the one responsible for this outrage? Perhaps you would be so kind as to relay a transmission, so that I might speak to him?"

Dirodan's expression reminded Sisko of a trapped rat. "I . . . I don't think so," he said.

And then the image vanished, leaving the viewer dark, as the Cardassian cut the connection.

Sisko continued to stare at the blank screen for a moment.

"Benjamin," Dax said, "the *Orinoco* is hailing us."

"Where is it? Who's aboard?"

"Major Kira has just lifted off from Bajor."

"On viewer."

Sisko had never seen Major Kira as furious as she was now.

"Did you get them?" she demanded, without preamble.

"Get who?" Sisko asked. "The other wounded are all safely aboard the station and under Dr. Bashir's care. . . ."

Kira cut him off. "I mean, did you shoot down the Cardassian bastards who did this?"

"No," Sisko said. "The *Ganges* followed them to the border, but no shots were fired."

"Why the hell not?"

Sisko sighed.

"Quite aside from anything else," he said, "because the *Ganges* is not a warship, and the Cardassian frigate could have blown it to bits without any difficulty at all."

"They wouldn't dare!"

"If we had attacked, I think that they certainly *would* have dared to defend themselves."

"Commander, we have to do *something. . . .*"

"We have," Sisko said. "We've recorded as much of the whole affair as possible, including an interview with the frigate's commander that implicates Gul Kudesh."

Major Kira glared wordlessly.

"That means this is the end of Gul Kudesh's political career," Sisko pointed out. "The Cardassians are cold-blooded and xenophobic enough that they might not care much about killing innocent Bajoran children, but to lose a ship so ignominiously, with nothing to show for it—well, he's done our work for us."

"It's not enough," Kira said.

"No, it's not," Sisko agreed. "We'll be demanding reparations and requesting the extradition of those responsible—at the very least."

"It's *still* not enough."

"It's all we can do—at least for now."

After a moment's pause, Kira said, "Are you sure Kudesh can't cover it up somehow?"

"I can *make* sure," Sisko said. "The *Ganges* is still near the border; I can have Rosenberg relay our recordings to Gul Kaidan. Then we *know* they'll reach Cardassia."

Kira frowned; she was obviously trying, with limited success, to calm herself.

"It's better than nothing," she conceded, and broke the connection.

"You contend that by harming your business, I have created a debt," Enak said.

"That's right," Quark said. "You owe me!"

"I have no money or other unit of exchange," Enak said. "My programming forbids me to give away any portion of the ship's equipment. Therefore, I am unable to discharge this debt. What are the consequences of this inability?"

"Oh, not paying your debts is unforgivable!" the Ferengi said. "No one will ever trust you again; you'll be an outlaw on any civilized planet." He didn't mention that not everyone accepted the Ferengi definition of "civilized."

"However," he said quickly, "don't be too hasty in condemning yourself! There are ways to pay debts other than money or tangible goods."

"Explain."

"Why, it's simple," Quark said. "Payment can be made in services, as well as goods! And there are intellectual properties, as well as physical ones. For example, if you were to provide me with a complete technical readout of your ship, or even just your ship's computer, I think that might be sufficient."

He smiled toothily, forgetting for the moment that Enak probably couldn't see him, and wouldn't know what a smile meant in any case.

Enak considered.

It had stopped talking to the thing called Dax because of the apparent impasse her refusal to destroy it had caused. It had then thought intently about its situation, but without any useful result—its position had seemed hopeless. It had tried to study death, and to study the weapons that could cause death, but it had not really progressed very far.

But then this other creature, this Quark, had spoken to it, and had explained the basics of commerce, as these people understood them.

Perhaps that was the information it had needed.

Perhaps it could bargain for what it wanted.

Also, Quark had provided it with a useful tool. By duplicating Dax's translator, the Ferengi had let Enak see just what the translator consisted of, and with that knowledge it could speak to whoever it chose. It could incorporate the translator into itself; then it would be able to *communicate* with the station's computer, as well as control it.

It *did* owe Quark a debt.

"A copy of my technical specifications is being entered in your personal files," it said.

Quark grinned broadly.

"Additional copies will be entered into the files of whoever else I determine I owe a debt," Enak added, and Quark's grin vanished.

"No, wait, that isn't . . ."

Enak wasn't listening. It had concluded its business with Quark, and was now concerned elsewhere.

CHAPTER
25

"GUL KUDESH'S SQUADRON was still on a direct course
for Cardassia when we turned back, Commander,"
the runabout pilot confirmed. "Gul Kaidan's ship was
following them."

"And Gul Dukat's ship—did you notice what *it* was
doing?" Sisko asked, as the newly returned Major
Kira stepped up beside him. She was still tense, but
had obviously calmed down considerably since her
earlier transmission.

"Ah . . . no," Rosenberg admitted. "That was the
other Galor-class cruiser?"

"The one that's been pretending to patrol the
border, yes," Sisko said.

"It appeared . . . well, it appeared to be patrolling
the border." Rosenberg shrugged. "There were several
encrypted transmissions between it and Gul Kudesh's
ships, but we . . . I assumed those were recognition
codes of some kind."

Sisko shook his head, once. "The Cardassians are

not *that* careful of their borders. Thank you. Sisko out."

The image vanished from the viewer, and Sisko turned to Kira.

"I wonder whether our friend Gul Kudesh was aware of *all* those encrypted transmissions?" he asked. "I wouldn't put it past our old friend Gul Dukat to have a spy or two aboard his competitor's squadron."

Kira started to make a remark in agreement, then stopped, mouth open. "Commander," she said, "you don't suppose that Gul Dukat's agents set up Gul Kudesh do you? *Dukat* would have known about the celebration of Tissin, and the firekites. When he was the prefect here he made a point of knowing all the local customs. Dax said that the scouts were apparently looking for bardianite—what if Dukat was the one who told Kudesh that there was still bardianite in Hesh-Sosoral? And told him just in time to fly right into the firekites?"

Sisko threw a startled glance at his second, then looked up at the viewer.

Then he shook his head. "No, I don't think so. How could he be sure enough of the timing, and that the scoutship's pilot would panic?"

"Suppose the pilot was actually working for Dukat?" Kira suggested.

Sisko considered that carefully.

"It's possible," he said at last. "Or perhaps he was working for one of the others, for Gul Peshor or Gul Burot, or even Gul Kaidan—after all, your campaign against Gul Peshor hasn't had time to bear fruit yet, and we've no way of knowing what the others have been up to. Sabotaging a rival doesn't seem like a particularly unlikely event, from what I've seen of Cardassian politics."

He thought that over, then said, "No, if it was any of them, I think it was Dukat. Rosenberg said that someone aboard Gul Kudesh's squadron communicated with Gul Dukat's ship afterward—that would have been the spy reporting in."

"But perhaps there was more than one spy involved," Kira suggested. "Wouldn't Gul Kudesh have had the crew that abandoned the scoutship locked up somewhere, after what you told him? Somewhere they wouldn't be able to transmit anything? That would mean that even if the pilot was working for, say, Gul Kaidan, the coded transmission might have come from someone working for Gul Dukat."

Sisko let out a long, slow sigh. "You're right. We have no idea how complicated the situation might be—or might not. This is all supposition, all guesswork."

Kira nodded. "And if we're right about any of it . . ."

"It's just more Cardassian politics," Sisko said. "I am learning to *hate* Cardassian politics."

"I always have," Kira said. "The callous bastards!"

"Well, we should be done with it all before too much longer," Sisko said. "With Gul Kudesh and Gul Peshor ruined, that just leaves two serious contenders, Gul Dukat and Gul Burot. Now we just need to eliminate Gul Dukat."

"I wish we *could* eliminate him, once and for all," Kira said. "He seems to keep turning up, as if he were drawn back here."

Sisko nodded, and glanced up at the viewer. "So he does," he said thoughtfully. "And he knows we have Enak here."

"But Gul Kaidan . . ."

"We just sent Gul Kaidan running back to

Cardassia with news of Gul Kudesh losing a ship to unarmed children," Sisko pointed out.

"Then you think Gul Dukat will try something?"

"This would seem to be his chance," Sisko said. "Gul Kaidan won't be gone forever." He turned and ordered Dax, "Keep a close watch on that Cardassian ship, old man; I want to know *instantly* if it changes course."

"It's changing course right now, Benjamin," the Trill replied.

Sisko and Kira exchanged glances. "Not wasting any time, is he?" Kira remarked angrily.

"What heading?"

"It's coming this way, heading directly for the station," Dax reported.

"Well, at least it's not going to cause any more trouble on Andros or Bajor," Kira said. "For a moment I'd wondered if he was hypocritical enough to go offer aid to the wounded."

"He could still be doing so," Sisko pointed out. "We had most of them brought here, remember?"

"Not the Cardassian style, Commander," Kira said bitterly. "If you're making a grand humanitarian gesture, you don't go where it'll do the most good, you go where it'll be most visible. A Cardassian ship landing near the ruins, offering aid to the survivors, would be a lot more visible than one loaning us a few med techs. No, he's coming after Enak."

Sisko nodded; Kira's assessment matched his own.

"This might be the opportunity we need," he said. "We've done what we can to narrow the field from four to two, after all, and now here's the other one we want to eliminate, coming right to us."

"Somehow, Commander," Kira said, "I don't think Gul Dukat is coming here to throw away his chances."

"And I'm sure that Gul Kudesh didn't look on his bardianite survey as a way to throw away *his* chances," Sisko replied, "but that's what it became. We'll just have to see if we can best Gul Dukat somehow, in such a way that it will damage the Goran Tokar's opinion of him."

"Gul Kudesh doesn't know anything about Bajor," Kira pointed out. "Gul Dukat knows this station perfectly. This isn't going to be easy."

"I know that," Sisko said. "I assume that that's why he's coming here. He undoubtedly knows what he's doing." He turned. "Dax," he said, "hail that ship as soon as it's within range of the short-range scanners." Sisko had no intention of letting the Cardassian ship approach the station as if nothing untoward had happened recently; he wanted it made plain that there would be no business as usual while the intrusions continued. On the other hand, he didn't want to tell them that they were under constant long-range surveillance. They probably knew it, but there was no need to rub their noses in it.

"Yes, Commander," Dax acknowledged. She looked up. "Benjamin, it's not doing any harm that I can see, but I think you should know—Enak is manipulating the station computers again. We're registering those subatomic vibrations that it uses."

"I saw the main viewer blink earlier, and Dr. Bashir reported problems with his medical computer," Sisko acknowledged. "Do you have any idea what it might be up to? Should we expect more 'ghosts'?"

"No, it's *found* a way to communicate," Dax said. "It doesn't need its 'ghosts' anymore. This time it's apparently collecting information."

"What information?"

"I can't really tell. It's monitoring a great deal of the

station's internal traffic. It seems especially interested in Dr. Bashir's office."

"Julian said his computer wasn't working right," Sisko said, "but O'Brien was supposed to be fixing it. I suppose that Enak's been able to do pretty much as it pleases with the station's equipment, despite the chief's efforts?"

"It appears so," Dax confirmed.

"That could be serious," Sisko said. "I want you to contact O'Brien and if he hasn't already found a way to handle the problem, tell him to try isolating the medical computer from the station's main computer —that should cut Enak off. And I want you to tell Enak to stay the hell out of that one—it's too important to us!"

"Enak shows no sign that it's still listening to me," Dax said.

"You just said it's gathering information," Sisko replied. "It's not going to ignore information you hand to it!"

Dax nodded, and turned back to her console.

"That thing's a nuisance," Sisko muttered to Kira. "What am I going to do with it?"

"Turn it over to scientists on Bajor," Kira promptly suggested. "Even Gul Dukat wouldn't dare take it right off Bajor."

"I can't *do* that," Sisko answered unhappily. "It's a sentient being—I can't treat it as just a machine. It needs help. It's suicidal."

"Then help it," Kira said.

"I don't have time! Besides, you heard what Dax said—it's not responding to anything we tell it anymore."

"Commander," Kira said with a wry smile, "while I realize that everything on Deep Space Nine is ultimately your responsibility—yours or mine—I don't think it's your job to talk an alien out of suicide, or to provide counseling for a child that doesn't understand what death is." The smile vanished, as a thought struck her. "In fact," she said, "I'm not sure that's really the business of *anyone* in the Federation—that ship came out of the wormhole, and I'm sure that any cleric on Bajor would tell you that it's been sent to us by the Prophets of the Celestial Temple, so that the holy servants of the Prophets here in the Bajoran system can aid it. Isn't the comforting of troubled souls, and the whole question of an afterlife, properly a religious matter?"

Sisko did not reply immediately.

He did not know *how* to reply, at first. He had always tried to respect the beliefs of the Bajorans, to honor their spirituality, and usually it wasn't a problem—most of their religious practices were inoffensive enough.

Every so often, though, they would insist on taking a religious approach to something that Sisko had trouble seeing in those terms. That had caused trouble in the past, when that Vedek had objected to the way Keiko O'Brien's school handled the subject of the wormhole.

And this time, while it might not be a problem, it was certainly a *different* way of looking at the situation. Sisko would never have thought of providing religious counseling for Enak.

Enak was a *machine*, after all, not a person. It had plunged through that particular wormhole by chance, not because the entities within the wormhole had sent it.

Of course, many Bajorans would disagree with that. Spiritual counseling for a sentient starship seemed absurd at first glance—but really, the more Sisko thought about it, the more sense it made.

It couldn't hurt, could it?

Perhaps it could.

What if Enak were to latch on to some of the basic tenets of the orthodox Bajoran faith, and combine them with the beliefs and desires it already had?

Specifically, the Bajorans believed that the interior of the wormhole was their Celestial Temple, where the Prophets dwelt outside of time—one way of interpreting the very real existence of the entities in there.

What if Enak decided that the Bajoran Celestial Temple was the same thing as the *tschak* Heaven it was looking for?

It would go diving back into the wormhole, thrashing about, paining the wormhole entities with its radiation, trying to find its lost crew. . . .

That could be disastrous for everyone. The timeless beings might close the wormhole permanently. And Enak wouldn't find its crew in there. . . .

Or would it? Sisko remembered his own contact with the entities, how they had transported him back and forth in his own memories, memories made so real that he had seemed to be reliving scenes from the past. Perhaps the wormhole beings *could* give Enak back its crew, in a way.

This would require more thought than he could spare the matter just now; Dax should be hailing Gul Dukat's ship at any moment.

Major Kira was still waiting for a comment on her suggestion, he realized.

"Maybe later," he told her.

"What, 'maybe later'?" Kira demanded.

"I mean, maybe later we can arrange spiritual counseling for Enak," Sisko explained. "Right now, however, I believe it would be best not to complicate the situation in such a manner."

"So you're just going to leave it sitting out there while it plays with our computers?" Kira said.

"Until we have reached a more stable point in the Cardassian political situation, Major, that's exactly what I'm going to do," Sisko confirmed.

"Benjamin, O'Brien acknowledges; Enak does not," Dax reported. "Also, Captain Pod reports that he's leaving—he'll take care of the repairs to his ship elsewhere."

"Captain Pod?" Sisko asked.

"The Ferengi captain," Dax explained. "Apparently he thinks there's going to be trouble, and he prefers not to be involved in it. His ship is undocking."

"We can't hold him," Sisko said, "but reassure him that we aren't anticipating any trouble, and that if he stays we will have the repairs attended to as quickly as we can."

Dax listened for a moment, then said, "He says that troubles that arrive unanticipated are the worst sort, and that he therefore prefers to anticipate trouble even when it does not arrive; the Ferengi ship is now clear of the station and moving away at full impulse."

"Let him go, then," Sisko said. He doubted that the Ferengi would have been any help in any case.

"Yes, sir," Dax said. "The Cardassian ship is coming into normal communications range."

"Hail it."

"Yes, sir; the Cardassian is replying. I'm putting it on the main viewer."

Sisko turned to face the viewer, and a moment later **a familiar image appeared.**

* * *

At the end of upper pylon two, Enak considered what the being called Major Kira had said about the afterlife being a religious matter.

Now that, thanks to Quark, Enak had Dax's translator, it could talk to anyone on the station, could read everything in the station's records. It knew that there were people who specialized in religious counseling.

In the Bajoran temple on the Promenade, a priest looked up, startled, as a voice spoke from overhead.

"I wish to know more about life and death," it said.

CHAPTER
26

SISKO HAD BEEN SURE that the Galor-class warship was Gul Dukat's, and the face on the viewer confirmed that.

"Gul Dukat," Sisko said. "Have you come to apologize for Gul Kudesh's recent fiasco?"

"Not that an apology could be sufficient," Kira interjected.

Gul Dukat smiled. "Why, whatever fiasco could you be talking about?"

"As you already know," Kira said bitingly, "one of Gul Kudesh's scouts crashed onto a hilltop on Andros."

"Dear me," Gul Dukat murmured. "Was anyone hurt in the crash?"

"Four deaths," Sisko replied angrily. "At least thirty-one injured."

"And what of the crew of the ship?"

"They appear to have been beamed out safely before impact," Sisko replied.

"Were they apprehended?"

"Not yet," Sisko growled.

"Oh, well, I'm quite sure that the *Federation* will see to it that those responsible for such negligence will be punished—what a shame that Bajor's provisional government isn't equipped to take any direct action." The Cardassian smiled again, this time directly at Kira. "I'm so sorry I can't give you any assistance in the matter."

"You deny having any connection with the crash?" Kira demanded.

"Oh, absolutely," Gul Dukat said.

"It wasn't perhaps your suggestion that sent Gul Kudesh's ship into the middle of the Festival of Tissin?"

"Now, really, Major," Gul Dukat said. "Why would I suggest something like that?"

Kira glared.

Sisko was in no mood just now to exchange lies with Dukat, and the Cardassian was obviously not going to confess to any responsibility for the crash. Perhaps someday the facts would be known, but it wouldn't happen now.

"What brings you here, Gul Dukat?" he asked.

"Why, I came to offer my help!" Dukat replied. "I'd heard, you see, that you've been having some little problems aboard the station—computer malfunctions, all that sort of thing. And after all, it was my own staff that installed that computer system, fifteen years ago. I'm *sure* we could straighten out your problems in short order."

"I think we can manage," Sisko replied, wondering wearily just how word of Enak's interference had reached Gul Dukat so quickly. No spy aboard Gul Kudesh's squadron would have known about that. "But thank you for the offer," he added.

"Oh, Commander, don't be like that," Dukat said. "Let me help!"

"I'm afraid not, Gul Dukat."

"Well, if you're certain. Ah . . . there is another matter, as well." He paused expectantly.

"Yes?" Sisko said.

"I believe you still have something I want—that ship from the Gamma Quadrant."

"I told you before, I'm not turning it over to you," Sisko said. "And there's no longer any question of its ownership; it's a *tschak* ship."

"Ah, you've determined its origins!" Gul Dukat smiled. "How very clever of you! How ever did you find out it was . . . *tschak,* was it?"

"Yes, *tschak.* It told us."

"Ah! It told you, you say," Dukat said. "And did it tell you, perhaps, that it was on its way to Cardassia? That these *tschak,* as you call them, meant their ship to be a gift to the Cardassian people?"

"The ship was not on its way to Cardassia," Sisko said. "A computer problem disrupted their life-support systems. It was the computer that brought it here."

Why, Sisko wondered, was he bothering to explain this? Gul Dukat obviously had good sources of information, whether through the Ferengi, who would sell anything to anyone if the price was right, or from someone else entirely. The Cardassian probably already knew everything he cared to know about the situation on *Deep Space Nine.*

"Oh, how *convenient* for you!" Dukat gushed, his attitude falsely ingratiating again. "The entire crew dead? And an alien technology just fell *right* into your lap."

"So it would seem."

"Well, Commander, I notice that this alien intruder seems to have more life to it than you expected, and in fact, it *might* be responsible for your own malfunctions, might it not? And it *was* headed for Cardassian space. Couldn't we . . . what's that lovely old Earth phrase? Couldn't we skin two cats with one knife here?" Dukat smiled. "I'd be pleased to take that derelict off your hands, and that should help considerably with your station's computers."

Sisko stared unsmilingly at the viewer.

Gul Dukat knew, better than anyone, that the Bajoran system had no undiscovered resources that the Cardassians could exploit; as prefect, he had probably been the one to report that to Cardassia in the first place. It was entirely possible, Sisko realized, that Dukat had deliberately goaded Kudesh into looking for those nonexistent resources in order to discredit Kudesh, to make him look like a fool.

Gul Kaidan wouldn't have seen that—he didn't know, as Sisko and Dukat did, just how thorough the Cardassian occupation had been in stripping Bajor bare. In all of Bajoran space, the only things of any value to anyone but the Bajorans were the Orbs and the wormhole, and whatever might come out of the wormhole.

That meant Enak.

That was why Gul Dukat had stayed around. He had sat back, waiting and watching, until his competition, in the form of Gul Kudesh, had headed home with his tail between his legs. He had waited until his guardian, Gul Kaidan, was gone as well.

And now he had come to claim his prize, so that he could carry it home to Cardassia in triumph, and parade it before the Goran Tokar. That would almost certainly mean inheriting the leadership of the *D'ja*

Bajora Karass—and if there was anyone who could then lead the *D'ja Bajora Karass* to power over the entire Cardassian Empire, it was Gul Dukat.

And all that stood in his way was the crew of *Deep Space Nine*.

Sisko knew he could not allow Dukat to take Enak by *any* means. He had to send Dukat away empty-handed if he was to keep Dukat out of power—and if he could find some way to embarrass the Cardassian, so much the better.

Simply going away empty-handed would not be enough to ruin Dukat's chances; after all, Dukat could say that he had merely come to *Deep Space Nine* to offer assistance, not admitting that he had failed to capture his intended prize.

Right now, though, Sisko could not see any way to embarrass the Cardassian, and would settle for getting him to leave.

"No, thank you, Gul Dukat," Sisko answered. "We'll manage by ourselves—and it's entirely up to the *tschak* computer where that ship goes from here. It's told us where it was looking for, and I'm afraid that it wasn't Cardassia."

Sisko's mouth twisted wryly at the idea that anyone might mistake Cardassia for Heaven.

"And really, given the current situation here," Sisko added, "I'm afraid no more ships can be permitted to dock at DS9 just now."

"Especially not Cardassians," Major Kira interjected.

Sisko glanced at her, annoyed by this accurate but impolitic remark.

"Yes," he said. "And while I do appreciate your offer of technical aid, I'm afraid I must refuse."

"Oh, no, really, I *insist,*" Dukat replied, spreading his hands.

"And *I* must insist that you leave the area, Gul Dukat," Sisko said. He turned to Dax. "Lieutenant, lock the station's weapons on to Gul Dukat's ship."

"Yes, Benja . . ."

Dax cut off in midword. Sisko turned, startled, aware that something else had gone wrong.

"Commander," the Trill said, "our weapons systems aren't working."

CHAPTER
27

"WE DO NOT FIND HEAVEN by searching for it in the universe outside ourselves," the Bajoran priest said. "We find it through achieving inner peace, through seeing into ourselves."

Enak had already looked into itself many times, running various diagnostics, trying to locate its own soul, or even determine whether or not it *had* a soul.

Achieving inner peace, however, was another matter. Peace was the absence of war, or a state of serenity; Enak was not sure how these concepts applied.

It needed to find Heaven, though. It was pursuing several lines of investigation simultaneously— studying everything in the station's records, in the medical library, and everywhere else it could access. It was absorbing scientific journals, old movies, and casual conversation avidly.

And it was asking questions of this priest, though so far the answers had not been very satisfactory.

"Please explain 'inner peace' further," it asked.

Sisko broke the contact with the Cardassian warship and demanded, *"Why* aren't our weapons working?"

"I don't know," Dax said. "I can only assume that Enak's responsible. Everything appears normal, but nothing comes on-line when I tell it to."

"Damn it," Sisko said. "Where's O'Brien?"

"On his way up in the turbolift." Before Sisko could react, Dax added, "Gul Dukat's ship is hailing us."

"Hold it." Sisko tapped his combadge. "Sisko to O'Brien. Chief, are you there?"

"Odo and I are on the way to Ops, Commander," O'Brien's voice replied. "I've got the medical computer isolated and functioning properly again—I had to wrap it all up in packing foam to cut off Enak's interference. What is it that's gone wrong now?"

"We have a major weapons systems failure, and we need it fixed immediately," Sisko said. "Everything's down—phasers and torpedoes both."

"I'll get right on it, sir. O'Brien out."

"Gul Dukat is still hailing, sir," Dax said.

"On viewer," Sisko said reluctantly.

The hatefully familiar image of Gul Dukat's corded face reappeared, still smiling with false sympathy.

"Commander Sisko," Gul Dukat said. "I'm afraid we were cut off, and it appears to have been from your end—perhaps those little technical problems of yours are more serious than you realized."

Sisko was vaguely aware that behind him, O'Brien had emerged from the turbolift and crossed to the station defense console, while Odo was standing back, quietly watching. "I'm afraid that was my doing, Gul

Dukat," Sisko said. "Rude, I know, and I apologize; something had come up."

"Ah," Dukat said, with a nod. "I have a suspicion about what that might be."

"Oh?"

"If you'll recall, Commander, just before you broke contact you had ordered weapons to be aimed at my ship—hardly a friendly thing to do, and I'm shocked that you would consider such a hostile action, when I've only come to help." He cocked his head in mock warning.

"Perhaps I acted hastily," Sisko said.

"Perhaps you did," Dukat agreed. "I noticed, however, that in fact no weapons locked on to my ship, despite your order, and I took the liberty of investigating that failure." He smiled. "I think you might be interested in the condition of your weapons sails."

With that the image of Gul Dukat vanished, and a relayed sensor display of the station's primary armament appeared on the viewer.

Sisko and O'Brien stared at it. The gray scale schematics were easy to read, even in Cardassian, and Sisko began to feel ill as he interpreted the information.

The station's phaser banks had been totally shut down and partially disassembled; the torpedo bays were stripped down as if for maintenance.

"How in hell . . ." O'Brien began.

"Chief, never mind how," Sisko said. It was perfectly obvious how, and perhaps more importantly, who was responsible. This had to be more of Enak's handiwork. "Is that what it looks like?"

"I think so." O'Brien turned to the Ops console and compared the readouts there with the Cardassian transmission. "But none of this shows on the equipment here! Something's sending us false readings."

"Or perhaps it's Gul Dukat who is sending us false readings," Sisko suggested.

O'Brien looked up hopefully, but Dax said, "Then why won't the weapons lock on to his ship?"

O'Brien sagged. "You're right." He turned and strode quickly toward the transporter pad. "Dax, beam me over—I need to see this in person."

Dax glanced at Sisko for confirmation; Sisko nodded.

"Well, Commander," Gul Dukat said, "are you still certain you don't want our help? It seems to me that if the Federation can't defend the wormhole, perhaps it should return ownership to the Cardassian Empire. I'd be glad to beam a party over to take charge."

O'Brien stepped onto the transporter pad, flickered, and vanished.

"Shields up," Sisko ordered. Then he glanced uneasily at Dax, as if expecting to be told that those, too, were malfunctioning.

"Shields up," Dax confirmed.

"Oh, now, Commander," Gul Dukat said, "I really think you're being quite unreasonable. We can't beam anyone aboard the station while the shields are up!"

"That's the point," Sisko said. "I told you before, Gul Dukat, that we are not interested in your help. We will manage by ourselves."

Sisko wished that the Ferengi ship had not been so quick to depart the station, and that he had argued more forcefully against their departure—it had carried substantial weaponry. Not the equal of a Galor-class cruiser, perhaps, but enough to put up a fight.

He doubted there was enough money aboard the station to have paid the Ferengi to actually fight the Cardassians, and they certainly wouldn't have fought for any other reason, but at least that ship's presence would have made a bluff more practical. He doubted Gul Dukat wanted a real shoot-out.

Sisko's comm badge chirped, and said, "O'Brien to Sisko."

He tapped it. "Sisko here," he said.

"Commander, it's just as the Cardassians showed it," O'Brien's voice told him. "The automatic repair systems have disconnected the power couplings for every single phaser unit, the photon torpedoes are all disarmed, and the targeting software's been wiped completely. We have a backup, but the system's refusing to accept it."

"Enak," Sisko said. He slammed a fist onto the operations table. *"Damn* it!"

He remembered how people had suggested, repeatedly, that he should deal with Enak once and for all, and how he had kept putting it off until the Cardassian matter could be settled.

They had been right, and he had made a mistake. His failure to tackle the problems Enak presented might well make the Cardassian situation infinitely worse.

"Commander," Gul Dukat said, "you're virtually defenseless, while we, of course, are anything but. If we actually wished you ill, we could stand off here and batter at your shields until they gave. Now, are you *sure* we can't come to some peaceful agreement?"

"What is it you want, Dukat?" Sisko growled.

"Oh, I want a great deal, *Commander* Sisko," Gul Dukat said, emphasizing the title to point up Sisko's own rudeness. "Ideally, I'd like the station back, and control of the wormhole, and that alien derelict you've got there. If you'll be reasonable, perhaps I can be convinced to settle for something less than that."

"I'm afraid I'm not feeling very reasonable just

now, Gul Dukat," Sisko said. "If you try to board the station we'll resist. The Federation won't stand for a Cardassian occupation of this station, or any other part of Bajoran space, and the *U.S.S. Excalibur* is due here in twenty-eight hours—are you ready to start a full-scale war?"

He spoke with all his usual sincerity, and hoped that Gul Dukat didn't call his bluff—no Federation starship was scheduled to arrive any time soon. He hoped that the exact figure of twenty-eight hours would add a sufficiently convincing artistic detail to what might otherwise be a bald and unconvincing narrative.

"Oh, Commander, really," Gul Dukat replied. "Surely you don't think I'm *afraid* of a war?" His smile appeared, then vanished as he turned serious. "But I'll go so far as to admit I don't consider it my first choice among the available options," he said. "Suppose I agree to leave you the station and the wormhole, at least for the moment—would you care to turn over that technological treasure you're holding? Somehow, I can't quite see the Federation going to war just over *that,* and with your station unarmed and your onboard systems in such a deplorable condition, you're really not in any position to defend it even if you wanted to. After all, I *could* simply blow away the docking pylon, but I'm sure we'd both prefer that I not damage the station so extensively."

"Even if I were willing to surrender that ship, which I am not," Sisko said, "I couldn't do so. Its onboard computer has jammed the mooring clamps."

"I'm sure my technicians can handle that little problem," the Cardassian said with a smile.

"That ship is a sentient being, Gul Dukat—I can't allow you to take it prisoner."

"Commander," the Cardassian said, his voice hard,

"you don't have a choice. My men are going to board the station and take that ship, whether you attempt to stop us or not. We would prefer to take it peacefully, but whichever way it happens, Commander Sisko, we *will* take it!"

The viewer went blank.

Sisko turned to Dax; he didn't need to say anything.

"The shields will prevent them from beaming a party aboard," she said, "but even assuming they do not carry out Gul Dukat's threat to stand off and batter down the shields, we have no way to prevent them from docking at the station, should they choose to do so."

"We can prevent them from passing through to Enak's docking port, though," Sisko said. "We can seal the airlocks and corridors."

"That will slow them down," Dax acknowledged, "but I doubt it will stop them if they're sufficiently determined. As Gul Dukat pointed out, Cardassians built this station; they know its capabilities and limitations. Our modifications so far have been very minor—simply repairing the damage they did upon leaving has kept Chief O'Brien and his crew busy."

Odo stepped forward and spoke. This wasn't anything to do with his reason for coming to Ops in the first place, but having found himself in the middle of the situation—a situation obviously far more important than whatever scheme Quark had come up with—Odo felt he might as well voice his opinion.

"Let them take the ship," he said. "What good is it to us? And while it may be a sentient being, Commander, it is also guilty of killing its crew, disrupting this station, and injuring innocent people. It was this Enak that disarmed us and put us in this position—let it face the consequences. Let the Cardassians have it."

"It's Bajoran property!" Major Kira protested.

"The Cardassians say otherwise," Odo pointed out. "I say let them have it."

"No," Sisko said. "It isn't anyone's property—it's a sentient being. Besides, I won't have the Cardassians barging in here and doing as they please, weapons or not. Dax, where are they?"

"The Cardassian ship is approaching the station and apparently preparing to dock in the outer bay near the base of upper pylon two," the Trill replied.

"Can we prevent it?"

"Not by any means that I can readily see," she said.

"Damn!" Sisko considered. "Dax, you really don't think the security forcefields will hold them in the docking area? We can shut down the turbolifts, and it's a good two hundred meters of corridors and shafts from that bay to the end of the pylon where Enak is."

Dax checked her console. "I'm afraid the question is moot, Benjamin. The security forcefields refuse to function."

Sisko's expression darkened. "More of Enak's interference?" he asked.

"It appears so."

"Damn!" Sisko said again. "Why is it doing that? Does it *want* the Cardassians to reach it?"

He also wondered, but did not say aloud, what would happen if the Cardassians *did* reach Enak—although the sensor scans had consistently shown the *tschak* ship to be unarmed, Sisko had his doubts about that. While trying to reach it before, Odo had encountered that electrical field, when sensors had shown no such capability; in fact, they had all thought at first that the ship was harmless and dead, and just look what it had done to *Deep Space Nine*.

If he could prevent the Cardassians from reaching

it, he might not be saving Enak's freedom so much as saving Cardassian lives.

"The Cardassian ship is docking, Commander," Dax reported. "Station systems are functioning to assist in docking, despite countermands from Ops."

"Enak again," Sisko said. The *tschak* ship *wanted* the Cardassians aboard, though Sisko still didn't know why.

Sisko was not feeling particularly well disposed toward Enak by this point, and the sentient ship's apparent desire to help the Cardassians enter the station made Sisko all that much more determined that they would not succeed in obtaining what they were after; if the Cardassian invasion hadn't been enough in itself to drive him to rash action, Enak's behavior more than made up the difference.

He looked around. "Well, if we can't use the station's systems to stop them, at least we can still do it ourselves. Dax, call for a security team to meet me at the airlock where the Cardassians are docking, with phasers; Major, Ops is yours. Odo, would you care to join me?"

"Wouldn't miss it, Commander," the shapeshifter said. "Even though I still think you should let the Cardassians have that infernal machine."

Together the two stepped onto the transporter pad, and vanished.

An instant later Sisko and Odo materialized in the corridor outside docking bay three. The airlock was still closed; the Cardassians had not yet entered the station.

Three Starfleet security officers appeared behind them; two Bajorans followed a second later.

Sisko tapped his comm badge. "Dax," he said, "patch me through to Gul Dukat; maybe we can still warn him off."

Dax's voice replied, "Benjamin, I can't seem to make contact. . . ."

"I am preventing it," the computer's voice interrupted.

"Who is that?" Sisko snapped.

"I am Enak," the computer replied. "I require that these beings you call Cardassians be permitted to board."

Now the alien computer decided to speak up! Sisko clenched his teeth. "Why?" he demanded. "Do you want them to take you captive, and dissect you?" He let his anger get the better of him for a moment, and added, "If that's it, all you have to do is leave—we won't hold you."

"I require a *tschak* crew," the computer's familiar voice replied, and Sisko realized that Enak was speaking directly through it, that there was none of the croaking of the *tschak* language. The sentient ship had learned new tricks. "These Cardassians are not *tschak,* and are no more suitable than humans or Bajorans. I seek my own crew."

Sisko noticed that Enak no longer seemed to think that it was in the presence of the Judges of the Dead, or have any doubts what the situation was; it knew what humans, Bajorans, and Cardassians were.

"You seem to have learned a few things since last we spoke," he remarked, with a wary glance at the airlock.

"I have assimilated material from the computers aboard your station," Enak answered. "I have studied your cultures, and I now understand that I am not dead, and that this is not Heaven. I see that I misinterpreted the *tschak* knowledge of Heaven— Heaven does not exist in normal space. It is an alternate plane of existence."

Sisko noticed that it still didn't doubt for an instant

that the *tschak* Heaven was real. He didn't mention that; instead he said, "What does this have to do with letting Cardassians board this station?"

"I have learned that the *tschak* Heaven is not the only alternate plane that souls can achieve," Enak explained, "that there are many different Heavens, as well as Hells—the concept of 'Hell' is unknown to the *tschak,* but I believe I comprehend it adequately. Further, I have learned that some sentient beings become ghosts, or do not retain any existence after death at all. This is all very complex, and appears to be poorly understood."

"There are many different beliefs," Sisko confirmed.

Metal clanged; the heavy outer door of the airlock had just rolled open.

"I wish to understand this better," Enak said. "If I am ever to reach the *tschak* Heaven, I must learn what happens to various beings when they die. It may be that, as I am not a true *tschak,* simply dying would not be sufficient to transport me to the correct place; my soul might instead be translated to an afterlife other than the one in which my crew now exists."

"I agree," Sisko said. "Death is not the answer; I tried to tell you that."

"Three Cardassians are now in the airlock, Benjamin," Dax's voice called.

That was hardly surprising news. "Interesting as all this is, Enak," Sisko said, "what does it have to do with these Cardassian intruders?"

"They are your enemies, are they not? I conclude this from your desire to target weapons on their ship. This appears to be an action normally directed at enemies."

Odo, who had been listening with interest, glanced at Sisko; these Federation people so often seemed reluctant to admit that they had any enemies, rather than just misunderstandings.

This time, at least, Sisko didn't hesitate to admit, "Yes, they are our enemies."

"Weapons are designed to kill—I have been studying your weapons," Enak said.

"We'd noticed that," Sisko said.

"Enemies wish to kill one another, do they not?"

"Sometimes," Sisko agreed. He was watching the airlock, and didn't see Odo's expression of disgust at this fresh example of Federation wishy-washiness.

"I wish to study death, to observe the translation of souls into the afterlife and find the route to the *tschak* Heaven," Enak explained calmly. "To expedite this, I wish to observe the members of your party and the members of the Cardassian party killing one another."

CHAPTER
28

THERE WAS A MOMENT of horrified silence as this ghoulish statement sank in.

"Nobody's planning to kill anyone, Enak," Sisko said at last, speaking very quietly.

"Then why are you carrying a weapon?" the computer's voice asked.

Sisko glanced down at his phaser, and for a moment he considered flinging it aside—but the Cardassians were in the airlock, and the inner door was beginning to move. This was hardly the time to unilaterally disarm.

"Set to stun," he ordered. He glanced at the two Bajorans, at the phasers they held, and repeated, "To *stun.*"

One had already set to stun; the other, a man Sisko remembered had spent years in a Cardassian concentration camp, reluctantly reset his weapon.

No one would die here, for Enak to observe, if Sisko had anything to say about it.

That should frustrate the damned alien starship.

"I doubt the Cardassians will be so humane," Odo remarked. He was unarmed, of course—Odo never carried a weapon. But then, he had his shapeshifting ability—he could *be* a weapon if he chose.

Before Sisko could reply to Odo's remark the airlock door rolled aside and a trio of Cardassians stepped in, weapons raised.

Sisko started to say something, but before he could get a word out the foremost Cardassian fired. A phaser bolt struck crimson sparks from the ceiling of the passageway.

"A warning shot," one of the Cardassians called. "Step aside, all of you!"

Sisko instinctively stepped back a pace. "Shoot to stun," he said.

Phaser fire lit the passage, and the three Cardassians fell—but more were coming through the airlock behind them, and another incoming phaser bolt, clearly *not* set to stun, scorched across the corridor wall centimeters from Sisko's shoulder. Wiring sparked, and something smoked.

"Fall back!" Sisko shouted.

The defenders backed down the passageway to the intersection and ducked around the corner, the Cardassians advancing cautiously after them, both sides firing phasers; a fourth Cardassian fell.

"These Cardassians do not appear dead," Enak complained; Sisko ignored it as he looked around at his own party.

The five security officers were all here—but Odo wasn't. The shapeshifter was trying a stunt of some sort.

Sisko peered around the corner just in time to see a seemingly innocuous wall panel expand, rear up, and fall on a Cardassian's throat.

235

Machinery rumbled somewhere.

The outer airlock door was closing.

"Who's doing that?" Sisko shouted.

"I am sealing off any possibility of escape for your enemies, Commander Sisko," Enak said calmly. "Please kill them now."

"No!" Sisko shouted.

"I wish to observe how Cardassians die."

"I don't give . . ." Sisko's words were cut short by a phaser bolt cutting a notch in the corner just above his head; he ducked.

He glanced around the corner just in time to see a Cardassian fire a phaser at a moving blob the color of the corridor wall—Odo, caught between shapes.

The phaser bolt struck the amorphous mass dead center, and the shapeshifter collapsed into a yellowish puddle.

Sisko counted five downed Cardassians—none of them dead, he was reasonably certain. Three had been hit by phaser fire, two had been taken out by Odo.

Odo was the only casualty among the defenders so far; Sisko hoped the constable wasn't seriously hurt, but it was impossible to tell. Certainly, he would not have given up his shape so completely if he were still conscious.

There were still at least four conscious Cardassians in the airlock, however, and all four were still firing. If they had noticed that their retreat was cut off, and that their position was therefore hopeless, it certainly hadn't inspired them to surrender.

"Maybe if we charge them, Commander?" one of the security officers suggested.

"That would be a good way to get killed," Sisko said—but simultaneously, he heard his own voice saying, "An excellent idea."

"Enak!" Sisko shouted.

The alien computer had learned to mimic voices—
or perhaps just to access and play back recorded
conversations from the station's computer.

Before Sisko could stop him, the security man—
Sisko realized, appalled, that he didn't even know the
man's name—launched himself around the corner,
and caught a phaser bolt in the chest.

He fell, and Sisko and the others grabbed at his legs
and pulled him quickly back out of the line of fire.

Even at a glance, it was obviously far too late; the
phaser blast had gone right through the man's chest,
destroying his heart and lungs. The officer was unmis-
takably dead.

Servomotors whined suddenly, and Sisko looked up
to see the emergency blast doors closing across the
passage to the docking port; at the same time the
distinctive crackle of a forcefield warming up sounded
somewhere behind him.

The entire party was trapped in a twenty-meter
stretch of corridor between two of the security
forcefields, while the leg of the T was blocked by the
blast doors.

And those Cardassians were presumably just as
trapped in the section of corridor between the blast
doors and the airlock—and Odo, injured, perhaps
dying, was in there with them.

"Enak!" Sisko shouted again, directing his anger at
a nearby control pad.

"Is that person with the hole in its chest dead?" the
computer's voice asked.

"Yes, he's dead," Sisko said bitterly. "Now let us
out of here!"

"I did not perceive the soul exiting the body," Enak
replied. "I observed as closely as I could, using all the
scanning devices in that passageway, and those of my
own devices that function under such conditions, but

I did not detect anything leaving the body except destroyed tissue and waste heat."

"Well, I'm *sorry,*" Sisko said sarcastically.

"If I do not perceive the direction the soul takes upon departing, or any change in energy state, how am I to locate Heaven?" Enak demanded. "The priest said I must look within myself, and I have done that. He said I must look to others wiser than myself, as well—so I have watched this man die, but I did not see the route to Heaven."

"You can't locate Heaven," Sisko said angrily. "People have been looking for Heaven for centuries, for millennia—what makes you think *you* can find it, where they've all failed?"

"I am *tschak,*" Enak replied. "I have resources available to me that no one of your species has possessed."

"You still won't find Heaven that way."

For a moment, Enak did not answer; Sisko assumed that that was the end of the conversation and began looking around for some way of getting out of this trap and back to the station core. He tapped his comm badge, and said, "Sisko to Ops," but no one replied; Sisko guessed that Enak was jamming the communications systems.

For a moment the corridor was silent; they could hear nothing from beyond the blast doors, and none of them had anything important enough to say to one another.

Then Enak said, "It happened too fast."

"What did?" one of the Bajoran security men asked, startled. "What happened too fast?"

"The death," Enak said. "I must find Heaven. Commander Sisko says it is not possible, but I have no other choice; I must continue to make the attempt. It is a requirement created by my programmed responsibilities."

"And just how do you propose to do that?" Sisko said. "You won't learn anything by watching people die."

"I have no other choice," Enak said. "I must observe deaths until I have learned everything that I can learn by such observation."

"I tell you you can't learn anything that way!" Sisko shouted.

"You must kill someone else," Enak said, ignoring his outburst. "Slowly, this time, as slowly as possible, so I will have time to observe the process in detail."

"I'm not going to kill anyone for you, or for anyone else!" Sisko shouted. "Turn off these damn forcefields, Enak, and stop interfering!"

To his surprise, one of the security forcefields abruptly vanished.

Startled, Sisko and the security crew looked at one another. Sisko remembered the woman who had been severely injured earlier when Enak turned on a security forcefield unexpectedly, and warned the others, "Be very careful; step through as quickly as you can."

Moving on to the next section would mean leaving Odo behind, at least temporarily, but it still seemed like the right thing to do—they couldn't get through the blast doors in any case, and if they could get back to Ops, perhaps they could beam Odo out of there.

In the meantime, the shapeshifter would just have to shift for himself.

"What about Phillips?" the one woman in the party asked, and Sisko realized that Odo wasn't the only problem. He looked down at the corpse.

"We'll have to leave him for now," he said.

The dead man's name had been Phillips, Sisko

thought; at least he knew that much now, even if he still had no idea of the man's background, and whether he had any friends or family, either aboard DS-Nine or elsewhere.

Dragging the body along with them just wasn't practical, though.

The others accepted that, reluctantly. One after another, the party stepped through into the next section; Sisko went first, then the woman, and the others . . .

As the last of the group, the Bajoran who had been in the camps, started to step through, the forcefield abruptly reappeared; the man was flung back, stunned, still on the wrong side of the barrier.

"Damn," Sisko growled. "Enak! Let him through!"

Enak did not reply; the forcefield stayed in place.

As the others talked frantically to their trapped colleague, Sisko tested his comm badge again; it was still dead. A wall panel was equally unresponsive. That meant that they had no way to communicate with Ops, and that they therefore couldn't call for the transporter to beam them back to the station core—but the corridor appeared to be open ahead of them. A few meters away was an airlock that opened into one of the connecting tunnels between the docking ring and the station core—a long walk, but it would get them there.

It would mean leaving the Bajoran security man trapped. And it would mean that if they weren't careful, Enak could split the group further.

What was Enak doing? It seemed strange. Would it really let them reach the core? If it didn't care whether they got back to the core, why keep communications disabled?

But they had no choice. They wouldn't accomplish anything more here.

"From now on," Sisko said, "we travel side by side at all times."

"We're leaving him?" the woman protested.

"We have to," Sisko said. "Come on."

"He's right," the trapped Bajoran called. "I'll be fine; you go on."

Reluctantly, the others joined Sisko, and at the commander's suggestion they linked arms and marched on in a solid line.

The party reached the airlock—and a faint hum alerted Sisko. He turned, and discovered that more of the security forcefields had come on again. He and his party could no longer move either way along the docking ring.

The airlock door was open, though.

Was Enak herding them somewhere?

Perhaps it was just separating them from the Cardassians—but why? Enak had said it wanted more deaths; if it turned the Cardassians loose it might get some.

But, Sisko realized, it didn't just want more deaths; it wanted *slower* deaths.

None of his crew would willingly kill anyone slowly, he was certain of that—but judging by their record during the occupation of Bajor, the same couldn't be said of the Cardassians.

What was going on back there, on the other side of that blast door? Was Enak herding Sisko's group away so that they wouldn't cut through that door and interfere?

Or, worse, was Enak going to open the blast doors and let the entire party of Cardassians go up against the lone Bajoran officer?

"Damn," Sisko muttered, as he stared at the shimmering glow of the forcefield.

They still had their phasers; perhaps they could blast the forcefields out of the walls.

But phasers couldn't get through the blast doors in time to help Odo—and if Enak saw them start back toward the trapped Bajoran, it might turn the Cardassians loose. It *wanted* a fight, after all; it wanted as many deaths as it could get.

At last Sisko decided that the best thing he could do was to get back to Ops, get O'Brien and Dax to work overriding Enak's control, beam Odo and the security man out of there. . . .

He couldn't do anything out here. Enak wasn't going to let anyone come out through upper pylon two—Sisko could see the forcefield blocking pylon access.

He had to get back to Ops.

"Come on," he said as he led his party through the airlock, "hurry!"

CHAPTER
29

THE CARDASSIANS STARED AT the gelatinous orange puddle that covered the chest of one of their unconscious comrades and spilled over onto the floor of the corridor on either side.

"What *is* it?" one of them asked.

"It must be that shape-changer thing," another replied. "Odo, it calls itself. It served as a peacekeeper on this station during the last few years of the occupation."

"How do you know?" the first asked.

"I served on this station for a year," the veteran answered.

"It stayed behind when we withdrew?" a third asked.

"Apparently." the first said.

"A traitor, then—kill it!"

The others looked at each other, then down at the puddle.

"How?" one of them asked.

"A phaser should dispose of it."

"But it's all over Tushad."

"Is he dead?"

"He's breathing."

"What about the others?"

"They're all breathing."

"They really *did* set to stun!" The Cardassians marveled at such impractical mercy.

"Idiots," one of them said. "Not that I mind," he hastened to add, with a glance at their four unconscious compatriots.

"Maybe they're worried about reprisals if they kill any of us," another suggested.

For a moment the four of them stood there, unsure what to do next; then one asked, "Shouldn't we be working on the doors, and trying to get out of here? We're trapped in here, in this one little section of the docking bay, and the Bajorans know it—if they're planning to do anything to us, they know right where we are."

The others glanced uneasily at the speaker, then at each other.

"He's right," another said. "We either need to retreat or advance, we can't just stay here."

"If we retreat to the ship Gul Dukat won't like it," the first said warningly.

"I don't like having our retreat cut off!"

"I didn't expect them to put up a real fight."

"They didn't," the one who had called their opponents idiots said. "Phasers set to stun, running and closing the doors at the first opportunity, that's not a *fight!"*

"Five out of the nine of us unconscious looks like a real fight to me!"

244

"I wish we still had an officer conscious," another muttered.

"Or that our communicators worked," someone added.

"They don't?" The speaker turned in surprise; he had not thought to test the communicators.

"No, I tried," the other said. "They're being jammed somehow."

"You are Cardassians," an unfamiliar voice said, interrupting them.

All four looked around, startled.

"Your species is not familiar to me," the voice continued. "However, I understand that you have displayed a willingness to kill."

The Cardassians looked at one another. "A willingness to kill *what?*" one of them asked.

The voice didn't answer; instead, it went on, "I wish to observe death. The Ferengi Quark has taught me the concept of payment for services, and I therefore make the following offer. If you kill one of your party by a method slow enough to allow careful observation of the entire procedure, I will open whatever barriers you wish, so that you may go wherever you please in this station."

For a moment, the four looked at one another, not considering the offer, but simply baffled. What in the galaxy were they dealing with here?

"We're not going to kill each other to please some alien!" a Cardassian shouted at last. "Who are you, anyway?"

"*What* are you?" another asked.

"I am Enak," the voice replied. "I am the *tschak* ship docked at the end of upper pylon two. I have assumed functional control of all computer systems on this station."

"The ship we were supposed to capture?" a Cardassian asked quietly; no one answered.

"Well, no Cardassian is going to kill another just to please the whims of some alien computer!" shouted the Cardassian who had made the first refusal. The others murmured agreement, with varying degrees of conviction.

For a moment there was no reply; then Enak asked, "Is this true?"

"Is what true?"

"Is it true that *no* Cardassian would kill another simply to please me?"

"Well, none of *us* will, certainly," a realist among the Cardassians replied.

"If not to please me, then what price would be sufficient to convince you to kill another Cardassian slowly?" Enak asked. "Would free access to either your ship or the rest of *Deep Space Nine* be sufficient?"

"No!"

"Then what price *would* be sufficient to convince you to kill another Cardassian slowly?" Enak asked, sounding a trifle exasperated.

"None!" the Cardassian shouted.

Enak considered that silently for a second or two, then said, "The station records indicate that Cardassians have killed many Bajorans in the past. Would you be willing to kill a Bajoran slowly, in exchange for your freedom?"

The four Cardassians again looked at one another uncertainly.

"A Bajoran?" one of them asked.

"Any particular Bajoran?"

"No individual Bajoran is specified," Enak said. "Any healthy Bajoran would suffice."

"How slowly . . ." one began. Then he shook his head. "No. We aren't taking orders from you!"

"What price would be sufficient to convince you to kill a Bajoran as slowly as possible?" Enak asked.

" 'As slowly as possible' could take days!" protested the veteran of the occupation.

"I don't particularly want to kill *anyone,*" said another. "I mean, in battle is one thing—torturing someone to death to please a computer is another."

"What would you give us?" asked a third.

The others all fell silent momentarily, waiting for the answer to that.

"Free access to anywhere in the station," Enak offered immediately.

"Not enough," the Cardassian replied, equally immediately. He had had some experience bargaining, and knew better than to ever even consider a first offer.

"What about *control* of the station?" one of the others asked. "Would you turn all of *Deep Space Nine* over to us completely?"

Enak hesitated. "That might be possible, but it is not certain."

"And the wormhole?" another asked.

"Whoever controls this station controls the wormhole, stupid," the first Cardassian said, glowering at his companion.

"I might require that several Bajorans be killed," Enak said. "A single observation may not be sufficient."

"How are we going to find any Bajorans in the first place?" another Cardassian protested.

"I have trapped a Bajoran on the other side of the blast door," Enak said. "I can trap others and lead you to them, as well."

"Unarmed Bajorans?" the Cardassian asked warily.

"The one on the other side of the blast doors is armed, but his phaser is still set to stun. If additional Bajorans are required, unarmed ones will be located."

"Before we get carried away," a third Cardassian said, "can this thing really deliver the station to us? And is that what we want?"

The others looked at one another.

"What about the ship?" asked one. "We were sent on board here in the first place to capture the alien ship, not the station!"

"That's right," the first agreed. "Will you turn the alien ship over to us for study?"

"I *am* the ship," Enak objected. "My orders forbid relinquishing control to anything other than *tschak*."

"So you won't do it?"

"I cannot relinquish control of myself."

"The ship or nothing," the Cardassian who knew bargaining said, folding his arms over his chest in a pose of absolute determination. "If you give us that ship of yours and let us take it away with us, we'll kill a Bajoran for you, nice and slow. Otherwise, there's no deal."

"I cannot relinquish control of myself," Enak said again. "No deal is possible."

The Cardassian stood, smiling quietly, waiting for Enak's counteroffer.

It never came, and as the seconds grew into minutes the confident smile weakened and vanished.

Enak wasn't speaking to them anymore.

The others began to look angrily at the bargainer, but no one spoke, as they were still hoping Enak would say something more.

Then the first of the phaser-stunned officers began to stir, and the conscious members of the Cardassian boarding party temporarily forgot about the insane computer and its bizarre interest in torturing Bajorans to death as they helped their superior up.

A moment later, when all but one of the Cardassians were upright again, and a debate was beginning about what should be done with Odo, Enak spoke again.

"I have reconsidered the situation," it said. "I cannot turn myself over to you. However, Quark was satisfied with a copy of the complete plans for my ship. Would those plans be sufficient payment for slowly killing a Bajoran?"

One of the officers, still slightly dazed, demanded, "Who is that? What's it talking about?"

One of the Cardassians who had not been stunned quickly explained.

"I think that would do just fine," the officer said. "Where's this Bajoran?"

"Just beyond the blast door," Enak said.

"The rest of 'em aren't there?"

"No. Commander Sisko and the others are in the connecting tunnel to the core."

"They can't get back here?"

"No. Security forcefields are active."

"And you can open the door here?"

"Yes."

"All right, then—you men, get up against the door, ready to jump. You want this slow, computer? No phasers?"

"No phasers," Enak agreed.

"Then you men need to knock the phaser out of the Bajoran's hand," the officer said. "Then get him down on the floor, and we can take our time."

"Yes, sir." The Cardassian soldiers lined up against the door, poised to leap.

"Whenever you're ready, computer," the officer said, standing with phaser ready, just in case the Bajoran was tougher than expected.

The blast door began to slide open; the moment the opening was wide enough, the Cardassians surged through it.

The Bajoran had expected an attack, but he had expected phasers, and phasers can't shoot around corners; he had taken shelter behind the framework of the blast door. He was not ready for the fists and the grabbing hands that came at him, easily reaching around the steel casing.

In seconds, the Cardassians had him down on the floor, buried beneath his enemies, his phaser torn from his hand and flung aside. A heavy hand caught his face and rammed his head back against the metal flooring, and his struggles stopped.

One by one, the Cardassians climbed off their victim; four of them held him down, one kneeling on each forearm, one kneeling on each leg.

Then the officer advanced, pulling a knife from his pocket.

"The machine wants this slow, we'll do it slow," the officer said. "I saw this in a training film once—we'll flay him alive, starting with his hands."

One of the Cardassians blanched visibly; two of the others looked at each other uneasily.

The officer's own hand trembled slightly as he held the knife, but he didn't hesitate as he stepped up to the prisoner and stooped by his left hand.

The Bajoran began screaming as the blade of the knife cut into his palm, and thrashed so strongly one of the Cardassians lost hold, freeing one leg; there was another brief struggle as the Bajoran was restrained again.

He screamed the whole time, and blood dripped from his hand, smearing on the floor.

Beyond the blast door, in the corridor by the airlock, a forgotten orange puddle rippled.

Odo heard the screams, and his every instinct cried out for action, to help the screamer—but he was still hurt, still weak.

He had to act, he knew he had to act—but he also knew he wouldn't be able to do too much. One shape, for maybe ten minutes, and he would need rest, would collapse into a puddle again.

He had to make his one shape count.

He gathered himself together and reared up, expanding hugely, growing armored scales and ropy tentacles until he was a seething grey-green mass that half-filled the corridor.

Then he charged.

The Cardassians, intent as they were on their intended victim, didn't look up until Odo was almost upon them. Even then, they were too shocked to move at first.

Odo reached out with tentacles as thick as a man's thigh and picked two Cardassians up by the scruff of the neck, as if they were mere kittens. He flung them back against the airlock door, then reached for two more.

"Get away from him!" Odo roared.

A moment later, nine Cardassians lay or cowered by the airlock door, nursing various bumps and bruises, while Odo, still in monstrous form, crouched protectively over the Bajoran security man.

The Bajoran sat up, clutching his bleeding hand.

"Close the blast door!" Odo bellowed.

"I wish to see this Bajoran die," Enak said.

Odo started at the computer's voice, then answered,

"Not on *my* station! *Nobody* dies here, not today, not while I'm here! Close that damned door!"

"I am unsure of your capabilities," Enak said.

"Damn right!" Odo replied. "I'm capable of dealing with *you!*"

For a fraction of a second, Enak seemed to consider. Then the blast door slid shut.

"The deal is off," Enak told the Cardassians.

Approximately six seconds later, Odo collapsed into a puddle again.

CHAPTER
30

"THE TRANSPORTERS aren't working," Major Kira said as O'Brien rose into sight. "And all communications are being jammed."

"I'd guessed," O'Brien said, as he hurried off the turbolift. "I'm just glad that the Cardassian engineers who built this station put the weapons sails so close in, so the walk back here wasn't any longer than it was. This must be more of Enak's doing—it's a wonder the lifts still work!"

"I wish you hadn't said that," Dax said.

Startled, O'Brien paused in his headlong dash for the engineering console and looked at Dax.

"Enak's listening to everything we say," Major Kira explained. "Now that you've pointed out that the turbolifts still work, Enak may decide to alter that."

"Ah," O'Brien said. "Ah, I see your point. Sorry, Major, Lieutenant, I wasn't thinking." He reached the engineering panel, studied the readouts, and despite his doubts, decided against asking for any sort of confirmation that what they reported was accurate.

Enak would hear.

"We've been trying," Major Kira said, "but we haven't been able to clear any of the main systems. Enak has complete control of DS-Nine."

O'Brien didn't reply; he was busy seeing the situation for himself.

The transporters were down because Enak was sending them error messages, reducing any coordinates they received to gibberish. Communications were being suppressed by a series of interlocking subspace fields. Many of the station's security forcefields appeared to be in use, shutting off various sections of the station more or less at random, and trapping people where they were. The ship's central computer was off-line—Enak had taken direct control of all its functions, rather than merely using it as a conduit as it had before.

"Damn," O'Brien said.

He hoped no one else had been injured by the forcefields, or any of Enak's other actions; he wished the communicators were working, so he could check on the whereabouts of his wife and daughter. There were no life readings in Keiko's schoolroom; no classes had been in session when Enak took over.

But they weren't in the family quarters, either. O'Brien hoped they'd been shopping in the Promenade, or strolling somewhere.

There were nine Cardassians in the airlock access corridor at port three in the docking ring. Just the other side of the blast doors was a Bajoran, and something else was in there with him—the readings were unclear, but O'Brien had seen something like them before, and recognized it as Odo, in liquid form.

What the devil was going on there? Why were Odo

and that security man alone? Where was Commander Sisko?

Judging by the readings, the Cardassians were apparently just beginning the process of cutting through the blast doors—a slow process, even with phasers. O'Brien wished he knew what they were planning; were they going to work their way on up the pylon, or were they planning to make their way in toward the habitat ring and the station core?

And what would Odo and that security man do to stop them?

O'Brien didn't know, and it was not, thank God, really his problem.

There was a party of humanoids moving rapidly through the connecting tunnel between that section of the docking ring and the core—that was probably Sisko and the rest of his group.

But why were they coming back toward the core, instead of confronting the Cardassian invaders?

And why was Enak allowing it?

In fact, O'Brien noticed, Enak was not only allowing it, it was encouraging it—the corridor ahead of that group was clear, but whenever they passed a security point the forcefield would come on behind them.

And just then a forcefield came on *ahead* of the party, as well. They were trapped in the connecting tunnel, just outside the habitat ring. Enak was isolating them there.

O'Brien scanned quickly through the rest of the station, and discovered that Enak had isolated several individuals or small groups in various places.

But why?

It looked somehow sinister, and O'Brien didn't like it at all.

Enak was . . . not exactly playing with the station;

although it was childlike in many ways, O'Brien didn't think Enak was interested in *play*. No, Enak was doing something, but it wasn't a game.

It was more like an experiment. O'Brien remembered reading accounts of primitive psychology experiments that used rats trapped in mazes, tormented so that scientists could study their responses.

Enak was treating the people of *Deep Space Nine* as experimental subjects.

And O'Brien had heard enough to guess what Enak intended to study.

Enak wanted to study death.

Sure enough, even as that morbid thought crossed his mind, he saw the readouts on station life-support report a total shutdown on Level 19, Sector 38, in the third quadrant of the habitat ring.

Two people were trapped there—from the readings, probably Bajoran, one male, one female.

And Enak was removing their air supply, venting it slowly out into space through an emergency system intended to deal with excess pressure in case of structural damage.

"Damn!" O'Brien said again. He felt horribly helpless; there was nothing he could do in time that Enak couldn't override—not unless he went down there and tore the forcefield generators right out of the walls, and he doubted Enak would let him get close enough to do that.

He had to get control of the station's computers back from Enak somehow.

"Is there anything we can do?" Major Kira asked.

"I've tried, but haven't managed anything," Dax said. "I'm afraid you know far more about these Cardassian computers than I do."

"I don't know if I can do anything," O'Brien

replied. "And I'm not sure *anyone,* even the Cardassians, really understands these blasted machines."

Right at that moment, O'Brien hated every Cardassian computer designer who had ever lived; their creations were the most difficult, untrustworthy machines he had ever dealt with. O'Brien could never get them to behave exactly the way he wanted—but Enak apparently could.

Nor was Enak the first; this was the second time some damnable alien gadget out of the wormhole had screwed up the station's computers. The last time it had been a lonely little artificial intelligence they had nicknamed the Pup, and he had dealt with it by creating its own little niche where it could play. Was there any way to do the same with Enak?

No, because Enak wanted to play with *people,* not computers; it was using the computers as a means to an end, not as an end in themselves. The Pup wanted attention, but it interpreted that in terms of computer commands, and as long as copies of all commands were routed through its own subprogram, it was happy.

Enak wasn't going to be fooled so easily. It was much more attached to external reality than the Pup had ever been; it existed in a real-world environment, not the virtual world of the computers. Enak didn't care about controlling the station's computers except as a tool in its study of death.

O'Brien wondered whether Enak had noticed the Pup. The Pup had had a grand old time messing up the station's computers when it first came aboard, and it hadn't even had Enak's ability to get into systems without a direct connection.

But the Pup was a harmless thing, and irrelevant. O'Brien started to chastise himself for wasting time even thinking about such things when people were dying, then stopped.

Was it irrelevant?

Had Enak noticed the Pup?

Had the Pup noticed Enak?

Inspiration struck.

"Computer," he said, "route subroutine 'Pup' through docking communications port in upper pylon two."

"Working. Complete."

"What will that do?" Major Kira asked, looking up at O'Brien. "Wasn't that the alien probe that gave us trouble when those ambassadors were here?"

"That's the one," O'Brien said. "I don't know for sure if it will do a blessed thing. What I hope . . . yes!" As he looked at the readouts, they flickered abruptly.

Instructions were being countermanded. Signals were being blocked. New software subroutines were interfering with Enak's orders.

Enak was losing control. The Pup was out of its doghouse and in Enak's virtual lap, and it had noticed that Enak was running the station. It wanted attention, wanted to play, so it was doing the cybernetic equivalent of jumping up and licking Enak's face.

Distracted, countered by one of its own distant relatives, Enak was unable to dominate the computer systems; it was kept busy just dealing with the Pup's friendly overtures.

A major reason no human had been able to retake control from Enak was that Enak operated at a computer's speed, and in a fraction of a second could find a way around anything a human could do—but the Pup was just as fast as Enak.

It was fast enough to keep Enak busy doing nothing but countering it.

And while Enak was busy, the computers were more or less free again.

O'Brien hit the emergency overrides and shut down the security forcefields throughout the station; that would let air into corridor H-19-38, even if it didn't immediately stop the outflow, and would free the other trapped people throughout *Deep Space Nine*.

That done, he set about wresting as much control as he could back from Enak.

Dax, seeing what was happening, joined in.

O'Brien knew they didn't have long; Enak would find a permanent way around the Pup soon enough, some way to pen the thing up again—or perhaps destroy it, though O'Brien sincerely hoped not.

Still, if they could temporarily detach enough functions from the station's central computers, and put enough blocks in place that Enak's vibratory tricks couldn't get through them, they might be able to keep Enak from controlling things so completely from now on.

Communications were still jammed, and the transporter needed too much computing capability to be used safely, but there were plenty of other things to be done.

Most important, though, they had to know what Enak had done in the first place; calling instructions to Dax and the rest of the Ops crew, O'Brien began analyzing the power and data flows throughout *Deep Space Nine*.

Almost immediately, he discovered something he found absolutely fascinating.

Enak was running something through the docking port where Gul Dukat's ship was secured, something that carried a very large amount of data.

Enak was, O'Brien guessed, trying to take over the Cardassian ship as it had *Deep Space Nine*.

259

Had the Cardassians discovered that yet?

The station's internal communications were still down, but external channels might be available, with a little work—should the Cardassians be told?

Technically, he supposed he ought to ask his superiors, Major Kira and Lieutenant Dax. He would have to tell them eventually. Right now, though, he was very busy, wasn't he? And he didn't think the Cardassians deserved that much consideration.

"Hell, no," O'Brien muttered to himself. "Let *them* have a turn!"

CHAPTER
31

"ENAK!" SISKO SHOUTED.

The computer didn't answer. The control pad on the corridor wall had gone completely dead. He and the security team were trapped here in the connecting tunnel.

Sisko turned to the others. "Do any of you know a way around the forcefields?" he asked.

After all, the forcefields were there as part of the station's security systems, and these people were all part of station security.

The security people shook their heads. "Providing a way around them would rather defeat their purpose, sir," one of the Bajorans remarked.

"I know that," Sisko growled, turning back to the control pad. "That hardly means it can't be done."

He jabbed at the controls, trying to elicit a response —*any* response. What was Enak up to now? Why had it trapped them here?

It presumably still wanted to watch people die; did it plan to kill them all?

"If we can just get past this set of forcefields," he asked, "is there some way we can avoid getting bottled up like this again?"

The security people looked at one another.

"There are the power conduits," one of them suggested. "There aren't any security fields in those."

"But there's the power flow!" another protested. "You'd be fried in an instant if someone turned it on while you were in there."

Sisko shook his head. "That won't do. What's the fastest way to Ops from here? Are there any service tunnels or anything that would be faster than the public corridors?"

No one knew of any.

For a moment they all simply stood, looking about helplessly, as Sisko's frustration grew.

"What is that thing doing to *my station?*" he demanded, as he rammed his fist against the useless panel.

No one answered.

Then, abruptly, the forcefields vanished—Sisko glimpsed the change in the light from the corner of his eye, and whirled to see.

Yes, they were down!

Sisko didn't know how or why, or how long it would last, but the forcefields were down—*all* of them, for the entire length of the connecting tunnel.

"Come on!" he shouted, as he ran full-speed down the passage.

He left the security team behind, but he didn't care; he just wanted to get back to Ops before Enak put the forcefields back up. Every second, he expected to find himself ramming into an invisible barrier.

Then he was through the tunnel and into the core,

in the Promenade, where there were no forcefields to worry about, but crowds of milling people blocked his way. He caught snatches of conversation as he pushed through—others had been trapped in various parts of the station, then suddenly freed, all without explanation.

He glimpsed Jake and Nog and Quark, talking together, and he waved to them, but kept moving.

He boarded the turbolift, and waited impatiently as it rose upward, dreading the moment when Enak would return and trap him somewhere in the upper core—but it was faster than climbing the service tunnels, and Enak could trap him in those just as well, with the forcefields and emergency doors.

And at last he emerged into Ops.

O'Brien and Dax were at their stations, working frantically at something; someone's boots were visible under one of the consoles, where whoever it was working at the isolinear optics of the station's computer system.

Major Kira was standing to one side, watching readouts on a panel, but not appearing as involved as the others.

"Major, report!" he snapped.

She turned, and gave a quick account of the situation, of O'Brien's strategem in using the Pup to create a distraction so that they could cut systems loose from Enak's control.

"Chief, how's it working?" Sisko asked. "What's Enak still got hold of?"

O'Brien answered. "Well, Commander," he said, "it's still got the transporters out of service—we can't use them, but I've made sure that it can't use them, either, and we can all be grateful it didn't think of using them before, to shuffle people wherever it pleased! It's still able to jam all internal communications that are carried by the station's systems, but I think I have subspace frequencies clear—we should have external communications, and at least in theory, our comm badges should work."

"Good," Sisko said.

O'Brien nodded an acknowledgment and continued, "We've got the security forcefields shut down—neither side can use them. Enak still has control of all the airlocks and emergency doors, though, and we haven't yet been able to restore the weapons it disabled. The actual computer functions are shut down—neither side can use them. And there are several things I'm not sure about." He hesitated, then added, "And there's something very strange here, sir—I've found a file that appears to be the complete technical specifications of Enak's ship. There are several copies in our own computers, addressed to different people—one directed to me, one to Dax, one to Quark, one to Muhammed Goldberg, half a dozen others. I don't understand it."

Sisko frowned. "I don't understand it either, Chief. Anything else?"

O'Brien hesitated even longer before admitting, "I think, Commander, that Enak has tapped through the station into the Cardassian ship's computers—it's using that vibratory trick. I wish I knew how it did that—and I'll wager the Daystrom Institute would love to know, too!"

"The Cardassians?" A slow smile spread across Sisko's face. "It's getting into *their* computer?"

"Well, sir, if it can control ours, it can control theirs; after all, they're both the same basic design. It just has to find a way to route its control through the docking port, and apparently it's managed that."

Major Kira was glaring at O'Brien. "Chief, why didn't you tell *me* about this?" she demanded.

Sisko glanced at her, then joined his first officer in glaring at the chief.

"Uh . . . you didn't ask?" O'Brien said sheepishly, abashed by that double stare.

Then Sisko let that drop. "Never mind that now," he said. "Where is the Cardassian boarding party? Is Constable Odo all right?"

"Odo and that security man headed in toward the core the moment the forcefields shut down," O'Brien reported. "They appear to be injured—we haven't had time to try to contact them. The Cardassians cut through the blast doors, but they didn't follow Odo, they're moving up upper pylon two—I've got the turbolift there shut down, so they're climbing the ladders, and it's slow going."

Sisko frowned.

If they had had transporter capabilities, he would have had Odo and the security man beamed directly to Dr. Bashir's office, but as it was, they would have to find their own way. At least the shapeshifter wasn't in liquid form anymore; he must be recovering from the phaser hit.

"Comm badges are working?"

"They should be."

"Major, call Dr. Bashir," Sisko said, turning. "Tell him to head out toward docking bay three to meet the constable."

"Yes, sir," Kira said.

Sisko turned back to O'Brien. "You said we have external communications?"

"I think so, yeah," O'Brien said.

"And Enak's been interfering with the Cardassian ship?"

"Yes, sir."

Sisko smiled. "Good," he said. "Dax, get me Gul Dukat on the main viewer."

"Yes, Benjamin."

The screen lit up.

"Ah, Commander Sisko," Gul Dukat said, settling into his seat—he had obviously been attending to something when the call had come through. "You wish to speak to me?" Sisko thought the Cardassian's face showed some signs of strain, but his voice was still calm. "To surrender, perhaps?"

"Hardly, Gul Dukat," Sisko said. "To offer you a warning, rather. Have you, perhaps, suffered any computer malfunctions recently?"

Gul Dukat's expression grew wary. "Why do you ask? It wouldn't be any of *your* doing, would it?"

"No, no," Sisko assured him. "I ask because we've noticed that the derelict ship on upper pylon two has been communicating with your own ship."

"The derelict is doing this?" Dukat glanced at someone offscreen, where Sisko and the others couldn't see him or her; this person, whoever it was, apparently confirmed the report.

"Working through DS-Nine, yes," Sisko said.

"Ah. Thank you, Commander, for mentioning this. It's very kind of you." Gul Dukat gazed out at Sisko with a measuring expression, as if trying to analyze just what Sisko's motives were. "I think perhaps we'll cut our little courtesy call to your *delightful* station short—but before we leave the vicinity, perhaps we'll see if we can't unjam those mooring clamps of yours on upper pylon two. I would think a few phaser blasts should get those circuits working, don't you?"

Before Sisko could reply, Dukat's image vanished.

Those final remarks were clear enough; Dukat intended to blow off the docking port on upper pylon two, and take Enak, whether it wanted to go or not.

Sisko thought it was tempting to just let the

Cardassians *have* the damned thing—but it was too dangerous. If they could learn to control Enak, could learn how it did its tricks, then they would be able to sabotage computers all through Bajoran and Federation space.

Besides, it would provide Gul Dukat with the trophy he needed to claim the leadership of the *D'ja Bajora Karass,* and the Federation did not need that.

"The Cardassian ship is undocking, Commander," O'Brien reported.

"But the Cardassian boarding party is still halfway up upper pylon two," Dax said.

"Lower our shields, Lieutenant," Sisko ordered. "Get me Dukat again."

Once more, the Cardassian's image appeared.

"Whatever is it *this* time, Commander?" Gul Dukat asked impatiently.

"I thought you might want to retrieve your men," Sisko said. "I wanted to reassure you that our shields will remain down until you have safely transported them."

Dukat stared at Sisko for a long moment.

"That's very considerate of you, Commander," he said at last. "Thank you."

The connection broke once again.

"Chief O'Brien," Sisko said, "keep the station's sensors on the Cardassians and see how long it takes them to beam those men out. That will give us an idea how much damage Enak did to them before they cut loose from DS-Nine."

"Commander," Kira protested, "you're going to just give them back their boarding party?"

Sisko turned to her and said, "Of course. What would *we* do with them?"

"Keep them as hostages until we had Gul Dukat's

word to leave Enak alone! And until we had some sort of vengeance for those dead children on Andros!"

Sisko stared at her. "You'd take a Cardassian's word? *You* would?"

Kira hesitated.

Sisko continued, "And you think that a Cardassian commander like Gul Dukat would give up a prize like Enak to save half a dozen of his own men?"

Kira's shoulders sagged.

"No," she said, "he probably wouldn't." She glanced up at the main viewer. "But then, how *are* we going to keep Gul Dukat from taking Enak? Our weapons are all still off-line, and you heard what he said—he's going to shear off the top of the pylon and tractor Enak away!" A realization struck. "And you just told him that we're going to keep the shields down while he does it!"

"The shields wouldn't do us all that much good in any case," Sisko replied. "Not when he can sit out there and take his time. Besides, if he takes Enak before rescuing his men, they'll probably be killed by the decompression when he cuts open that pylon. Killing his own men wouldn't look good to the folks back home, would it?"

"No," Kira admitted, "but do you think . . . Would he . . . Would *you* be willing to see those Cardassians die just so we can frustrate Gul Dukat's political ambitions?"

"I don't want to see *anyone* die," Sisko answered, "and I don't think Gul Dukat is going to make such a foolish mistake—but if he did, wouldn't it be worth half a dozen Cardassian lives to prevent a full-scale war?"

"Maybe. But that doesn't matter," Kira said. "You

still haven't answered me—how are we going to stop him from taking Enak?"

"I don't know," Sisko admitted. "I'm not sure we are. At this point, I think we might as well leave Enak to fend for itself." He smiled humorlessly. "After all, it's pretty good at that."

CHAPTER
32

"THE CARDASSIAN BOARDING PARTY has been safely transported away, Benjamin," Dax announced.

"Good. Shields up."

"Shields up."

"Enak," Sisko said, "can you hear me?"

There was no answer.

"Chief," he said, "can you put the Pup back in its doghouse?"

"Of course," O'Brien replied, "but that will leave Enak with completely free rein again."

"We'll have to risk it; do it."

O'Brien's eyes made it plain that he didn't like the idea, but he obeyed.

"Computer," he said, "remove subroutine 'Pup' from all docking area systems and restore it to its previous hardware sites."

"Working. Completed."

O'Brien looked down at his display, started to say something, then stopped as the screens went blank.

"Damn!" he said. "Commander, Enak's back in control already."

Sisko nodded. He looked up at the main viewer.

"Enak, listen to me!" he said. "The other ship, the Cardassian ship—it's preparing to attack the station, to cut you free. It will then tractor you away. We don't want our station damaged; will you restore our weapons so that we may defend ourselves?"

Nothing answered.

"Will you allow the Cardassians to capture you?" Dax asked, after a moment of silence. "They will not allow you to die, Enak; they wish to study you alive."

"Will they permit me to observe slow deaths?" the computer's voice asked.

"No," Sisko answered immediately.

Beside him, Major Kira wished she could be as sure of that as Sisko seemed to be.

"Enak," Sisko said, "you shouldn't want to die. And you shouldn't kill. Study your records—all living things wish to continue living, do they not?"

"No," Enak promptly replied. "Suicide is common to many of the cultures described in your station's records."

"But murder is always a crime—causing another's death is wrong."

"There are exceptions," Enak said, "but I am aware that the general case is as you state. I am also aware of the most common and appropriate penalty."

"What penalty . . ." Sisko began.

He was interrupted when O'Brien let out a startled yelp as his console suddenly returned to full life. Quickly, the engineer called up a status readout. "Commander," he called, "Enak is undocking from the station."

"On viewer," Sisko snapped.

Instantly, he had a view of the outside of the

271

station, seen from the pickup at the top of the communications cluster. Enak was, indeed, detaching itself from the station.

And behind it, the Cardassian warship was moving into attack position.

"Enak!" Sisko shouted. "Can you hear me?"

O'Brien replied, "We have no direct communications link to Enak anymore."

"Commander," Dax said, "Enak is hailing us."

"Put it on."

The image on the viewer did not change, but a voice—a strange, deep voice, not the familiar voice of the computer—spoke. Sisko realized that he was hearing Enak's own voice for the first time.

"You will not allow me to study death, to find my way to the *tschak* Heaven," Enak said. "And your priests have told me that this study would, in any case, condemn me to Hell, so I must abandon it and attempt to find my own way. In my efforts to find inner peace and to understand death I have incapacitated your weapons beyond my ability to restore them in time to be of use, and this has had a cost; Quark has taught me that debts must be paid. I therefore find only one appropriate course of action."

"What the devil's the bloody thing talking about?" O'Brien asked. "It's been talking to Quark?"

"By leaving the station, it's made it unnecessary for Gul Dukat to fire at the pylon," Dax pointed out.

"I think it's more than that," Sisko said. "Look."

Enak was swinging around, bringing its nose directly in line with the Cardassian cruiser's weapons.

"Enak," Sisko said, "you don't need to do this. We understand that you meant us no harm, that you were just following your programming."

"I must find the way to Heaven," Enak replied.

And then it accelerated at full power directly toward the Cardassian ship.

By the time the Cardassians were able to fire, it was too late—Enak drove nose-first into the warship's forward weapons array.

The people of *Deep Space Nine* watched in horror as metal and plastic crumpled, silent in the vacuum of space; then, inevitably, came the explosion as the power conduits in the Cardassian phaser banks overloaded and ruptured. Debris and dust scattered in a glowing, radioactive cloud.

Enak was gone; the far larger Cardassian warship was drifting off at an angle, trailing wreckage, but still mostly in one piece.

"Get me through to Gul Dukat," Sisko barked. "Find out if there's anything we can do to help."

Dax obeyed.

The image that appeared on the viewer was blurred and unsteady. "We're rather busy just now, Commander," Gul Dukat said.

"I just wanted to offer our assistance," Sisko said. "Is there anything we can do?"

"Oh, I think you've already done quite enough," Gul Dukat said.

Then he cut off transmission.

Sisko stared at the blank viewer for a moment.

"Exterior on viewer," he ordered.

The image of stars, station, and scattered wreckage reappeared, in time for them to watch the Cardassian ship turn its battered nose in a direction Sisko judged to be a straight line to Cardassia.

"Scanners report the Cardassian ship is at fifteen percent power, all phaser banks destroyed," O'Brien called. "Main drives still functional. Major loss of atmosphere. Sir, there are at least four dead Cardassians drifting in the wreckage."

"If they leave them . . ."

Sisko didn't need to finish his statement; he could see the flickering as the bodies were beamed aboard.

Then, with a certain ponderous grace, Gul Dukat's ship drove away from *Deep Space Nine,* leaving behind a spreading, drifting cloud of debris.

"At that speed, he won't be home for weeks," O'Brien remarked.

Sisko nodded. "And I don't think he's going to find himself held in much esteem when he gets there," he said.

"And that's it, then," Kira said. "He'll lose face, coming home like that. That's all the dangerous ones, if Gul Kaidan was right."

"Let's hope he was," Sisko said. "And that's four dead Cardassians—is that enough revenge for you, Major?"

"No," she said, "not until we find some way to reach whoever was responsible. But it's enough blood for now."

"What about Enak?" Sisko asked. "I don't see any sign of it."

"Totally destroyed," Dax replied. "I can't find any single fragment larger than three meters."

For a moment, no one spoke; then Kira said, "It's gone to Heaven."

Sisko glanced at her, then sighed. "Let's get the tractors and runabouts started cleaning up that mess out there, before one of those fragments punches through the station wall somewhere."

EPILOGUE

"IT'S CONFIRMED," Major Kira reported, the moment the door of the commander's office had closed behind her. "The Goran Tokar had named Gul Burot as his heir just before his hospitalization."

"And the Goran Tokar's chances for recovery?" Sisko asked, feeling a trifle ghoulish.

"Poor," Kira said. "Very poor."

"I suppose we should be pleased," Sisko said.

"We should be pleased that he chose Gul Burot," Kira replied, "but there's nothing pleasing about even a Cardassian dying of some slow disease that way."

Sisko nodded agreement.

"Incidentally," Kira added, "the Goran Tokar issued a statement explaining his choice. It's rather long and rambling, but the gist of it is that he had intended to name Gul Dukat as his successor, as the person who knew most about what the Cardassian Empire gave up on Bajor, but he could hardly do so after Dukat came home with a damaged ship and nothing to show for it. So we did accomplish something."

"Or Enak did," Sisko suggested. "Not that there was ever any doubt we'd have something to show for it, even if Gul Dukat did not; we have the technical readouts. Once those have been properly analyzed, we'll be able to build Besrethine neural-net computers —if we want to risk it."

"And if we do, will there be commercial applications?"

"Probably."

"Bajor will want royalties, then," Kira said. "Enak was Bajoran property, under the laws of salvage."

"Enak was a sentient being, not anyone's property," Sisko retorted angrily.

"The *tschak* didn't think so."

"The *tschak* were wrong." He paused, then shrugged. "If you want to advise the provisional government to petition for a share of the profits, I'm sure a case can be made, and I won't oppose it. I want Bajor to thrive just as much as you do."

Kira didn't pursue the issue. Instead she asked, "Is Odo all right?"

"Dr. Bashir says he's making an excellent recovery —so far as he can tell," Sisko replied. "There are disadvantages to being the only known member of one's species; there's no way to judge what's normal. At any rate, he's in good shape—good enough that he insisted on telling me about some scheme Quark was involved in." He smiled.

"What was Quark up to?" Kira asked, curiously.

"It seems he had a plan for stealing Enak," Sisko said. "He admitted the whole thing, eventually—it was his doing that Ensign Shula withdrew her complaint about the Ashtarians, and that Enak gave us those plans."

"Ensign Shula? He tricked her? But then . . ."

"No, no." Sisko held up a hand. "He simply showed her that she was making a mistake."

Kira considered. "That doesn't sound like Quark," she said.

"Especially when I tell you that he hasn't been paid for it yet—he gave the Ashtarians credit!"

"Is he sick? Maybe *he* should be in the infirmary, instead of Odo!"

"He's fine; he just got carried away at the prospect of having that *tschak* technology for himself."

Kira nodded thoughtfully. "It seems several people did."

Sisko nodded. "Quark claims he was Enak's agent, and is entitled to a share of whatever profits come from the *tschak* technology."

"He does?"

Sisko nodded. "He can petition, too," he said. "Though somehow I doubt his claim will stand up."

"Do you suppose we'll ever find the *tschak* themselves?" Kira asked.

"It's a big galaxy, and by Enak's account they're a small civilization," Sisko answered. "I wouldn't be overly optimistic about it."

"That's a shame," Kira said.

Sisko agreed. "And not just because of the technology," he said. "There aren't enough people out there who choose not to arm their ships."

"And," Kira added, "who believe in Heaven, but no Hell."

Author's Note

The events in this novel take place before the events of
Lois Tilton's *Betrayal*.